"I do know I'm curious ⸻
on mine. And I think y⸻
notions of chivalry...pr⸻ ⸻ ⸻ promotions...all
prevent you from acting on that curiosity. But I don't
let myself be bound by those considerations." Her eyes
followed the track of her finger as it continued to trace a
path to and fro along his lip. "Well, perhaps sometimes I
do, but not always. Let's not be bound by them right now.
What do you say, Charles?"

He didn't say anything. He couldn't. It was as if his
breath had left his lungs, making speech impossible. And
even if the ability to speak hadn't deserted him, he didn't
wish to interrupt the way she softly caressed his mouth.
His will had crumpled before it.

She cupped his chin lightly, her thumb now simply resting against his mouth. "Shall I kiss you then?" She paused,
and as the question hung in the silence, a hint of a smile
tipped up the corners of her mouth. "You're not protesting, which isn't quite the same as permission. But does it
imply permission?" Her other hand curled around his neck
as she raised herself up onto her toes to bring her mouth
level with his. "Let's make it clear. Meet me halfway,
Charles," she whispered. "Please. Meet me halfway."

SAY YOU'LL BE MY LADY

ALSO BY KATE PEMBROOKE

Not the Kind of Earl You Marry

SAY YOU'LL BE MY LADY

*An Unconventional
Ladies of Mayfair Novel*

KATE PEMBROOKE

FOREVER
New York   Boston

Copyright © 2022 by Kate Pembrooke

Cover design by Daniela Medina. Cover art by Alan Ayers. Cover photography by David Wagner. Cover copyright © 2022 by Hachette Book Group, Inc.

Forever
Hachette Book Group
1290 Avenue of the Americas, New York, NY 10104
read-forever.com
twitter.com/readforeverpub

First Edition: February 2022

Forever is an imprint of Grand Central Publishing. The Forever name and logo are trademarks of Hachette Book Group, Inc.

The publisher is not responsible for websites (or their content) that are not owned by the publisher.

The Hachette Speakers Bureau provides a wide range of authors for speaking events. To find out more, go to www.hachettespeakersbureau.com or call (866) 376-6591.

ISBNs: 978-1-5387-0377-9 (mass market); 978-1-5387-0379-3 (ebook)

Printed in the United States of America

OPM

10 9 8 7 6 5 4 3 2 1

To Wendy and Chris Anna—talented writers, but even better friends.

Acknowledgments

Once again, it's time to acknowledge those who've played a part in getting this book into your hands, Dear Readers.

I want to thank the fabulous team at Forever who work tirelessly to help transform the initial manuscript into an honest-to-goodness book. I'm indebted to my fantastic editor, Junessa Viloria, for being the steady hand who shapes my words into a much better story. And thanks to Leah Hultenschmidt for also providing invaluable guidance. Many thanks to Jodi Rosoff for working her publicity magic to get the word out about *Say You'll Be My Lady*, and to Daniela Medina for creating such a lovely book cover. I'm also grateful to my copy editor, Shelly Perron, for supplying that final polish to make the story sparkle.

Thank you to my agent, Rebecca Strauss, for not only dispensing sage advice, but also for being such a wonderful cheerleader. You put a smile on my face.

Hugs and a huge thank you to Shannon Gilmore for always being ready to brainstorm, help with research questions, talk books, or tweak a graphic for me. And I would be remiss if I didn't mention my assistant, Kelly Oakes, who helps me in so many ways. You rock, Kelly!

And finally, I couldn't do this without the support of my husband. Thank you, sweetheart.

SAY YOU'LL BE MY LADY

Chapter One

~

And that concludes this week's business portion of the Wednesday Afternoon Social Club." Lady Serena Wynter, one of the club's founders and the de facto leader, smiled at the two dozen or so ladies who'd attended today's gathering and gestured toward the far end of the room, where platters of finger sandwiches and desserts had been laid out on a long table. "So let's do justice to these refreshments, ladies. I've been told Edwina's cook has made a batch of her lemon-raspberry tartlets for us today."

Those present needed no further urging. Edwina, Lady Beasley, hosted their meetings at her Upper Grosvenor Street residence, and the membership had come to look forward to the delicious treats her kitchen staff prepared for them each week. A line began forming at the rear of the room and the hum of conversation grew louder.

Serena made her way to where some of her closest friends were gathered around Charlotte, the Countess of Norwood. Besides Edwina, who sat in a chair adjacent to Charlotte's, there was Grace, the Duchess of Rochester, her niece, Phoebe Talbot, and a close friend of Phoebe's, Julia Keene.

"What a delightful surprise that you could join us today. I thought you weren't returning to London until next week," Serena said, giving Charlotte an affectionate kiss on the cheek.

"That was William's plan, not mine." Charlotte patted the rather considerable girth of her stomach. "Honestly, this baby has turned my husband into a veritable mother hen, and frankly, it's driving me mad. I recovered from my cold over a week ago, so there was no reason to delay our return when I feel perfectly fine." She laughed and framed her abdomen with her hands. "Well, as fine as one can when one's belly is the size of a large melon. I move about with an ungainly waddle these days, but it doesn't mean I'm incapable of carrying on as usual."

"That goes without saying," Serena agreed. "Nonetheless, I'd be happy to get some refreshments for you if you don't feel like leaving that armchair." Charlotte looked quite comfortable reclining against the well-padded chair cushions with her feet propped up on a matching ottoman.

"Please, don't fuss over me. I get more than enough of that at home." She gave them a wry smile as she awkwardly got to her feet.

They made their way over to the refreshments table and made their food and drink selections. Fortunately, their recently vacated seats hadn't been claimed by anyone else yet. As Charlotte once again settled herself in an armchair she said, "I can't wait to catch up with everyone. I see so many new faces here today. For heaven's sake, I missed only the first few weeks of the Season, but I already feel behind."

"You know Serena. She doesn't let the grass grow under her feet," Grace remarked. "I was surprised to show up at our first meeting in the new year and find over two dozen ladies in attendance."

"It helped that Edwina and I stayed in London throughout the summer and fall when much of the *haut ton* depart for the countryside," Serena said. "Even with that seasonal exodus, by Christmas there were over twenty of us meeting weekly. Word about us continues to spread, and now that the Season is in full swing..." With a sweep of her arm, Serena gestured about the room. "As you can see, we're filling up Edwina's drawing room."

"The more, the merrier," Edwina said. "If necessary, we can hold our meetings in the music room. That's where my family used to host large gatherings when I was young."

"This house belongs to your family?" Charlotte asked. "I assumed it had belonged to your late husband."

"No. My husband's younger brother lives in the home I shared with Beasley. We're on good terms, and I have a standing invitation to stay there any time I wish. However, I don't wish to be the importuning relation always underfoot. My parents no longer spend time in London, nor does my sister, Constance, who wouldn't stay here in any case, as she and her husband have a large residence just off Berkeley Square. So it works out for me to live here."

"It also works out quite well for us ladies of the Wednesday Afternoon Social Club," Grace said. "So much so that I forbid you to ever quit the group, Edwina. Because seriously, where else would we be able to plot our schemes and misbehave?"

Serena smiled in acknowledgment of this truth. A widow like Edwina was the obvious choice to host their meetings because despite the innocuous-sounding name they'd chosen to give themselves, much of society— and this would include all but the most enlightened of husbands—would frown upon a group like theirs.

The Wednesday Afternoon Social Club embraced the notion that females needn't be relegated to only the lesser roles in life, but were fully capable of being contributing members of society, even in a world structured to grant far more rights to men. Not to mention the ladies in the club discussed these contributions while wearing trousers (if that was their preference) or partaking those traditionally male libations such as brandy or whisky. To be sure, plenty of cups of tea were also consumed at the meetings—with a splash of strong spirits if the lady wished.

The point of the group wasn't simply to copy the behavior of men, but rather to give ladies, for an afternoon anyway, a choice as to how they wished to comport themselves. Whether that took the form of what they wore or what they consumed or what they discussed, they had the freedom to choose.

The duchess continued, "Rochester is quite broad-minded and doesn't seem to mind my penchant for wearing trousers in a discreet setting now and again"—she gestured to the pair of trousers she currently wore, which showed off her tall, slender figure to great advantage— "but I'm not sure even he would countenance similar behavior in a large group of ladies meeting in his home. Nor do I think he'd approve of ladies drinking strong spirits, should that be their inclination."

"There are those of us so inclined, but still prohibited from it, Aunt Grace," Phoebe Talbot remarked. She sat in a chintz-covered armchair with her legs draped over one of the chair's arms, managing to look demure and shockingly unladylike at the same time. She fanned herself with a folded copy of the latest issue of the *Advocate*, a radical newspaper published by Edwina's beau, Jason Latimer.

The duchess turned to her niece with a wry smile. "My darling Phoebe, you know that I'm risking your mother's censure just by bringing you to these meetings. We both know, she'd consider them thoroughly unsuitable for a young lady. And while I disagree with that, I'm *not* going to introduce a seventeen-year-old to liquor. I promise you that next year, when you make your official come out, I'll allow a cup of spiked punch. Until then, you'll have to be satisfied with tea or lemonade and the ability to wear trousers, if you wish."

"Trousers proved unexpectedly disappointing and, in my opinion, more bother than they're worth, considering one must change into them after arrival," Phoebe said. "A wee nip of whisky would be a lovely consolation."

"Next year, my darling, you may enjoy the rum punch."

The girl gave an exaggerated sigh, but her smile was good-natured. "That's the story of my life. Wait until you're older. Wait until you're married." She twirled one slim hand in the air. "Wait until...insert some other reason."

Serena gave Phoebe a sympathetic look. She recalled being Phoebe's age, filled with anticipation as the future beckoned just around the corner, eager to move past the preparation for adulthood and start living her life as an adult. The choices she'd made then had shaped everything she'd done since.

"Speaking from the ripe old age of three-and-twenty," Serena addressed the girl, "I can remember those days of what seemed to be endless waiting, but I promise the time will pass more swiftly than you realize, and I'm sure your aunt will agree that staying busy is the perfect antidote."

"Exactly right," the duchess agreed.

"I could use assistance maintaining the inventory ledgers for the leased properties," Julia Keene spoke up. She'd joined the group in May of last year. A petite girl with black hair and dark eyes that hinted at a Welsh ancestry, she'd quickly become a member they could rely on. "I've only just started compiling the ledger for our third property and now with a fourth one..." She sent a questioning look in Phoebe's direction.

"I don't mind helping with that," Phoebe replied. "As long as Aunt Grace has no objections."

"None whatsoever," her aunt replied.

"Ooh," Charlotte said, grimacing and placing a hand on her abdomen. "Someone is making their presence felt. This one kicks so fiercely at times, I wonder if it thinks it can kick itself right out of my belly."

"A feisty child," Grace remarked. "So who does it take after. You or Norwood?"

"William says the baby must take after me, because, of course, my husband is the soul of amiability." She rolled her eyes in amusement. "Or so he claims. I, however, remind him of the morning we met when he was anything *but*. At least, initially. *Ouch*," she added, giving her stomach a look of mock sternness. "Boy or girl, this one is hard to ignore."

A sudden pang of bittersweet longing came over Serena. Six years ago she'd put aside dreams of marriage and motherhood, and forged a different path for herself. One that was usually fulfilling and satisfying. She rarely felt any pangs of regret unless something came along to remind her of those old hopes and plans. But a young man's death on the field of battle in Spain had put an end to the future she'd envisioned back then.

As she always did, she pushed away those memories. The past was the past, unchangeable, irreversible, and therefore, something she willed herself not to dwell upon. *Her* life hadn't ended, which meant replacing old hopes with new ones. She'd found new purpose—one shared by the ladies in this room today.

Charitable work had long been a passion of hers, and it was the other important facet of the Wednesday Afternoon Social Club. What had begun as a few friends who'd been determined to make a positive difference in the world had grown into this vibrant group of ladies, united by a shared vision to take action when they saw a need.

Almost as if reading her thoughts, Edwina said, "Charlotte, I don't believe you've heard the latest news about our war widows project, although Julia just alluded to it. We finally signed a lease for a fourth property."

"That *is* wonderful," Charlotte said. "And to think that less than a year ago we were readying that first location on Red Lion Square."

"I'm excited about our newest endeavor to provide educational opportunities for children," Grace said. "Although the vote was close between that and supplying warm clothing for those children who live on the streets of London."

"I voted for the educational opportunities. I believe education will stay with them always, whereas warm clothing could be taken from them and sold for the profit of someone else," Julia Keene said.

"Sadly, the exploitation of children in that way, and in so many others, is not uncommon," Serena said. "We can't right everything that's wrong in the world, but we can make an effort to improve what we can."

"Which project did you vote for, Serena?" Charlotte asked.

"The option which came in third," Serena replied. A distant third, somewhat to her disappointment.

Charlotte nodded sympathetically. "Housing unwed pregnant girls would also have been a worthy endeavor. Perhaps it can go on the ballot next year."

"Perhaps," Serena said. Though she was already considering what she could do on her own.

Charlotte turned to Edwina. "You must give my compliments to your cook, Edwina. These sandwiches are heavenly, and normally I don't even like liver paste sandwiches."

"One of the vagaries of pregnancy," Grace said. "I craved pickled eggs when I was expecting my first baby, but couldn't stand the sight of them during the next two, and then craved them again with our last child."

"It's odd, isn't it?" Charlotte said. "I've come to like things I usually don't, and yet I can't abide some things I normally like. And it's not even just food. I had to tell my maid to quit spritzing my clothing with rose water. The smell simply doesn't appeal to me anymore."

"Your preferences may return to normal once the baby is born," Grace said.

Charlotte shrugged, then turned to Serena. "Speaking of preferences, how is Mr. Townshend these days?"

Serena laughed. "I'm not sure how preferences and Mr. Townshend are related, but he's fine I suppose."

Charlotte exchanged a look with Edwina and Grace. The three of them had made no secret they favored a match between Serena and that gentleman. And if she were presently interested in finding a match, Serena supposed she could do a good deal worse than Charles Townshend. She considered him a friend—even if they'd had their fair share of disagreements in the past.

"Oh, no. You've had an argument, haven't you?" Charlotte looked dismayed.

"A small one," Serena admitted. "He was being his usual overprotective self."

"Well, after that incident in Seven Dials, I can't say I blame him," Edwina said.

Charlotte's eyes widened. "Wait? What incident?"

Seven Dials was notorious as a crushingly poor, crime-ridden area of London. Going there hadn't been one of Serena's wiser decisions, although at the time it had seemed urgent. She'd been trying to rescue a young pickpocket from the clutches of someone named Mother Duggan, who ran a ring of child thieves. Mattie and Serena's paths had crossed when the girl had tried to steal Serena's reticule one day when she was putting up flyers with information about the jobs and housing they offered to war widows.

In the end, Serena had succeeded in rescuing the girl, but it had been dicey for a while, and the footman accompanying her had suffered two black eyes when some of those sympathetic to Mother Duggan's "rights" concerning Mattie had expressed their displeasure. Serena herself had sustained some bruises before they could make their way back to the coach.

"It's a long story," Serena said, not wishing to rehash that day. "Suffice it to say, I learned my lesson about going to Seven Dials."

"I should hope so," Edwina said. She turned to Charlotte to give her a brief recap, concluding with, "Serena and a footman suffered relatively minor injuries, but the point is, it could have been much worse."

Charlotte frowned. "When did this happen?"

"Last autumn," Serena said.

Charlotte shook her head. "Mr. Townshend must have been beside himself when he heard about it."

"He expressed his displeasure most emphatically," Serena said dryly.

"Well, you are going to have to make up with him because I wish to have a dinner party so that we can all catch up, and I intend to put him on the guest list."

And no doubt, she would make sure Charles was seated next to Serena during dinner. Her friends weren't particularly subtle when it came to their efforts to throw the two of them together.

"I will do what I can," Serena said. "As soon as he gets back from Bath. He's been there the past two weeks. His employer, Sir Roland, suffered a severe bout of rheumatism and wished to take the waters. Charles insisted on accompanying him over the old gentleman's objections."

It was actually this trip that had led to their argument. Charles had called on her to let her know he'd be out of London for a while, and to extract a promise that she wouldn't go to any dangerous neighborhoods while he was gone. A promise she could have easily made, since the incident in Seven Dials had cured her of heedless risk taking. Yet, despite her reformed attitude toward her safety (and, by extension, those of her servants), she'd taken exception to his demand, and one thing had led to another and they'd had a spat.

She regretted the argument, especially since she knew it was mostly her fault. She'd been cranky that day, and she'd taken it out on Charles. The truth was she'd started missing him soon after his departure. He annoyed her, but he also amused her, and lately, she'd begun to feel an undeniable pull of attraction. Even during their last disagreement, it had been there underneath her sharp words. No doubt her friends would be ecstatic to hear this, but she had no intention of admitting it and have them redouble their matchmaking efforts.

"When is he expected back?" Charlotte asked.

"I don't know. I haven't heard from him." She gave them a sheepish smile. "I told him not to bother writing me while he was gone, which was unfair of me, I admit, since he does have my best interests in mind."

Charlotte gave a sad little shake of her head. "Well, when you hear he's back, let me know, and I will issue you all invitations to dinner."

"I expect he'll turn up soon," Serena said. "He's so frightfully conscientious. I can't see Charles neglecting his parliamentary duties for any longer than necessary."

She didn't add that the real question in her mind was had she treated him so shabbily that he'd wish to neglect their friendship instead.

Chapter Two

~~~

*A*rriving home from an afternoon spent running errands, Serena was greeted in the front hall by their butler.

"Mr. Townshend is waiting to see you in the drawing room," Menken said.

"Oh, what a pleasant surprise." She removed her bonnet and gloves and handed them to him. "Please have refreshments sent in, Menken."

"Of course," the butler said before turning and heading down the hall to carry out her request.

Serena tried to ignore the little flutter of excitement at seeing Charles again. The truth was she'd felt his absence keenly these past two weeks, and not only because it had effectively stalled her efforts to find tradesmen willing to offer apprenticeships to the sons of the war widows (though it had). Serena had enlisted his help in approaching businesses that took on apprentices. She was eager to begin pairing those boys who wished to learn a trade with a skilled tradesman.

"The prodigal returneth," she observed as she swept through the door of the drawing room. "When did you get back? How was your time in Bath? And how is Sir Roland faring after taking the waters?" Ever the gentleman, Charles came to his feet and remained standing until she'd taken a seat.

"I'm very well, thank you. And you?" His expression was solemn, but he couldn't quite hide the amusement in his eyes.

As an outright rebuke, she would have found it annoying to have her rudeness pointed out, but as a bit of gentle teasing…? She liked his humorous side a great deal.

"I thought I'd save you the bother of observing the social niceties, but I see you're having none of that. I'm perfectly well, and am exceedingly glad to hear you're the same." She folded her hands primly in her lap. "You'll be happy to know that somehow I managed to stay out of trouble while you were gone."

"Always happy to hear that. To answer your barrage of questions in order, yesterday evening, for me, about a week too long, but I'm happy to report Sir Roland's aches and pains are much improved. He appears glad to be back in London." Something flickered in the depths of his blue eyes before he added, "I know I am."

Another tiny fillip of emotion danced inside her. He hadn't explicitly said that he was glad to be back because he'd missed her, but surely the sentiment lay buried beneath his words. Or was that just wishful thinking on her part? Surely, at the very least, it was an olive branch.

"I'm glad you're back as well," she said. "In case you were wondering, given how...awful I was before you left."

One corner of his mouth lifted. "I took it as a good sign when Menken didn't turn me away at the front door."

She gave him a teasing smile in return. "Yes, well, I'm waiting on that list of tradesmen you promised me, though with Parliament in full swing, I expect you'll have some catching up to do before you can attend to that."

"Some," he agreed. "But I'd arranged to have anything of importance brought to me by courier, so I was able to stay current with the things that truly required my attention. I even made a brief three-day trip home at Sir Roland's insistence, since the journey to Frome is so much shorter from Bath than if I were traveling from London."

"I'm sure your family was delighted to see you, although I expect they were disappointed it couldn't be of a longer duration. It's been, what? A year since you visited them?"

"Not quite a year," Charles replied. "It was a pleasant visit, but quite long enough to suit me, considering Mama has acquired...notions concerning myself and a certain Miss Lewis."

"That's a common affliction among bachelor sons," she said. "I'm just thankful Papa has become reconciled to having a spinster for a daughter. I take it you don't share in her inclination toward Miss Lewis?"

For some reason, the idea of Charles courting someone made her feel an uncomfortable stab of jealousy, which was ridiculous, because she had no claim on his affections beyond that of friendship. Certainly she always pushed back when her friends suggested she behave in a manner that would encourage his attentions. But there was no denying the way she'd felt just then.

He shook his head. "Don't get me wrong. Miss Lewis is a perfectly nice girl, but I'm not really at a point where I'm ready to acquire a wife, and it would be most unfair of me to expect Miss Lewis to wait until I was." He shrugged. "And even if I were at that point, there wasn't any particular connection between us. I hope I convinced Mama to drop the matter, but I'm not sure that I did."

Serena couldn't deny that his words brought her a measure of relief. "She'll come around, and you do have the advantage that living this far from your family effectively spikes her guns when it comes to pushing a match between the two of you."

"Yes, although I suspect that Miss Lewis will be a frequent topic in any letters I get from Mama. She can be annoyingly tenacious when she gets an idea in her head. But I won't bore you with that any longer, when I have something that will surely be of more interest to you." He smiled and picked up a folded paper from the table beside his chair. "While I was in Bath, I made some inquiries and compiled a list of apprenticeship opportunities, although I don't know if you intend to send any of the boys that far afield."

"I hadn't thought of it, but it might be good to give them a choice beyond London."

"In that case, my labors weren't in vain." He rose and taking the few strides necessary to reach her chair, handed her the piece of paper. As she took it from him, her fingers briefly brushed against his—far too briefly to justify the tingle of awareness that prickled along her skin. Had he felt it too? He gave no sign of it, but then to her knowledge, neither had she. It wasn't as if either of them was likely to exclaim out loud "Did you feel that?" Though it would make male–female relationships so much easier if people did.

"Those tradesmen expressed a willingness to take on some of the boys," he said as he settled back in his chair. "Only some have a current need for an apprentice, but those that don't said they would in the future, and they promised to contact me when they do. However, it wouldn't be amiss to inquire again in a few months, just in case they forget their promise, or mislay the contact information I gave them."

As Serena unfolded the sheet of paper, she caught the faint scent that clung to it, a mixture of citrus and spice and clean linen dried in the sun. She liked that he didn't favor overpowering colognes as some men did.

She scanned the list of about two dozen names of tradesmen along with the names and addresses of their places of business. "This is wonderful. Thank you."

"I'll work on getting you a list of more businesses here in London. I've compiled a short list, very short, in fact, which is why I haven't shared it with you yet. But I will once I make some more progress on it." He leaned back in his chair and crossed one leg over the other. "So what have you been up to in my absence? Besides staying out of trouble, that is." He smiled and two shallow furrows formed in his cheeks, not quite dimples, but features that Serena found...appealing.

"The usual. The Norwoods have returned to town, so I've been spending time with Charlotte. We've been continuing on with our work for the war widows. The Duchess of Rochester is hosting another subscription ball for us this Season to raise funds for our newest venture, so we've begun planning for that. Papa has hosted several dinner parties, mostly for his political cronies."

"Sounds as if you've been quite busy," he remarked.

"You know me. I don't like to be idle. Would you like to hear about the latest project for the ladies of the Wednesday Afternoon Social Club?" Serena asked.

"As a matter of fact, I already heard about it."

"Really? From whom? We just voted on it the day before yesterday."

"My source is Mr. Latimer. We sparred together at Gentleman Jackson's early this morning. I like to keep my form sharp. If I don't line up some new form of employment, I may have to resort to earning my shillings in the ring again."

Serena knew that while he studied at Cambridge, Charles had boxed to earn money to help with his living expenses, but she didn't believe for one minute that he seriously intended to take it up again as a profession.

"Do you intend to leave Sir Roland's employment then?"

"I think I must, once my term in the House of Commons ends. The plan was always that I'd serve as the MP for the borough of Rainsley only until Ambrose-Stone's younger brother came of age to run for the seat. Brosey arranged the job for me as his uncle's secretary while I serve in Parliament. Sir Roland has made it clear that he'd be willing to continue to employ me in that capacity, but the truth is the old gent has less need of a secretary these days than when he took me on nearly four years ago. It's time to look for a position elsewhere."

"Perhaps Sir Roland could recommend you for a position within the diplomatic corps. I'd think he could with his contacts." She almost regretted making the suggestion because a diplomatic posting could send him heaven knew where. Which shouldn't matter, but somehow it did.

"I've thought of that, and Sir Roland has mentioned on more than one occasion that he'd put in a good word for me should my inclinations ever head in that direction. I'm not sure they do, but I'm considering it. Among other things."

"You don't want to run for a different seat in Parliament?"

"I would but for the electioneering involved. It's one thing to temporarily occupy the seat in the pocket of Ambrose-Stone's family. Brosey made it clear that I was his candidate, and probably paid his constituents the usual bribes." He gave her a pointed look. "Although if he did, I've no knowledge of it. The arrangement worked because he never tried to influence my votes in Commons in any way, so whether he bribed the voters or not, my conscience was at ease. However, I couldn't stomach what it would take to win some other seat. I'm ready to move on."

Serena couldn't help thinking it was a shame Charles didn't hold a title and therefore have a hereditary claim to a seat in the House of Lords. Despite their tendency to butt heads at times, she respected his integrity, and England needed men of integrity leading it. Perhaps someday the country would reach a point where there'd be men *and* women in positions of leadership, but that day, she was certain would come well after her lifetime.

"Would you like me to speak to Papa on your behalf? He might have some connections that could be useful as you search for a new position."

"It's kind of you to offer, but don't bother your father about my need for a job. I'm sure he has more important things to occupy him."

"He's never too busy to further the cause of a man with promise." Especially if she were to request it on Charles's behalf. "I'll leave the offer open."

"I appreciate that." He gave her a wry smile. "If I get desperate enough, I may take you up on it."

A short silence sprang up between them. Serena nibbled on a tea cake and watched Charles eat. Watched the way he held a dainty ham-and-butter sandwich in one well-shaped hand, aware that it had been a very long time since she'd found the sight of a man's hands so fascinating. It was hard to imagine his hands bruised and swollen as they must have been when he boxed.

For that matter, it was hard to picture him as a boxer in the ring. He had a lean, athletic build that had more in common with the lithe form of a fencer, rather than the hulking body of a boxer. She tried to envision him in the ring, light and nimble on his feet, a boxer who relied on his brains rather than his brawn, but it was still hard to reconcile the mental image of him sporting the bruises and blood one associated with a typical boxing match with the thoughtful, unassuming man seated across from her.

Whatever injuries he'd endured in those days, they'd left no lasting marks upon him. Not any that she could see, and this made her unaccountably glad. It would be a shame if his nose, straight and patrician as it was, had suffered a hit that left it crooked and mashed in. Or to see gaps in his mouth where teeth had gotten knocked out. Or…

He gave her a strange look and she realized she was staring.

Why was she looking at him like that? He couldn't tell what it meant. Was she affronted or angered because he'd rejected her offer of help? Possibly, though it wasn't like Serena to take offense over something like that.

And now that they were back on good terms, he'd like to keep it that way. Once upon a time, he'd rather enjoyed needling her, but at some point their relationship had become less combative and he found he preferred that even more. To be sure, he still aggravated her at times, but it was mostly unintentional.

Perhaps she'd taken offense to his remark about accepting her father's help if he got desperate. He'd meant it to be funny, but it could have come across as rude. And now he was the one staring as he tried to interpret her expression.

The thought occurred to him he could just be forthright and ask.

"Have I offended you?" he said. "If I have, tell me. Or if I've unwittingly committed some glaring social *faux pas*, enlighten me so I won't do it again."

"I...I've no idea what you're talking about." And suddenly she was the one who looked uncomfortable.

"Oh," he said, more nonplussed than ever. "My mistake, but you seemed to be looking at me rather strangely. I thought...it meant something."

She blushed.

Serena.

Had blushed like a schoolgirl. *What the devil...?*

"No. No, nothing. My thoughts wandered is all." She glanced down at her hands, which held her cup of tea, then back up at him with a look of wry chagrin. "If anyone should apologize, it is I, for a moment of inattention."

"Apology accepted. If that were, in fact, an apology."

A burble of laughter escaped her. "It was. A poorly executed one."

And just like that the moment had passed and they were back on safe, familiar ground. But he still wondered what that blush was about.

He leaned forward and took two more tea sandwiches from the platter on the tea tray. "Fill me in on the latest doings of the Wednesday Afternoon Social Club. Tell me about your new endeavor."

"I thought you said Mr. Latimer already had."

He inspected the filling of a sandwich prior to taking a bite (it appeared to be curried chicken, a favorite of his), but he lifted his gaze long enough to say, "He did, but I'm sure you can tell me more about it. He didn't exactly inundate me with details."

"It's early days yet. There's not a whole lot to tell, other than I have high hopes we can help bring educational opportunities to children. A committee will look at the possibilities and make recommendations."

"You don't sound as enthusiastic about this new venture as you usually do," he remarked. While Latimer had been spare with the details, Serena was typically quite effusive, waxing on and on passionately, sharing more than most people cared to know. Charles never minded, however. He admired her wholehearted devotion to her causes. That she'd confined her description to only a few sentences was, for her, remarkably close-lipped.

"Well, you're mistaken. I think it's an extremely worthwhile endeavor." She leaned forward and studied the tea tray a moment before selecting a small triangle of cheese.

He still wasn't convinced there wasn't something she wasn't saying. He could hear it in her voice, and he found her reply very telling. He hadn't questioned if she thought it worthwhile because, naturally, she would find anything worthy that improved the plight of others. He didn't contradict her though, just nodded and finished another of those delicious chicken sandwiches.

She must have (correctly) interpreted his doubtful silence because she added, "Oh, very well, if you must know, it's not that I'm *not* excited. I backed a different idea, but the votes went as they did, and I accept that."

"You voted. How democratic of you. And very sportsmanlike of you to accept the outcome. But what did you favor?"

She didn't answer right away. "Something you wouldn't approve of," she said at last.

"No surprise there," he said, leaning forward to deposit his now empty plate back onto the tea tray.

"No, it's not, considering you seem to think I need to be wrapped in cotton wool."

He opened his mouth to protest, then closed it again because he didn't wish to argue.

"If you had your way, you'd prefer I never leave the safety of my home. Or, at least, the safety of Mayfair."

He simply couldn't let that pass. "That's not true. But for the love of heaven, at least admit there are times you've recklessly ignored your own safety. If you're going to insist on going to places that put you at risk, at least do so with the proper protection. I've offered to accompany you anywhere you might need an escort capable of deterring trouble, but you have yet to accept my offer."

Her gaze dropped and for some unfathomable reason, seemed to be focused on his hands, which now that he'd finished eating, were resting on the arms of his chair.

He flexed his fingers slightly. "I assure you, I can

deliver a punch with the best of them. You needn't worry for your safety. Not that you do, which is why we're having this discussion, but the point is I'm capable of protecting you should the need arise."

"I never doubted that you were. I don't like to be a bother to others, and expecting you to dance attendance on me as a bodyguard would be a bother. Admit it. It would be supremely annoying."

"It would be...somewhat annoying," he admitted reluctantly, hating to bolster her argument in any way, but unable to lie to her.

"Exactly. But if it eases your mind, I take a footman with me if there's a question of going somewhere unsafe."

"That helps mollify my worries, but it *doesn't*," he emphasized, "eliminate them entirely. I'd be happier if I knew you always traveled with a footman for protection. Two would be even better."

"Two strikes me as a bit ridiculous, but I will take it under advisement."

He was fairly certain this meant she had no intention of traveling with two footmen. "You still haven't enlightened me about what idea you preferred for the Wednesday Afternoon ladies to take up."

"Does it matter? I was outvoted."

This ought to be true, but he wouldn't put it past her to proceed on her own. Her prevarication only deepened his suspicion that, outvoted or not, she didn't intend to abandon whatever it was, and he wanted to know what sort of dangerous circumstances she might face.

"Call it idle curiosity then."

"I prefer to call it meddlesome nosiness."

He inclined his head ever so slightly. "I won't dispute

that characterization." When she didn't say anything, he made a sweeping motion with one arm. "So please, satisfy my meddlesome nosiness."

"Oh, very well." She rolled her eyes, a gesture he'd seen many times before when he'd irritated her. "But only if you promise not to lecture me."

"Promise." He drew an X over his heart with one hand.

"There was an incident last fall. Early one morning, Edwina and I were riding in Hyde Park near the Serpentine." Her brow furrowed and her eyes took on a distant look. "A young girl was pulled from the water. She was dead...and obviously pregnant. It was a deliberate act on her part. She must have left a note because her employer, a merchant's wife, was present after having raised the alarm." She shook her head. "Anyway, I haven't been able to forget it. The tableau of the people gathered around her lifeless body, a mixture of censure and pity on their faces. Girls like that need another option, and that's what I voted for. That we could support these girls through their pregnancy, and help place the child in a home if keeping it was not an option."

"That's a very worthy cause," he said. "But so is the one you're embarking on."

"Oh, I know," she said. But her voice sounded a little hollow. "I just can't shake the feeling of impotence and frustration from that morning."

"Of course not. But you can't save the entire world."

"Townshend! Good to see you again."

They both turned toward the sound of the familiar voice. The tall form of Lord Huntington, Serena's father, stood in the doorway. He wore a hat and carried a leather portfolio, as if he were about to go somewhere. Or perhaps had just returned, although Charles rather thought he would have already given his hat to the butler or a footman in that case.

"I didn't know you were back in London." He grinned. "Sir Roland back in fighting form then?"

"For the moment," Charles replied.

"Glad to hear it," Lord Huntington said. "I hate to see the old rascal laid low by the infirmities of age. Always a bit of a firebrand back in the day. Never suffered fools gladly."

"He still doesn't," Charles said. "He refers to the two secretaries in his employ prior to me as 'those nincompoops.' Although, these days I think his bark is a great deal worse than his bite. I haven't been threatened with dismissal in, oh, six months or more."

Lord Huntington nodded in amusement. "Good old Rollie. Give him my best. The two of you must come to dinner sometime." He turned toward his daughter. "Serena, my dear, can you add two more to the guest list of our next dinner party?"

"Of course, Papa."

"Good enough." Lord Huntington's gaze swung back to Charles. "Hope to see you both then. I'd love to stay and chat, but I have an appointment at Whitehall." He dipped his head in farewell and disappeared from the doorway, only to reappear a few seconds later.

"Do you need a ride anywhere, Townshend? Be happy to drop you off if you do."

"I appreciate that, sir. I could, actually, if it's not too much trouble. I have a meeting in an hour."

"Not at all. Not at all. Come along and we'll get you where you need to be."

Charles rose and turned to Serena. "Thank you for the refreshments. I didn't mean to depart quite so abruptly, but your father's offer is too generous to pass up. Riding in a private carriage is by far preferable to taking a hackney."

"I understand. Riding in comfort triumphs the pleasure of my company." When he started to protest, she brushed this aside with a careless wave of one hand. "I'm teasing. Don't give it another thought."

But, of course, he would give it another thought. Because thoughts of Serena were never far from his mind.

It was a state he'd lived with for some time now.

Arriving at White's, Charles headed to the coffee room to kill some time until his appointment with Ambrose-Stone's younger brother, Ronald Dixon. He thought it too early in the day for a whisky or a brandy, though there were gentlemen present who exhibited no such inhibition. Instead, he ordered a cup of tea and settled into a chair to drink it and read the *Times*.

Young Dixon arrived thirty minutes late, and offered no apology for his tardiness. This was no surprise. Previous encounters with the young man had shown him to hold an unjustifiably high opinion of himself and a tendency toward snobbishness. Charles found him much less likable than his older brother and far more vapid. Ambrose-Stone was nobody's fool, but Charles couldn't say the same for his brother.

He hoped Brosey intended to keep a modicum of control over Dixon's representation of the seat the family controlled in the House of Commons. He doubted the young man would show much inclination to act in the interests of his constituents without his older brother insisting he do so.

The reason they were meeting today was that Ambrose-Stone had requested Charles's help in preparing Dixon for taking over the seat prior to the general election. But an hour later, during which young Dixon's attention was constantly drawn away by new arrivals to the coffee room, Charles decided to call it a day. He'd arrange to meet Dixon again, perhaps at the man's suite of rooms at the Albany, one of London's hotels that offered living space to London's well-to-do bachelors. With fewer distractions, maybe he could impart some information about the borough Dixon would represent.

Hungry now, Charles decided to order lunch in the club's dining room. Entering it, he spied the Earl of Norwood and his brother-in-law, Phillip Hurst, and ambled over to their table to offer his greetings.

"Join us, Townshend," Phillip Hurst said. "I need the presence of another bachelor. Now that Norwood here is happily married to my sister, he's joined the ranks of those married men who feel compelled to urge those of us who aren't to hasten our own journeys toward wedded bliss."

Norwood grinned as Charles took a seat at the table. "He's exaggerating. I merely urged him to consider attending a ball my oldest sister is hosting. And I simply pointed out that his social life is largely centered around male-dominated bastions such as White's, where he could hardly hope to meet an eligible young lady, *and* I will add that I only offered this observation when he remarked that marriage seemed to agree with me."

"He's right, Hurst. If you do, er, intend to journey to a state of wedded bliss, you've got to attend the social functions where young ladies gather." Charles turned to Norwood. "And Hurst is right. Marriage does seem to agree with you."

Phillip Hurst's bluestocking sister and Norwood had been brought together when one of the earl's political rivals had a fake betrothal announcement published in the newspaper. What had started as a temporary engagement to squelch a potential scandal, had ended in marriage nearly a year ago. And despite the unorthodox way their union came about, no one would dispute that the earl was hopelessly besotted by his wife, and she equally so with him.

"Will you be attending Libby's ball?" Norwood asked. "Charlotte mentioned you were on the guest list."

Charles didn't answer right away, surprised by the question, since he was only infrequently invited to such a grand social function as a ball. His social calendar was most often filled with events he attended with Sir Roland, and those were usually gatherings with a political focus: dinner parties or salons hosted by members of the House of Lords, with the occasional invitation to a rout or a soirée. "To be honest, I haven't had a chance to go through all of my correspondence since returning to London, but as long as there's nothing Sir Roland wishes me to attend with him that night, I expect you'll see me there."

It was on the tip of his tongue to ask if Serena planned to attend. She was close friends with Norwood and his wife and almost certainly would receive an invitation. He didn't, though, because he didn't want to reinforce what he knew the earl already suspected—that he harbored a secret *tendre* for her.

"It's not until next week, so you have time to reply.

I know Libby always fusses about getting enough gentlemen to attend so that the ladies will have plenty of dance partners."

"Precisely why you won't catch me there," Hurst stated. "Dancing is not my strong suit."

"Then expect a visit from Charlotte, who is determined to convince you otherwise," Norwood said with a rueful smile. "Actually, she wanted me to convince you otherwise, but clearly I've failed."

A waiter arrived to take Charles's lunch order and the talk turned to politics. There was to be a gathering in France that fall attended by the four allied powers—England, Prussia, Austria, and Russia—which had fought against Napoleon's armies. Talks would focus on the potential withdrawal of those countries' armies from France, as well as a renegotiation of reparations on the part of France.

"If you have an interest in going as the attaché to one of England's diplomats, I could put in a good word for you," Norwood offered. "It would really be a glorified secretarial job, but it could potentially lead to a more important position."

"How soon would you need to know?" Charles asked. "I'm not yet sure where I'd like to land once my time as an MP is finished. And if Sir Roland wants a new secretary, I'll stay on and train the man, although I'm hoping my departure from his service will prompt Sir Roland into a complete retirement. He says otherwise, but I'm working on him."

"I'd say sooner rather than later, as there are those already vying for the assignments. Even so, if you can let me know within the next month or two, your chances at landing a spot would be all but certain. The plummiest placements will go fast though."

"Thank you," Charles said. "I'll give it serious consideration."

"You couldn't pay me enough to go," Phillip Hurst remarked. "Gad. Those diplomatic missions consist of talking, talking, and more talking for days on end. I can't imagine a more tedious way to spend time. Not to mention you'd be subject to lots of dinners featuring that French style of cooking I can't abide. Too much reliance on fancy sauces. Give me a good unadorned beef steak and potatoes any day." He waved a forkful of roast beef in the air to emphasize his point.

"That roast beef is drenched in gravy. Hardly what one could call unadorned," Norwood said.

"Fair enough," Hurst said, once he swallowed his food. "But what's the basis of the gravy? The drippings from the meat, therefore it's really just an extension of the meat with a few ingredients added. Not a lot of cream and butter and fancy spices that just serve to obscure the true taste of the food you're eating. Butter and cream have their place, to be sure, but not covering up the taste of my meat and vegetables."

"You give much more consideration to food than I do." Charles turned his attention to his newly arrived plate, where a pair of thick pork chops rested in the center surrounded by steaming mashed potatoes.

Hurst shrugged. "I like to eat, but the experience is far more pleasurable when I *like* what I eat."

"You eat more than any other slim man I know," his brother-in-law remarked. "How you do it is a mystery to me."

Hurst grinned. "It's a mystery to me as well. But I'm not complaining."

Lunch passed pleasantly before Charles, mindful of his duties for Sir Roland, took his leave of the other two gentlemen.

Chapter Three

～

"I don't think this neighborhood looks promising." Charles frowned as he looked out the window of the hackney cab.

Serena shared his reservations but was reluctant to give voice to them. She'd expected the area to be run-down, which was why they'd traveled here in a hackney rather than the fine carriage her father owned. A hackney would be less conspicuous. "Let's wait until we actually see the block where the building is located," she said, injecting far more optimism into her voice than she felt.

This was the third property they'd visited in her quest to find a potential property to lease to house girls who found themselves pregnant outside of marriage. A sense of restlessness had gripped Serena ever since she'd told Charles about witnessing the recovery of the body of the drowned maid from the Serpentine.

She couldn't shake the feeling that even if the Wednesday Afternoon Social Club had chosen a different project to focus on, she needed to start exploring what could be done to help girls like that maid—pregnant, unwed, and so desperate they resorted to such a solution to deal with their situation. She intended to use a sum she'd inherited from a spinster cousin on her father's side to fund the endeavor. Her plans were still evolving, but finding a building seemed the logical first step.

The first two they'd looked at had needed far more rehabilitation than her budget could support, although their locations had been less shabby than this one.

Shabby was a kind descriptor for this area. The brick exteriors were stained black with grime, shutters were missing or hanging askew as they framed small, dirty windows. An air of poverty and neglect hung over everything—and everyone—they passed. It broke her heart.

She'd hoped the environs might improve at some point, but it didn't look as if this would be the case. The land agent had described this property as "sound as a whistle, a great bargain at the price." Even if it turned out to be in habitable shape, she couldn't picture it as a potential haven for pregnant girls awaiting the birth of their babies.

"You can't seriously be thinking of bringing women and their families here," Charles said, echoing her thoughts. Although he was still under the impression it was for the war widows, since she hadn't enlightened him about her true purpose. True, she hadn't actually *said* they were scouting another place for the war widows, but naturally he would assume that's what they were doing. Once her plans were further along she'd correct his misapprehension.

"We've come this far. I'd still like to see it," she said.

He turned away from the window and gave her a steady look. "If that's what you want."

"I'm not disagreeing with you. It will probably turn out to be exactly what we expect, but it's been offered at a very reasonable rate, so I feel it's worth a look even if it ultimately disappoints."

"I'm just not very optimistic," he said.

"Really? I couldn't tell by your crossed arms and frowning face as you looked out the window," she teased.

One side of his mouth quirked up. "As long as I'm not too easy to read." He uncrossed his arms and rested one across the seat back. "Is this better?"

"You're now the picture of a gentleman at leisure," Serena said, thinking he looked very appealing. If they hadn't been so respectably seated across from each other with a footman there to lend countenance and an extra measure of brawn, she might have been tempted to nestle her head against his shoulder.

Edwina and Charlotte would be encouraged by the direction of her thoughts. Thoughts that made her restless and fidgety as her body thrummed with a sudden heightened awareness that Charles was a damnably attractive man. To cover her response, she pulled the land agent's note from her reticule and pretended to study it.

Her mind, however, was firmly fixed on the man across from her. His recent mention of his mother's hopes that something would develop between him and Miss Lewis had given rise to a certain curiosity regarding his love life. Had Charles ever seriously courted a girl? As long as she'd known him, he'd never mentioned that he was seeing anyone. His main interests seemed to be serving in the House of Commons and his work for Sir Roland.

And keeping an eye on her doings. For some reason, he'd taken that duty upon himself, and oddly enough, she found his concern less...maddening as time went on.

The hackney stopped and Charles turned to look out the window again. "What was the house number?" he asked.

"Number forty-three," she supplied.

"Then it looks like we've arrived," he said.

The footman, who'd been dozing in his seat, stirred and blinked his eyes a few times. "I'll get the door, my lady." He clambered out of the hackney and lowered the step, extending a hand to help Serena out.

Climbing down after her, Charles instructed the driver to wait for them. The man glanced around uncertainly, but when Charles offered him a few coins, he gave a reluctant nod of agreement.

Number 43 looked just as faded as the rest of the buildings on the block. Rusted wrought iron railings framed the steps leading to the front door. Serena pulled the key supplied by the land agent from her reticule, inserted it into the lock, and after a few minutes of fiddling with it, managed to unlock it and open the door.

Charles told the footman to stay by the entrance. At Serena's questioning glance, he said, "It's just a precaution. We are attracting the curiosity of the onlookers, some of whom might be tempted to seize an opportunity to lighten our pockets. I imagine they don't get many swells like us visiting the neighborhood. Also, it's added insurance our driver won't abandon us."

She nodded and they proceeded to tour the premises. The house wasn't quite as sound as the land agent had led her to believe. Water had obviously leaked in through several of the poorly fitted windows, and the upper floors sagged as if some of the support beams needed shoring up.

They saved the yard off the back for last. In Serena's opinion, this was the property's best feature, a private area where the occupants could take some fresh air. Separated from the neighboring yards by brick walls, it was small and untidy, but in the summer, at least, it would be a welcome oasis amidst the drab architecture of the environs. Dead plants—weeds she supposed—and bushes just beginning to bud crowded the space. Some green shoots were poking through the litter of last year's growth.

A lone tree stood in the back corner like a sentry. At its base, partially obscured by the branches of a bush, she noticed what appeared to be a pile of rags tucked among the tree roots and went over to inspect it.

"Oh!" she gasped, horrified to realize the pile of rags was in fact a sleeping child. An old moth-eaten wool blanket was wrapped around the curled form, but to her relief the blanket rose and fell with the child's breathing. Only a mop of tangled, dirty curls was visible above one edge of the blanket.

"Charles." She spoke in a low voice so as not to startle the child awake. She waved one hand urgently to motion him over to her. Kneeling down, she gently drew back the blanket to reveal a thin face. A little boy, she thought, since the curly hair didn't quite reach his shoulders.

"Poor thing must be exhausted," she whispered as Charles knelt beside her. "Thank heavens the weather is mild today, but we can't leave him here. We'll have to determine who he belongs to and take him back home."

"A child sleeping in the yard of an abandoned building may not belong to anyone," Charles said. He shrugged out of his jacket and laid it over the raggedy blanket. "First things first. You stay with him. I'll go purchase some food, since those thin cheeks indicate he or she doesn't get regular meals. I'll also inquire if anyone knows anything about the child. If he wakes up, keep him here, even if you have to restrain him to do so. If he's been on his own any length of time, his instinct may be to bolt in the presence of a stranger. Although, hopefully the promise of food will be inducement enough for him to remain with you."

"Of course," Serena said. "So you don't think he's merely wandered away from home for a bit of play and fallen asleep here?"

"Certainly that's possible. Children do that." He studied the sleeping boy a moment. "I don't know. Maybe it's that raggedy blanket he's drawn around himself, but I don't think that's the case here."

After he left, she was tempted to reach out and brush a hand across the child's curls, but she didn't want to risk waking him.

She contented herself with studying the child's skin, pale except where it was smudged with dirt, the delicately winged brows, the twin fans of dusky lashes, the rosy lips, the narrow pointed chin. He would probably look quite cherubic when he was cleaned up.

The child continued to sleep and she continued to watch until Charles returned. He'd bought some buns and a meat pie. Even though the pie was wrapped in brown paper, she could identify it by the smell wafting from it. He knelt beside her and set the food on the grass beside the child.

"Still sleeping, eh?"

He'd no sooner asked the question than the child's nose wiggled—perhaps in response to the rich smell of the meat and vegetables—and his eyes fluttered open. Upon seeing them, those eyes widened. He sat up, threw off Charles's jacket and scooted away, halting only when he spotted the food, whereupon his gaze flitted uncertainly from them to the food and back again.

"Go ahead," Serena prompted. "It's for you." The child remained frozen in place, so Serena reached out and unwrapped the meat pie, placing it beside the child. It was hard to guess his age, since malnutrition often inhibited a child's growth making them seem younger than their actual age. He *looked* to be seven or eight, but it was possible that he was a few years older than that.

Large gray eyes regarded them warily, but after a few seconds, hunger won out because the child snatched up the meat pie in dirty hands and began eating, biting into the crust, oblivious to the dark gravy running down his chin.

"Did you discover anything about the child's identity?" Serena asked in a low voice.

"Yes and no. I received conflicting stories, so it's a question of who told me the truth." He also spoke in a quiet voice meant for Serena's ears only. For a moment, his jaw tightened and his mouth pressed into a straight line. "The publican at the establishment where I bought the food said he's a wayward child and prone to running away from home. But if the woman I spoke with is to be believed, he's lived on the street for the past couple of months since the death of his guardian." He gave her a meaningful look. "From her I gathered there are certain parties with an interest in sheltering him, but only if he serves their own nefarious purposes."

Serena wasn't sure what "nefarious purposes" he meant, but whether he spoke of petty crime or, worse, child prostitution, she had no intention of leaving the boy to that sort of fate.

"We can't let that happen," she said. "We can take him with us and figure out what to do later."

At her words, the child looked up from his half-eaten pie. He didn't say anything, just studied them with a solemn gaze, still wary and uncertain. Cautious, rather than truly frightened. After a moment, he went back to devouring his food.

"What's your name?" she asked the boy. "My name is Serena."

Once more, he turned his attention away from his food and studied them with a grave expression. Those gray eyes of his framed by long, dark lashes were such a striking feature in his face. Dirty and disheveled as he was, it was obvious he was a very handsome child.

"Jem," he said at last.

"Just Jem?" she prompted.

He blinked and his eyebrows twitched, as if he were uncertain what she meant.

"My full name," she continued, hoping to clear up his confusion, "is Serena Wynter. Wynter is my last name. Do you have a last name?"

Jem shook his head and she glanced at Charles, who was studying the boy with an intent look. Charles knelt down, resting one knee on the ground. "Your last name isn't Murphy, is it?"

Jem frowned in confusion and shook his head. Charles studied him a moment longer, but he seemed satisfied with the boy's answer, and didn't, as Serena had expected, ask him anything else. The name Murphy must have come up when he inquired about the child.

"Well, it's really not important," she said. "Jem is a very nice name all on its own."

Before she could continue in this *let's-get-acquainted* vein, Charles spoke up. "I expect the driver is getting restless. He asked me how much longer we'd be. I assured him not too much longer, and that he'd be well compensated for his time. Still we shouldn't press his patience too far."

"Ah, of course," she replied. They should leave, but would the child willingly come with them after being in their company for such a short time? From the boy's perspective, he shouldn't trust them, but she hoped he would, that he understood they only wished to help him.

"Jem, we'd like you to come with us. This is Mr. Townshend, and he was told that you don't have anywhere to live. Is that true?"

"I just live around. Here and there," Jem said. He'd finished the meat pie and had already eaten one of the buns. He looked around. "I like this place."

"Yes, I imagine you might," she agreed. The yard, surrounded by the brick wall and with its tangle of plants probably did give him a sense of safety. "Do you ever go inside?" She indicated the house she and Charles had toured.

He shook his head.

"But surely you can't sleep outside when it's cold," she said, quite appalled by the thought.

"Old Croaker lets me sleep in the stables them nights," Jem said.

"I'm very glad to hear that," Serena said. "But if you're willing to come with me and Mr. Townshend, you could stay with me for a bit and sleep in a bed and have plenty of food. We'd like to help you find a real home. Will you let us do that?"

Posing it as if he had a choice might be a mistake, because even if he said no, there was no way she was leaving him here.

The boy took a bite of his bun and seemed to mull this over as he chewed. He swallowed and said, "If I had a real home, could I have a kitten?"

"I'm sure we could find you a home where you could have a kitten and a mother and father. Would you like that?"

"I'd like the kitten." He wiped his mouth with the back of his sleeve. "I never had one. Never had a mum or dad neither."

Obviously, he'd had parents, although it was possible he had no memory of them. For children like Jem there were any number of reasons he'd never known them. He might have been orphaned. Or given away as a baby if his parents lacked the money to care for him. His mother could have died, leaving his father unable to care for an infant...his father could have abandoned his mother prior to his birth...his family history was anyone's guess.

One thing she did know. She wished she could just gather him up and hug him right then.

"Then I promise to make sure you'll have a kitten. Perhaps even a pair of kittens, if you'd like."

Again, he took his time answering, and Serena waited while he considered her offer. There was a certain gravity in his manner that seemed oddly adultlike for a child.

The boy's gaze turned to Charles. "I'll come with you," he said.

It struck Serena as a little odd that the boy had directed

his acquiescence toward Charles, who'd hardly spoken this whole time, but she wasn't one to argue with a *yes*.

Jem clutched the raggedy blanket around his shoulders with one hand and carried the remaining bun with his other as they made their way back through the house, collected the footman who'd remained on guard duty this whole time, and then Serena made sure to lock the door behind them. Charles helped her and the boy into the hackney, after which Joseph, the footman, raised the step, and once he'd secured the door, they set off.

To Serena's disappointment, Jem curled against Charles and promptly fell asleep, still clutching the bun in his dirty hand. She'd pictured herself cuddling with the child on the way home, helping him feel wanted and secure.

She'd purposely omitted mentioning to Jem that one of the first things she intended to do upon returning to her house was to give him a bath and clean him up, fearing that mention of a bath might dissuade a child who clearly didn't wash often. She wondered what Charles thought of such a dirty little thing pressed up against him. He didn't look as if he minded. He had one arm wrapped around the boy to keep him secure on the seat while he slept.

"I'm surprised that you haven't quizzed me yet on what else I found out about the boy's background, given that he's sound asleep," Charles said. Jem was softly snoring now, tiny puffs of air.

"I was going to ask about it when we got back to my home, but since he's asleep, we can talk now. One thing about him that struck me is that though he speaks with the accent of the working class, his grammar could pass muster in Mayfair. Did you notice that?"

"I did. I think the answer must lie with the background

of the person who was raising him, an older female by the name of Old Mam according to the woman I spoke with. She told me Old Mam and Jem moved to this neighborhood three years ago, that Jem and his guardian weren't blood relations, but that she seemed to treat the boy kindly. She described Old Mam as standoffish and hoity-toity, that she seemed to think she was better than other folk because she could read and write a little. But if she had some education that probably explains the boy's grasp of correct English."

"That's not much information to go on," Serena mused. "And how tragic that there was no one who wished to take care of him when Old Mam died."

"Jem's origins are murky, as is so often the case with these children. On the other hand, the publican from whom I bought the food claimed Jem's mother was a woman named Mrs. Murphy. That's why I quizzed the boy about the name Murphy."

"I assumed you had your reasons."

"After I bought the food, the woman I spoke with followed me out and under the pretense of handing me something I'd dropped, which was actually only a piece of litter she'd picked up from the ground, informed me the publican was lying, that Mrs. Murphy runs a ring of child criminals. The woman seemed nervous, and I suspect she feared retaliation if he were to find out that she tipped me to the truth. That, plus Jem's disavowal of the name Murphy, makes me think she's more credible than the publican. But either way, I'm not sure which was worse for the child—to be forced to commit crimes or to have to fend for himself on the street."

"Neither is a choice any child should have to face,"

Serena said fiercely. "Though it's not uncommon that they have to. I tend to agree with your conclusion of who is more likely telling us the truth. Which makes deciding what to do about Jem a bit easier. I would have been hesitant to return him to a parent who neglected him to the point of letting him sleep in the open. Certainly, Jem didn't indicate he had any family ties when we asked him."

"What do you plan to do with the boy?"

"My immediate plans are to clean him up and feed him. I suppose I'll keep him with me for a few days while I figure out what would be best for him. I'm sure Papa won't mind. He's remarkably tolerant of my whims. I expect I could find a home for Jem with one of the tenant families that lives on my father's properties."

"One with a kitten or two," Charles said.

She laughed. "Of course. I promised."

Later, after Jem had been bathed by a pair of maids, he was dressed in one of Lord Huntington's shirts that had been hastily altered to function as a nightshirt for the boy. The sleeves had been shortened, but the garment hung down past his knees, making him look even more cherubic, like a pink-cheeked young angel in a white robe. Serena and Charles kept him company while he ate an early dinner. After Jem finished his meal, Charles tried to take his leave and let Serena get the child settled for the night. But Jem, who'd been remarkably sanguine about everything they'd asked of him so far, became so upset at the thought of Charles leaving, that Serena had urged him to stay a bit longer.

"At least until he's gone to sleep," she said.

Charles agreed to stay, and the next thing he knew, he

was carrying the boy upstairs as he followed Serena to the room that had been prepared for the child.

When he lowered Jem to the mattress of the bed, the boy's eyes rounded with wonder. He ran a hand over the coverlet and gingerly poked at the mattress and the pillows, declaring them softer than a bunny's belly. Charles and Serena shared a smile at the boy's unique comparison.

"Does a ghost live in there?" Jem asked, pointing to the wardrobe.

"Oh, no," Serena assured him. "There are no ghosts anywhere in this house."

Despite this reassurance, Jem frowned and looked doubtful, so Serena opened the doors of the wardrobe and invited him to inspect the interior. He scooted off the bed and proceeded to give the wardrobe a thorough going-over. Next he asked to look into each individual drawer in a tall chest of drawers. (Charles obligingly lifted him up so that he could look into the topmost ones.) Jem repeated the process with the drawers in the nightstand and the writing table. He finished by checking under the bed and behind the draperies. Finally satisfied that the room harbored no ghosts, he clambered back up into the bed.

"Would you like me to read you a story?" Serena said. Jem nodded, and she pulled a book of nursery rhymes off the nightstand. It looked new, and Charles wondered if she'd sent one of the servants out to purchase it after they'd returned with the boy.

She glanced at a chair in the corner.

"I can move that closer to the bed, if you like," Charles offered, remembering his own narrow childhood bed and how his mother sat in a worn armchair pulled right beside the headboard as she read to him at night. In those days, before her marriage to his stepfather, she'd been employed as a companion to an elderly widow. Charles looked back on that time with a certain fondness, despite the genteel shabbiness of their lives back then.

"Actually, if it's all right with Jem, I'll just settle in beside him on the bed."

Jem nodded his agreement and patted a spot on the counterpane. An almost shy smile of pleasure curved Serena's lips as she slipped off her shoes and climbed up beside him.

Charles had never seen that expression on her face before...she looked carefree and girlish, her cheeks pink with pleasure, a few tendrils of hair falling loose to frame her face.

He was particularly fascinated by one tendril that curled softly along one side of her neck, ending right at the base of her throat.

He swallowed, keenly aware that seeing Serena in this setting, almost as if the three of them were a family, represented the deepest desires of his heart.

Hopeless desires in which the two of them had a life together.

Of course, there was no *them*, nor would there ever be. But if there were a *them*, he imagined it would be a lot like this—completely ordinary and quite wonderful.

"You too," Jem said, smiling and patting a place on his unoccupied side.

"No," he protested. "It wouldn't be proper. I'll watch from here."

"It's fine, Charles. I trust you'll behave as a perfect gentleman, and no one will ever know. Surely we can allow Jem this request."

Two pairs of gray eyes regarded him steadily—Jem's beseechingly, while Serena's gaze had a challenging light to it. *Don't be such a prude, Charles,* it seemed to say.

He still felt that he really oughtn't, that as innocent as it was, it was still improper. But then again, he'd already crossed the bounds of propriety by even coming up to the bedroom with them, so did pushing past them a bit further even matter?

Maybe not for Serena's chastity, because there were some lines he simply *would not cross*. His peace of mind, on the other hand, was definitely in jeopardy.

He wavered a moment, but the truth was he'd be as disappointed as anyone if he didn't say yes.

So he nodded and was rewarded with beaming smiles from the pair of them.

Was he being unwise? Most probably. Where Serena was concerned it wasn't prudent to allow himself to ... imagine the possibilities. The chasm between them was too great, which he'd do well to remember.

"Who am I to say no when clearly the majority says yes?" he asked as he joined them on the bed. He settled in next to Jem, careful to keep his legs angled so that his booted feet hung over the side.

He could smell the scent of lemon soap that clung to the little boy now that the dirt had been scrubbed away. The odor of jasmine teased his nose too. Serena's cologne. He'd smelled it earlier in the carriage, but it was stronger now that they sat so close together with only one small boy between them.

Serena smiled at him over the boy's curls, then she opened the book of nursery rhymes and began to read. Jem fell asleep before even ten minutes had passed, his head resting against Serena's side, one of his hands tucked around Charles's elbow.

Serena stopped reading and studied the sleeping child for a few moments. A fond smile softened her face and Charles took the opportunity to study her, wishing he had the right to push back an unruly tendril just so he could feel the soft skin of her cheek beneath his fingertips.

She looked more content and relaxed than he'd ever seen her. Usually she radiated with energy and an endless drive to get things done, to plow forward, meeting and overcoming any obstacles that dared to block her path. Even when she wasn't physically moving she gave off a sense of being in motion, her expressive face betraying the liveliness of her mind.

She looked up and caught him staring. He could feel the heat of embarrassment creep up his neck, because he could only hope the longing he felt for her hadn't shown on his face. That, unexpectedly caught in an unguarded moment, he'd managed to conceal his true feelings before she could read them in his eyes. Realizing he was holding his breath, he let out a slow exhale.

For a second an odd expression flickered across her face, but then she smiled and said, "Somehow I expected getting him to bed would be a more difficult process. That's the impression I get from Grace at any rate."

Relief flooded through him. If Serena had noticed anything, she'd probably have said so. "The Duchess of Rochester puts her children to bed?"

"Don't look so shocked. Like me, Grace can be unconventional. To be sure, she employs nursemaids, but she doesn't consign her children to the nursery, only to interact with them infrequently."

"How admirable, if rather unduchesslike of her."

She nodded absently. "He's such a handsome child. I wonder who his parents are. Or were. Was he abandoned or orphaned? And how did he come to be in the care of Old Mam?"

"I doubt we'll ever know, but I can make further inquiries. In case the truth isn't what we believe it to be. I'll see to it, if you want. Poke around a bit more. Taking a closer look at this Mrs. Murphy ought to either confirm the publican's story or reveal him for a liar. Plus I can try to find someone who might know more about Old Mam and why she was raising him."

"That would be fine," she said slowly. She unwound Jem's curl from her finger and ran her hand over his hair before she carefully moved so that his head came to rest on one of the bed's plump pillows. In the process, Jem's hand slipped from around Charles's arm.

She placed the book of nursery rhymes back on the nightstand before gingerly climbing off the bed. She slipped her shoes on.

Charles eased himself to the edge of the bed, trying not to jostle it too much, although the child was sleeping so soundly he didn't think it would matter if he did.

"I'll leave the door open in case he wakens. The light from the candles in the hallway will keep it from being too dark for him to identify where he is." She bent down to place a quick kiss on Jem's cheek.

"Let's hope if he does wake, he doesn't imagine a ghost has wandered into the room," he joked.

She chuckled softly, then asked, "Would you like to stay to dinner? Or do you have plans for the evening?"

They were in the hallway now.

"I don't want to be an imposition," he said, joining her on the main staircase. "You don't have to feed me."

"I believe I'm the one doing the imposing, running you hither and yon this afternoon. It was good of you to stay with Jem this evening and help put him to bed." She gave him a sidelong glance. "He seems to have formed quite an attachment to you."

Charles shrugged this off. "He's been through a lot of change today. More than he probably realizes yet."

They'd reached the foyer, and Serena turned to him. "You never really answered my question. *Will* you stay to dinner?" She lightly touched his arm. "Please say yes. I'd like the company."

That gesture and her request set off a host of reactions. His pulse speeded up, every nerve in his body seemed to light up at her simple touch. Alarm bells jangled in his mind. For the preservation of his equilibrium, it was time to go.

"It will give us an opportunity to further discuss what should be done about Jem." She smiled, and the look in her eyes urged him to stay.

"Yes," he said.

Clearly his heart was overruling his mind, but he seemed incapable of flipping that around.

Oh, well.

In for a penny, in for a pound.

Chapter Four

*M*ay I have a moment of your time, sir?" Charles asked. He stood in the doorway of his employer's office. "I have a favor to ask."

Sir Roland looked up from the book he was reading, slipped a leather bookmark at the current page, and closed it. He pulled off his reading spectacles, folded them, and set them to the side. Putting his elbows upon his desk, he leaned forward, giving Charles his signature look, the one where he tried to divine the nature of a person's business before it was even stated. Sir Roland was devilishly good at reading people, which was why he'd had such a stellar career in the diplomatic corps.

"I suspect you wish to take the rest of the morning off to deal with some private business. In which case, the answer is yes, although I confess I'm curious as to the particular nature of your business because I know how loath you are to make such a request." He held up one hand, as if to forestall any reply Charles cared to make to that statement. "Not that you need feel obligated to satisfy my curiosity. I dislike nosiness on principle, even though I experience it myself now and again." His mouth twisted into a wry smile and he added, "Whetted no doubt, by the recent arrival of a footman wearing the maroon-and-gold livery of the Huntington household. Unless I'm reading the tea leaves all wrong?"

Sir Roland had never explicitly asked Charles about the nature of his relationship with Serena, though he had indulged in some gentle probing. Charles wasn't sure exactly what the old gentleman thought he saw in the tea leaves, but he had already intended to share the reason for his request to take the morning off.

"I'm sorry, sir, to have to ask, but I've been summoned to the Huntingtons'. During my free afternoon yesterday I was accompanying Lady Serena on an errand when we came across a child living on the streets. She brought the child back to her home, and..." He decided to gloss over the extent of his involvement in settling Jem in at the Huntingtons'. "For some reason, the boy exhibits a strong attachment to me. He's been asking after me this morning, and he's become quite agitated at my absence, even though she's explained to him that I don't live there, so naturally I wouldn't be present at breakfast this morning. Her note says she's unable to calm the boy's fears and she's requested that I come over and attempt to do so."

"And so you must," Sir Roland said. "How well I remember the misery of my first months at Harrow away from my family. I can only imagine what the lad feels. As horrific as life can be for children like him, it *is* what they're familiar with. If he finds your presence soothing, then you must calm the child. Take as long as you need. The rest of the day, in fact. Take it off. That's an order."

"But I thought you wanted your reply to Lord Peevey to go out this morning posthaste. I've only just begun the final copy, but I could finish this afternoon. I don't want to neglect my work for you. Merely delay it a bit."

"Pffft. My reply to Peevey can wait, and we both know it. I like to *feel* I possess some measure of importance, but we both know my days of true relevance are behind me. I can pretend otherwise, but..." He shrugged. "Now off with you. And give Lady Serena my best."

"I will. Thank you, sir."

The exchange bolstered Charles's opinion that Sir Roland had little need to employ a secretary, that he continued to do so more for Charles's sake than his own. After all, members of the House of Commons either had to have a source of income or be independently wealthy. Or have the financial support of their families, as in the case of Ronald Dixon, the man slated to serve in the seat Charles currently held.

He felt a rush of affection for the old gent. He knew the time had come for him to look elsewhere for a living, but he'd miss the man when he left his employ for good. The gruff exterior Sir Roland presented to most of the world hid a kind heart.

Arriving at the Huntington residence, Charles was ushered to the doorway of the sitting room where he stood in surprise for a moment as he surveyed the state of disarray that reigned therein. Wooden alphabet blocks were scattered across the floor, as were several of the pillows that usually resided on the sofas and armchairs. A blanket was draped over the backs of four wooden chairs to form a droopy-roofed tent of sorts. Charles could see a pair of tasseled pillows peeking from beneath the structure.

There was, however, no sign of Serena or Jem.

"Good morning?" he said, stepping into the room. He accidentally kicked one of the alphabet blocks, sending it skittering across the Aubusson carpet.

"Oh, Charles." Serena's voice, sounding slightly muffled, seemed to be coming from within the blanket tent. "You've arrived."

And then, to his shocked delight, a pair of stocking-clad feet emerged from the tent opening, followed by a vision of a very shapely backside as Serena crawled backward from the tent. He hastened over to help her to her feet and a familiar jolt of awareness raced through him when their hands touched. For a moment their gazes locked, and as a knowing expression crept into her eyes, he mentally kicked himself for doing such a poor job of hiding his feelings.

Her fingers tightened their grip on his hand, preventing him from letting go of her own. As she studied his face, a slow smile formed on her own. He felt his cheeks grow hot and he stepped back abruptly, stumbling backward when his foot came down on one of the wooden blocks.

"Charles," she gasped, holding tight to his hand when it became clear he was about to tumble down on his backside. "Careful."

With her help, he managed to regain his balance, but only just. His backward momentum as he fought to regain his footing combined with Serena's efforts to pull him toward her had somehow ended in the two of them colliding, though it happened so fast he wasn't sure whether he'd pulled her into him, or vice versa.

Either way, that brief contact between their bodies seemed to have set every one of his nerves alight with heightened awareness. So while he managed to stay upright, his emotions were now entirely off-kilter.

"Thank you," he said, twisting to glance backward so he might safely step away, and avoid a repeat performance. She let go of his hand and he moved to put a more proper distance between them. He gestured to the numerous blocks scattered about. "You saved me from a painful landing."

"It was the least I could do, considering the mess Jem and I have created in here makes navigating the room a bit hazardous."

"You're being too kind about my clumsiness." He looked around for Jem, having momentarily forgotten the whole reason for his visit. He spotted the boy at the entrance to the tent, a wide grin on his face. He'd evidently not only enjoyed Charles's bumbling performance, but also had gotten over whatever distress he'd experienced earlier in the morning. Not too surprising, given that the disheveled state of the room was due to it being turned entirely over to play.

Charles grinned back at the boy. "I suppose you think I looked pretty funny."

The boy's eyes sparkled as he nodded, before ducking back into the tent.

"Yes, well, I don't blame you for finding it amusing." Turning to Serena, he murmured, "It appears the crisis is over."

"For the moment," she replied in a low voice. "It comes

and goes. As you can see, I tried a number of ways to distract him, but nothing lasts for very long."

Charles felt the need for a distraction himself. Although he'd brought a measure of control to his unruly emotions, he was still far too aware of Serena's stocking-clad feet, even as he kept his gaze fixed anywhere but on them. It implied an intimacy between them that shouldn't exist.

Couldn't exist.

Fortunately, just then Jem's head reemerged through the tent opening and he scampered over to Charles, holding out what appeared to be a worn, stuffed mohair rabbit. It had the condition of a much-loved toy, and Charles wondered if it had originally belonged to Serena. Whatever its origins, Jem seemed to have adopted it as his own, because after briefly holding it up for Charles's inspection, he hugged it tightly to his chest, as children do with their favorite toys.

"Does he have a name?" Charles asked, indicating the rabbit.

"Sir Rabbit," Jem said. "He used to belong to Lady Sera, but now he's mine."

"Lady Sera?" Charles asked, directing an inquiring glance at Serena.

"I've acquired a nickname," she said, answering his unvoiced question. "As has Papa, who's become Lord Hunt. Menken has been dubbed Menks, which to the surprise of the staff, he doesn't seem to mind at all. Although, I doubt anyone else will have the temerity to address him thusly."

"No, I shouldn't imagine they will," Charles agreed. He'd never seen the butler display anything but the utmost dignity.

"In case you're wondering, you've become Mr. Towns.

I've been confronted many times this morning with the question 'Where is Mr. Towns? *Where* is Mr. Towns?' Frequently, this was accompanied by tears when my explanations proved unsatisfactory. I know you may find that hard to believe, given the relative tranquility you found when you arrived, but I assure you I was at my wit's end when I sent that note to summon you." She gestured toward the sofa and chairs. "But since you're here, let's have a seat. Perhaps you can make Jem understand why you weren't here when he woke up. I've failed to do so."

Charles smiled at the boy, who was following their conversation with interest. "I can try."

She took a seat on the sofa, so Charles chose one of the armchairs. Jem settled himself on the floor at Charles's feet, leaning against his legs. Sir Rabbit perched on Jem's lap.

"It's simple, really, Jem. I wasn't here this morning because I don't live here like Lady Serena or her father, Lord Huntington."

"You were here last night," the boy said, a distressed look coming over his face.

"Yes, but that was only because I'd been helping Lady Serena yesterday. I'm sorry if we weren't clear and you thought this was my home. I can see why you might, since you fell asleep before I went back to where I live."

"I live here now. Why can't you?" Jem asked.

Charles's gaze pivoted toward Serena. Had she let the child believe he was to live here? That wasn't the solution to Jem's situation they'd discussed in the hackney.

She must have divined his thoughts, because she frowned slightly and gave a brief shake of her head. He took this to mean she hadn't explained things to Jem yet.

"Well," he said, turning back to Jem. "You see, I'm not part of Lady Serena's family. I'm only her friend, and it wouldn't be proper for me to live here."

"But I'm not family either." Jem rested his chin on Charles's thigh and gave him a pleading look.

"Yes, well, I think Lady Serena is still considering what's best for you when it comes to finding you a home. We talked about it yesterday, remember? You wanted to live somewhere with a kitten. And Lady Serena promised to find you a home with a kitten. And a mother and a father and maybe even some brothers and sisters."

"I thought she forgot about the kitten," Jem said.

"No," Serena said. "When I make a promise, I keep a promise. You're here while we look around for the best home for you."

Jem turned toward Serena. "So I won't live here with you?"

She shook her head. "Not if I can find you an even better home."

"And I won't live with you?" Jem asking, looking at Charles once more.

"No, I'm afraid not."

Jem looked down at the floor as he considered this. "But I'll still get to have a kitten?" he said finally, his voice tinged with resignation.

"Most assuredly," Serena said. "And you won't have to live anywhere that you don't wish to live. All right?"

Jem nodded. Then he got up and gathering up several of the wooden blocks, began building a four-walled structure around Sir Rabbit. After a few minutes of building, he looked up and asked, "Can Mr. Towns go to Greenwich with us today?"

Chapter Five

W hy I think that would be a fine idea," Serena said.

"Greenwich? You mean to go to Greenwich today?" Charles asked in some astonishment.

"It was Papa's suggestion, actually," Serena said. "He thought a trip to the Royal Observatory would provide a welcome distraction"—she tilted her head in Jem's direction—"and the weather this morning *is* exceptionally fine. Once the idea took hold in his mind, he sent a footman off to see about procuring a boat to take us down the Thames, requested that Cook prepare a picnic lunch for us, and had his secretary cancel his appointments today. I'm not sure what he's presently doing."

She'd barely finished uttering this sentence when her father appeared in the sitting room. "Getting ready, my dear, that's what I've been doing. Ah, Townshend, I see you got my daughter's summons. Fortunately, things calmed down, more or less." Papa cast a frowning glance around the room. "Although the price seems to be a general anarchy in here."

Her father turned his attention back to Charles. "Did Serena invite you to come along to Greenwich with us?"

"Yes," Charles said. "But I don't want to intrude upon your outing."

Papa waved this off. "Nonsense. We'd welcome your company. Especially young Master Jem here, who seems to have taken quite a liking to you." He gave Charles a pointedly amused look. "In fact, I suspect you'd be doing us a favor by accompanying us."

"When you put it that way, how can I refuse?" Charles said.

"Good man." Her father rubbed his hands together. "We should make haste. We've a full day ahead of us."

"Should we send a footman to Sir Roland's to let him know you're not returning to work?" Serena asked.

"No need," Charles replied. "He gave me the rest of the day off."

In a remarkably short time, they were boarding the boat for the trip to Greenwich. In addition to the four of them, three footmen had been enlisted to see to the picnic hamper of food and the other items her father had deemed necessary for the outing.

The steady breeze allowed them to make good time as the captain ordered the sails to be unfurled, and no doubt the oarsmen on board were happy to allow the wind to power their journey. However, the choppy, whitecapped water of the Thames gave Ned, one of the footmen, a case of seasickness that had him hanging over the railing for much of the trip.

Jem, who'd never sailed before, seemed to be a little uncertain about the rocking motion of the boat, but it didn't take long for his nervousness to turn into excitement. He peppered the captain and the first mate with questions until Serena, fearing he was making a nuisance of himself, drew him away and endeavored to keep him entertained and out of the crew's way for the rest of the trip.

It was shortly before lunchtime when they pulled up to the dock at Greenwich and disembarked. Charles insisted on carrying one of the parcels to give Ned, who still looked like he was in danger of casting up his accounts, a chance to recover.

Perched on the hill above the dock was the Royal Observatory, a red brick building with decorative white quoins along its corners and towers topped with their distinctive domes.

Spying it, Jem exclaimed, "Is that a castle on the hill?"

"No," her father replied. "That's the building where they keep the Troughton Transit, the large telescope I was telling you about." He took Jem's hand and began leading the way up the hill. Serena and Charles followed behind them, and the footmen brought up the rear.

"Besides the food, what has your father deemed necessary for this trip?" Charles asked.

"I'm not an entirely sure," Serena said. "He mentioned something about playing battledore and shuttlecock, but beyond that and the food, I've no idea what he thought necessary to the outing today."

"I can attest that the contents of this basket I'm carrying

weigh more than a few small rackets and a feather-trimmed cork."

Despite this statement, Charles wasn't at all winded as they climbed toward the crest of the hill, and as she walked beside him, she couldn't help noticing the muscular breadth of his shoulders beneath the tight-fitting lines of his jacket. In consequence of which, she couldn't blame her own breathlessness entirely on the exertion of the climb. Though hopefully, if Charles noticed, he would attribute it to that.

As they neared the crest, Papa stopped and appeared to say something to Jem, who nodded enthusiastically. "We think this looks like a fine spot for a picnic," Papa announced. "We'll have the hamper unpacked and we'll eat before we tour the grounds further.

Charles set the basket he carried on the grass. When the footmen reached them, they placed their burdens down as well and began to unpack the picnic items.

Ned, looking less pale than he had when they docked, unpacked a large wool blanket and unfurled it on the grass. Soon they were all informally seated upon the blanket, enjoying a selection of cold meats, cheeses, crusty rolls, and apple spice cake. There was a stoppered bottle of milk for Jem, two bottles of white wine, and a crockery jug of pale ale. Serena poured herself a glass of wine and offered to do the same for her father and Charles, but to her surprise Papa said he preferred to have some of the ale. Charles ended up choosing that as well, and with the three footmen also sharing in it, the jug was soon emptied.

As they ate, Papa regaled them all with his knowl-edge of ships and navigation, sheepishly admitting at one point that it had been his youthful aspiration to join the Royal Navy.

"I wish we could see the Troughton Transit," he said, referring to the ten-foot telescope that had been installed at the Royal Observatory a mere two years ago. "But they don't let just anybody wander into the transit room, and a visit would have had to be arranged well ahead of time. Still, we'll have a fine time walking about the grounds and enjoying the views of the Thames from the heights around the observatory."

After the remains of their al fresco picnic were packed away, Papa said only one footman at a time needed to remain with the baskets, and that they could decide among themselves how to divide up that duty. But he warned them, "You'll need to be back here at three o'clock sharp because the captain intends to set sail at half past three."

However, only Ned elected to go off exploring. The other two were content to remain at the picnic spot and take their leisure.

After a half an hour of wandering the grounds, Jem started to become bored with looking at the scenery, and her father offered to take Jem back to where they'd picnicked. "We can get out the battledore rackets or the cricket bat, and have a bit of sport," he said. Jem immediately perked up at this suggestion, and Ned chimed in that he wouldn't mind a bit of play himself.

"What's your pleasure, Charles?" Serena asked. "Shall we wander a bit more, or would you rather join in a game?"

He inclined his head in a courtly manner. "I'd be happy to do either, so I will leave the choice up to you."

That didn't require much thought on her part. She'd

far rather enjoy his company without the distraction of the others. "Let's continue our rambles a while longer."

Charles proffered his arm to her, and she slipped a hand around his elbow. They set off in the opposite direction as the others, heading toward a copse of trees whose branches showed the faint greenish cast of newly furled leaves. Beneath the trees, pink and purple hyacinths grew thickly in some areas, creating islands of bright color in a sea of green grass. Reaching them, Serena couldn't resist picking one of the sweet-smelling flowers.

Charles watched as she closed her eyes and breathed in the fragrance of the hyacinth. Even though she wore a stylish bonnet, the breeze whipped loose tendrils of her hair about her face in a manner that he found particularly distracting. But then again, his equilibrium had been off since earlier, when his preoccupation of her stocking-clad feet had led to his nearly falling and to that collision between them that had sent his senses reeling and his emotions rocketing off in directions in which they had no business heading.

Awareness thrummed through him and it took all his willpower not to reach out and trace a finger along the curve of her cheek.

She sighed, and as if drawn by some invisible force, he swayed toward her. She chose that moment to open her eyes (of course) and her lips parted in surprise.

"Charles?"

For the second time that day, his feelings for her had revealed themselves. Not only revealed themselves, but he'd very nearly acted upon them. And once again his instincts prompted him to place some distance between them, lest he give in to his deepest inclinations.

He took a step backward, his heel finding a small depression in the ground, but this time Serena wasn't able to prevent his fall and to his chagrin, he ended up on his backside. At least the grass provided a reasonably soft landing so that the only thing bruised was his pride.

"Charles!" Serena knelt beside him, concern written across her face. "Are you all right?"

"I'm fine," he said, his disgust at his own clumsiness evident in his voice. Although better to fall and look like a clumsy fool, than to have given in to that impulse to lean in and brush his lips against hers. Besides, landing on the ground had at least jarred some common sense back into him. "Just hell-bent on making a fool of myself at some point today apparently."

She smiled at that. "Perfection is so overrated, don't you think?"

"Only in others," he said wryly.

"Well, I like a little imperfection in my friends," she said. "Probably because I'm so full of imperfections myself."

A smile tugged at his lips. "Am I supposed to refute that statement?"

She gave him an arch look. "Surely you know me well enough to know I wouldn't ask an honest man to compromise his principles." She tossed her flower to the side and reached out a hand. "Can I assist you in arising?"

"As a gentleman, I think that should be my line," he said, dusting some grass and dirt from his hands.

"I'm not so sure," she murmured. "*I'm* not the one so off-balance today."

They both came to their feet and brushed themselves off. He suspected the back of his gray trousers now sported a grass stain or two, and he could only hope that his jacket covered the worst of it.

Charles pulled his pocket watch from his waistcoat. "It's nearly two o'clock. Perhaps we should rejoin the others rather than wander farther afield."

"I suppose you're right," she agreed. "Let me just pick a bouquet to take back. I do love the fragrance of hyacinths."

As they headed back toward the observatory and their picnic spot, Charles said, "What do you intend to do about Jem?"

"Do you mean how do I intend to go about placing him with a family?"

"Yes," he said. "I think it would be best to find a good home for him soon, before he gets too attached to living with you. It will only get harder the longer he remains with you."

"I wouldn't worry about him being too attached to *me*. It seems to be *you* that he's so taken with. You didn't see him crying for you earlier."

"That only reinforces my point, don't you think?"

"I don't disagree, Charles, but I'm not going to hastily choose someone and come to regret it. I think taking the time to find the right home is the more important consideration."

"Important, yes, but surely no more important than ensuring that his move out of your household is as pain free as possible."

It wasn't only Jem's attachment to her that worried him. What if Serena became so attached to the child that she didn't want to send him elsewhere to live? Society would be sure to look askance at such an arrangement, given Serena's status as an unmarried female. Not that she would let the prospect of unsavory gossip deter her from that course if she decided to take it.

"I recognize your concerns and they are valid. But it's only been a day since we found him. Surely you didn't expect me to ship him off somewhere in only a day or two."

"I'm not saying that," he said. "I just want to know that you have a plan in mind, that's all."

"Then you may set your mind at ease. I intend to start by looking at the families who are tenant farmers on Papa's estates. I know many of them, but not all. I'll need to take some time to consider which ones might provide a good home for Jem, and then contact them to see if they'd be willing to take him in. Naturally, Papa would provide a stipend for his care. Does that sound like an acceptable plan to you?"

"Very," he said. "As long as you don't forget the most important consideration of all."

"And that would be ... ?" she asked.

"Why the kitten, naturally."

She laughed. "Well, of course. I doubt Jem will let me forget that."

They were within sight of the others now, and it looked as if her father and the three footmen were trying to introduce Jem to the principles of cricket. Cricket gear must have comprised part of the contents of the three large hampers. Two wickets had been set up and Jem stood before one of them, holding the bat in his hands. Papa stood nearby and appeared to be giving him instructions. There was no batsman in position in front of the second wicket, nor did Serena see another bat lying about anywhere. No doubt the low number of players dictated this lack of a second batsman.

Spying them, Ned, cricket ball in hand, called out, "They're back, sir."

Her father turned and waved them over. "Ah, we were hoping you'd return soon. We're in sore need of reinforcements. This young fellow has a real aptitude for making contact with the ball." Jem grinned broadly as the earl patted him on the head. "Regrettably, my best days as a fielder are well behind me, so I'll take over for Ned as bowler."

Serena sat her bouquet upon the ground and began undoing the ribbons of her bonnet. "I'll have to risk a few freckles if I'm to field with any effectiveness. The brim on this bonnet doesn't allow for a wide field of vision." She turned to Charles. "You may as well do as the others and remove your jacket, Charles."

He hesitated before shrugging out of the garment and laying it on the picnic blanket.

"What happened to your pants?" Jem called out. A noticeable greenish stain marred the back of Charles's trousers where he'd landed in the grass earlier.

"I tripped and fell," Charles replied.

Jem giggled. "Again?"

"Yes, again," Charles said. At Papa's questioning glance, he added, "I tripped over a block in your sitting room earlier, and I stepped into a small depression and lost my balance on our walk. Apparently, I'm beset with clumsiness today."

"Ah," her father said. "You can hardly be blamed for either of those spills. I took a tumble myself a little while ago thanks to the uneven ground." He glanced toward Serena, and as if reading her mind said, "I'm fine, daughter. No harm done."

Serena dropped her bonnet onto the picnic blanket and headed across the grass to take up a defensive position about ten or so feet away from where Charles stood. Her father strolled in the direction of Ned, who tossed him the cricket ball before loping off to choose a spot from which to field Jem's hits. They formed a semicircle behind her father. None of them stood as far away from the batter as they might in a real match. A youth-like Jem wasn't going to hit the ball as hard as a grown man.

Papa was a decent bowler, but Jem swung and missed at the first two balls thrown to him. He made solid contact with the third and the ball went sailing in a high arc toward Serena who darted over and made the catch. Jem, who'd been running madly toward the other wicket, threw up his hands in frustration.

"Don't look so glum," Lord Huntington said. "We're not playing a real game. You can keep batting a while longer." He mopped his brow with one of his shirtsleeves. It was warm in the afternoon sun.

Serena threw the ball back to her father and resumed her place in the field. She noticed that Charles had rolled his sleeves up to his elbows, and she found the view of his exposed arms to be unaccountably distracting. She backed up a few steps the better to enjoy this provocatively male display of muscled forearms.

The sharp sound of bat meeting ball rent the air as Jem's hit sent the ball hurtling straight toward Charles. She watched as he fielded it, cleanly scooping it up with one hand. Goodness, the man had a fine set of shoulders. He waited a few seconds before throwing the cricket ball back to her father, giving Jem time to reach the second wicket.

"Can I be a fielder now?" the boy asked.

"If that's what you want," her father said. He glanced over his shoulder toward Serena. "Would you like to take a turn at bat? Townshend can come in as bowler for a while."

"I'm happy to let one of the footmen have a turn." She turned an inquiring look toward the three servants.

"Thank you, Lady Serena, but we've all taken a turn already," Ned replied, giving her a grin that bordered on cheeky. "Let's see what you can do."

"Very well, gentlemen." She walked over to Jem and relieved him of the bat before heading to the wicket. Assuming a batting position, she called out, "All right, Charles. Let's see what *you* can do."

One side of his mouth lifted, but he didn't reply to her challenge, just wound up his arm and threw the ball to her. It was a slow toss though and she easily made contact, thwacking the ball past Ned, who turned and chased it down.

"Come on, Charles," she said. "I think you were taking it easy on me with that last one."

He eyed her a moment, then wound his arm around and delivered a much faster bowl this time. She barely managed to swing the bat in time to make contact with it, but the ball sailed right back to Charles who caught it with one fluid motion. She was out, but since they weren't really playing she supposed she could take a few more swings.

"Better?" he asked as she resumed her batting stance.

"Yes. Now bowl the ball, Townshend," she said. With

her competitive nature, she dearly wanted to get one good hit off him.

To her chagrin, she missed his next throw entirely and the ball hit the wicket. In a real game, she would be dismissed.

She fetched the ball, threw it back to him, and prepared to bat again.

He bowled again, but this time Serena was able to channel her frustration into a solid hit, but once again it headed toward Charles. Serena gathered up her skirts and ran toward the other wicket. From the corner of her eye, she could see Charles chase down the ball and run for the wicket. He tossed the ball toward it, but missed, so she wasn't out.

"Nice one," he said.

She gave him a demure smile, despite this hoydenish run to the wicket. "Thank you, sir."

"Perhaps we should end on that," her father said. "We still need to pack the picnic away and haul everything back to the boat."

"Nice play, Lady Serena," Ned said before heading over to the picnic area.

"Thank you, Ned," she replied.

Charles began pulling the stumps from one of the wickets out of the grass. She went to the other wicket and Jem ran up and helped her pull out its stumps before he scampered back to the picnic area.

Ned pointed out which hamper to put the cricket gear in. Once everything had been packed away they made their way back down the hill to the river. It was just shy of three o'clock when they all trooped up the gangplank, and the captain ordered the mooring lines to be thrown off once everything had been stowed away for the journey back.

Her father and the captain chatted as the boat made its way to London. The river was much smoother, a circumstance that Ned undoubtedly appreciated. But since they were heading upriver, they made much slower progress, as it was up to the efforts of the oarsmen to move the boat through the water.

"You have a sunburned nose," Serena told Jem, who was snuggled beside her on the padded bench seat. Charles sat on the other side of him. "We'll have to put some vinegar on it tonight to take away the burn."

Jem wrinkled his nose. "Vinegar? On my face?"

"Yes," Serena said. "That way your skin won't hurt so much." She turned to Charles. "You might consider using some as well. You're looking a little red in the face yourself."

"I think we all are," Charles replied.

"I'm sure I'll develop some charming freckles," Serena said. "But it was worth it."

"Does vinegar help freckles?" Jem asked.

"No, but you know what does?" she asked.

Jem shook his head.

"Lemon juice," she replied.

"Does it?" Jem asked, giving Charles a quizzical look.

"If Lady Serena says so. I guess she would know because I don't see any freckles on her cheeks." Her breath caught in her throat when his gaze lingered on her face as he studied her features. It made the third time that day that she'd felt a current of awareness pass between them.

"Jem!" Her father's voice interrupted the moment. "Come here. You, too, Serena and Townshend. Take a look at the Royal Hospital for Seamen through the spyglass. Designed by Wren, it's a marvel of classical architecture. Perhaps the finest of any comparable structure in Europe."

Serena was less than enthusiastic to view Corinthian columns and whatever other embellishments the hospital boasted, but her father was clearly excited for them to study its architectural details. At any rate, Jem and Charles had already risen from their places on the bench. Jem scampered over to her father and the captain, while Charles waited and gestured for her to precede him.

With a small sigh she rose as well. Her father's summons had severed whatever connection had passed between them. Jem was already scanning the riverbank with the spyglass and Charles had reverted to his more reservedly polite self.

But there'd been *something* in his expression earlier, and coupled with her own shifting feelings, she was determined to find out what.

Chapter Six

To Serena's relief, after the trip to Greenwich, there were no more tears or anxious questions about Charles. Once Jem grasped that Charles wasn't part of the Huntington household, but that he would still see "Mr. Towns" from time to time, he readily adjusted to his new situation.

Even with this improvement, Serena wanted advice on how best to deal with the child while he was in her care. Charles's warnings were fresh in her mind, and she shared his concerns about finding him a permanent home soon. Truly, she did.

However, it appeared unavoidable that Jem would be with them for the next few—or maybe even the next several—days while she tried to find a good home for him. She liked children, but with no nieces or nephews, she rarely had the opportunity to interact with them. She felt woefully unprepared to deal with the one who was suddenly in her charge. Since her own mother had been deceased for nearly a decade now, Grace, with four children of her own, seemed the obvious person to turn to for advice.

So two days after the Greenwich outing, Serena called upon Grace. While Jem romped with the duchess's younger three children in the back garden, she and Grace, seated under a large plane tree, enjoyed cups of tea and watched the youngsters play.

Grace, with her good sense and matter-of-fact attitude, set Serena's mind at ease. "A child's needs are fairly basic," the duchess said. "Beyond food, clothing, shelter, a few toys and books, they need love and security. In fact, a child supplied with those last two can usually survive a deficiency of the others, to some degree at least."

"You make it sound easy enough," Serena said.

"It is, and it isn't," Grace admitted with a little smile. "But at Jem's age, it's mostly straightforward and uncomplicated."

"It seems to me that Jem's situation could make it more complicated." Serena related what they knew about the child's background so far.

"It sounds as if one of his greatest needs at the moment is a feeling of security and belonging. I know you can supply that."

"Yes, but his stay with me is only meant to be temporary, until I can find a good family to take him in. Charles is urging me to do it quickly because that would be best for the boy. But I don't want to be too hasty. It's an important decision."

Grace appeared to consider this for a few moments. "Mr. Townshend has a point, but as long as you're honest with Jem and he understands what you're doing…well, then, I don't see why you couldn't take the time necessary to find the right place for him."

"It makes me feel better to hear you say that," Serena said.

Grace reached over and gave Serena's hand a reassuring squeeze. "Jem couldn't hope for a better champion."

"Do you think I should hire a nursemaid while Jem is with us?" Serena asked. "Right now I have one of the housemaids in charge of him. Ellie has six younger brothers and sisters, so she seems to know what she's doing, and Jem likes her well enough."

"Ellie sounds like she has the perfect background to act as a nursemaid," Grace said. "If, however, you decide to hire someone else, I can give you some recommendations."

"If you think someone with Ellie's background is sufficient, I'll continue to have her act as his nursemaid. She hasn't said so, but I suspect she likes it better than her usual duties."

"I'm sure she'll be fine. He seems happy enough, which is a strong argument to let the arrangement stand."

"I think I'll try to place him in a family with children," Serena said. "He's so happy being part of the group. I found being an only child a lonely existence."

"I liked having built-in playmates," Grace said. "Not that my sister and I were ever that close. She's ten years older, and besides we're so different. But my brothers and I…now we were a merry crew."

"I'd like Jem to be part of a merry crew. My concern is he'll be considered the outsider, since he wouldn't be born into the family."

"Not necessarily," Grace replied. "It really depends. In one family, that might very well be true, while in another he'd be accepted without reservation."

Serena was only partially reassured by this statement. Deciding where to place Jem was a huge responsibility, one that would determine the child's future happiness. Her stomach knotted up at the thought of making the wrong choice.

As if reading her mind, Grace said, "I'm confident you'll make a good choice."

A loud cry drew their attention back to the children. "Peregrine," Grace called. "Why is your sister on the ground crying?"

"She tripped, Mama."

"So it had nothing to do with that large stick in your hand?"

"No, Mama. It's my sword. I was just holding it high while I led the troops"—he motioned to Jem and his sister—"in a charge of the fortress." He pointed to a tree house where his younger brother's tousled head poked through an open window.

"I see. Well, help Aggie up and dust her off." She turned back to Serena. "If she's really hurt, she'll come tell me about it. Especially if her brother had anything to do with it."

"It looks as if the charge is reforming, so I expect she's fine," Serena said.

She watched Jem and Agatha line up behind Peregrine at the far side of the yard before Peregrine raised his stick "sword" once again and the three of them rushed toward the tree with the fort. Childish shouts filled the air.

Grace turned back to Serena. "We'll see how long the bonhomie lasts," she said wryly.

"Where is Phoebe?" Serena asked. "I thought she might join us today."

"She went shopping with Julia Keene, but I expect they'll be back soon. Although knowing Phoebe, there will be a lengthy stop at a bookseller's, so it might be some time still. I suppose it will depend upon whether Julia enjoys perusing the bookshelves as much as my niece."

Serena looked toward the tree house. Apparently the charge had succeeded because all four children now occupied the structure. Spying her watching them, Jem waved vigorously through the window opening of the tree house.

"She shops for books with the same fervor many females exhibit for trips to the modiste or the milliner," Serena said.

Grace smiled over her teacup. "Don't I know it. She would prefer getting a new book over getting a new gown or bonnet any day."

"One can hardly criticize her for that," Serena said, and Grace nodded in agreement. "Is your sister still happily ignorant of all the latitude you give Phoebe?"

"Anne is resigned that I won't hover over Phoebe to the same degree that she would, but she's so eager to have Phoebe 'exposed to the right people,' as she terms it, that she's willing to overlook that." Grace's pained expression reflected her distaste of her sister's snobbishness. "Anne and I are opposites when it comes to that. I married Miles *in spite of* his ducal title."

"Does she even know you allow Phoebe to attend the Wednesday Afternoon Social Club?" Serena took a sip of her tea.

"She does, although I never bothered to tell her the exact

nature of the meetings, or that I generally don trousers for them. She believes the Wednesday Afternoon Social Club focuses largely on charitable works, which it does, but you and I both know it's rather more than that. Of course, she's aware I occasionally wore trousers as a girl when I joined my brothers on rambles about the countryside, but I'm sure she thinks I outgrew that behavior." A mischievous smile played about her lips. "I won't let Phoebe do anything that *I* consider inappropriate for a seventeen-year-old girl, and that will have to be good enough for Anne."

A bellow of rage rent the air, followed by Agatha tossing the stick-sword from the tree house's window.

Grace gave Serena a *what now* glance. "Agatha Marie, why did you do that?"

"Peregrine is being bossy." The girl crossed her arms and thrust out her chin. "He won't let anyone else be the captain. Not even Jem, and he's our guest."

"Why do I suspect the real grievance is that Peregrine won't let *her* be captain?" Grace murmured. To the children, she called, "Would Jem like a turn being the captain? Since he's your guest that would be the thoughtful thing to do."

Agatha whirled around, apparently to pose this question to Jem. The girl's once neat braid was coming undone and the tails of her hair ribbon hung down her back, no longer tied into a bow. After a moment, she turned back to the window. "He says he would."

"Then there you go," her mother called. Grace turned to Serena. "Problem solved... for the moment."

The children continued to play amicably enough as the ladies finished drinking their tea. About a quarter of an hour later, they were joined by Julia Keene and Phoebe.

Noticing the girls' arrival, Grace's daughter came running over. "Did you get my book?" she asked.

"Agatha. Manners," the duchess gently scolded her daughter.

"Yes, Mama. Good afternoon, Miss Keene. I hope you and Phoebe had a lovely time shopping at the book-seller's."

"Quite lovely," Julia said, slanting a sly glance in Phoebe's direction.

"Mr. Bagshaw had a large selection of used children's books this week," Phoebe said. "So we were able to purchase quite a few to add to the libraries at our properties."

Everyone in the Wednesday Afternoon Social Club was well aware that Phoebe was in the habit of spending much of her weekly pin money on books for the children of the war widows they housed in their properties.

"Did you get *my* book?" Agatha asked again.

Phoebe laughed good-naturedly. "Yes, poppet, I did. It should be in your room waiting for you."

The little girl threw her arms around her cousin's neck. "Oh, thank you. Thank you! Peregrine always turns down the corners of the pages when he reads, and it drives me mad." She ran back to rejoin her brothers and Jem, apparently satisfied that Phoebe had made the purchase on her behalf.

"She's been very annoyed at what she sees as Peregrine's careless treatment of her favorite book, an illustrated edition of *Aesop's Fables*," Grace explained to Serena. "She's been saving up for two months to obtain her own copy. In truth, he turned down the corners on only two pages, and he quit when I told him to use a bookmark, but my daughter wanted a pristine copy."

"I can't say I blame her," Serena said.

"Fortunately for Agatha, there was a tall gentleman who could pluck the book from a high shelf, since neither of us could reach it," Julia said, her eyes sparkling with mischief.

"Oh?" Grace said, turning an inquiring glance at her niece. "I'd prefer you ask Mr. Bagshaw or his clerk for help rather than a stranger."

"I would have but they were occupied with a customer nearly the entire time we were there," Phoebe said. "As it was, we had to wait fifteen minutes before his clerk could total our purchases for us. And the man isn't exactly a stranger, Aunt Grace. You're familiar with him. We see him frequently when we shop there, and usually exchange polite nods, even though we've never been introduced."

"The dark-haired gentleman who often stands by the window and reads?" At Phoebe's nod, Grace turned to Serena. "He seems well mannered, and is clearly from good family, but still, we don't know him."

"If it makes you feel any better, I didn't *ask* him for help," Phoebe said. "He noticed we couldn't reach a book, so he came over and got it down for us."

"He got it down for *you*," Julia said. "I was already browsing elsewhere in the shop."

Phoebe blushed. "Don't be silly. You're giving Aunt Grace the wrong impression."

"Is he a good-looking gentleman?" Serena asked. Given Phoebe's blushes she suspected he was.

"Very," Julia said. "Dark hair, brown eyes, pleasing features. I wish he would cast glances my way as much as he does Phoebe's. Not that it would do much good if

he did. I've never seen him before, so he must not attend
many social functions."

"Honestly, you're mischaracterizing the whole encounter," Phoebe protested. "I don't encourage his attentions
at all."

"Beautiful girls don't have to," Julia murmured, although there was no malice in her voice. She was simply
stating the truth.

"No one's accusing you of encouraging him," Grace
said, studying Phoebe with an assessing look. "But I think
it's past time I ask Mr. Bagshaw about the gentleman's
identity, since we seem to see the man fairly regularly
when we visit the book shop."

"Plus, if we find out who he is, someone could invite
him to"—Julia waved a hand in the air and smiled
cheekily—"some social function. A ball, preferably. Then
he could ask us to dance."

Phoebe rolled her eyes and shook her head, but
Serena suspected that for all this show of indifference,
she was more intrigued by this young man than she was
letting on.

"Oh, no," Grace said. "I think the children might be
squabbling again." All four of them had climbed down
the wooden planks nailed into the tree trunk to serve
as a ladder, and solemn-faced, were crossing the yard
toward them.

"Jem wants to see the cats," Peregrine said. "May we?"

"Do you care if they visit the cats in the mews?" Grace
asked. "The children consider them their pets, although
we can't keep them in the house because they send Miles
into fits of sneezing."

"I don't mind," Serena said.

"Then come along," Grace said to the children. "Fall in and let's go see those kittens."

"Julia and I will go inside," Phoebe said. "Cats make her sneeze too."

That visit to the mews was how Jem became the proud possessor of a three-month-old kitten which he dubbed Tabitha upon being told she was a tabby cat.

On the carriage ride home, Tabitha contentedly slept on Jem's lap as he dozed against Serena's side. As Serena slipped an arm around him and kissed the top of his head, she idly wondered what Charles would say about the kitten acquisition.

Chapter Seven

Charles had thought he was arriving unfashionably early to the Peytons' ball, but his hackney was caught in a snarl of traffic as well-turned-out carriages clogged the street where the Peytons resided. No doubt when tonight's affair was written about in the society sections of the papers, it would be declared a "crush," that coveted designation every hostess desired, and was the bane of guests who didn't enjoy being crowded cheek-to-jowl with their fellow guests.

As he alighted the conveyance at the entrance, he noticed some of the other newly arrived guests eyeing him with a mix of curiosity and astonished amusement, due, no doubt, to his being the only guest to arrive in a hackney. He returned the looks with a friendly nod, and adopted what he hoped was an insouciant attitude, and made his way up the steps to the front door.

He crossed the elegant foyer with its black-and-white parquet floor and joined the line of guests working their way up one of the wide, curving staircases that led to the next floor, where they would be announced before entering the ballroom. He kept an eye out for Serena as he waited. He hadn't seen her since the trip to Greenwich three days ago. Evidently, Jem hadn't suffered from any more distress on Charles's account.

The line moved along quickly and within half an hour of his arrival, he'd been announced, had greeted the Peytons, and was presently headed to a far corner of the ballroom where a group of bachelors with little interest in dancing were gathered. Once there, he accepted a flute of champagne from a passing footman (no one could accuse the Peytons of skimping on the refreshments).

Despite this avoidance of the dance floor, Charles continued to look around for Serena. He wasn't positive she was even attending tonight, but there seemed to be a good chance she would. Every time a lady with dark brown hair and of a height similar to Serena's caught his eye, a little spark of anticipation ignited within him, only to be swiftly replaced with a dull sense of disappointment each time he realized it wasn't her.

He ran a finger under the edge of his cravat. The ballroom, as ballrooms were wont to be, was uncomfortably warm from the profusion of candles lighting the space to a brightness akin to midday. As people continued to crowd inside, it was certain to grow warmer, even though every window along the back wall was open to let in the cool night air. He finished his champagne and snagged another glass from a footman's tray.

He spotted Phillip Hurst making his way toward the cluster of dance-averse gentleman. Hurst hurried past a line of hopeful young ladies, and their equally hopeful mamas and chaperones. Charles couldn't help chuckling at the way the man kept his gaze aimed dead-straight ahead, determinedly avoiding the fluttering lashes and coquettish gazes directed at any eligible gentleman who wandered past.

By the time Phillip Hurst neared his corner of the ballroom, Charles could see a sheen of perspiration on the other man's forehead, although he couldn't tell whether it was because of the temperature of the room or—and this seemed an equally probable reason—because of nervousness caused by parading past the ladies.

"You survived," Charles remarked when Hurst came to stand beside him.

The other man pulled out a handkerchief and mopped his forehead. "Good gad. I don't know why I let myself be talked into coming to these things."

"Because you want to make your sister happy?" Charles said.

"Be nobler of me if that were the reason," Hurst said. "I mean, of course, I want Charlotte to be *happy*. What kind of brother would I be if I didn't want that? But, no, I'm here because it seemed easier than the alternative."

"Which was?" Charles prompted when he didn't expand on the thought.

Hurst gave him a long-suffering look. "My sister can be an awful pest when she wants to be, and lately she's never peskier than when she wants me to attend some social function. Eventually I reach the point where I agree to her demands." Frowning, Hurst glanced around. "Devil take it. Where's a footman with a tray of drinks? I'm parched."

"Here." Charles offered him his glass. "I haven't drunk from this yet, and you look like you need it more."

"You're a capital fellow, Townshend." Hurst drained the champagne in one long swallow. "That's more like it, though I could use another one. Or two." He mopped his forehead again. "It's deuced hot in here."

"I expect it's only going to get worse as more guests crowd in. The dance floor is relatively empty at present," he said, tipping his head in that direction.

"And by that I suppose you're suggesting I find a dance partner and avail myself of all that space." Hurst eyed the dance floor with a disgruntled expression. "Oddly enough it's not the dancing I mind. It's the asking a girl to dance that I hate, and always make a hash of." Hurst gave Charles a rueful glance. "I know. Ridiculous, isn't it? That I'm apparently incapable of articulating a sentence as simple as 'Miss So-and-so, may I have the honor of this dance?' But I am. Whenever I try to talk to a young lady, I stutter and stammer, the wrong words fall out of my mouth, and I invariably manage to make myself look like an imbecile."

"Have you considered that it might come easier with practice?"

Hurst laughed. "Past experience shows that repetition only makes it worse. It defies conventional wisdom, but there you are."

A footman came round with more champagne and they both helped themselves to a glass.

"But don't let my ineptitude at conversing with the ladies make you feel like you must keep me company.

Dance if you wish. I'm happy enough to stay tucked out of the way drinking this excellent champagne."

"For the moment, I am as well," Charles replied.

However, as the evening progressed he found himself getting more and more restless. He hadn't spotted Serena yet, and the hollowed-out sense of disappointment he felt only seemed to grow with each passing minute.

Maybe she hadn't planned on attending. Or maybe she'd changed her mind and decided to spend the evening with Jem instead. Although, surely the boy went to bed early enough that she could wait for him to fall asleep and still arrive well before the ball would conclude in the wee hours of the morning.

Maybe, he chided himself, *you shouldn't have bothered coming if your sole objective had been to see Serena.*

After another three quarters of an hour of fruitless waiting, during which he consumed quite a few flutes of champagne, he decided to find where they were serving refreshments. Between the warmth of the room and continually quenching his thirst, he was feeling floaty and light-headed.

There was a bottleneck at the large double doors that were both entrance to and exit from the ballroom. Latecomers were still being announced and trying to gain entry, while guests like himself were leaving to search for food or (for the gentlemen) a place to smoke or one of the retiring rooms set aside for freshening up.

Just as Charles managed to make it out into the hallway, he spotted Serena and her father halfway up the staircase as they waited to be announced.

Serena looked beautiful—in his opinion more beautiful than any other lady in attendance.

A diamond among glass.

The thought drifted through his mind. An imprecise metaphor, since she wore an emerald-colored dress, her dark hair piled into some elaborate arrangement. A long, lone curl hung loose, laying against her neck in a seductive spiral, drawing his gaze to the creamy décolletage exposed by the line of her bodice.

He tried to ignore the spark of attraction the sight of her ignited in him. After all that champagne, he didn't trust himself not to behave foolishly around her. He'd nearly given in to an ill-considered impulse the other day in Greenwich, and that was after only one glass of ale, which had been accompanied by a hearty lunch, so he could hardly blame his actions that day on drink.

Tonight, however, was a different story, and he didn't wish to test the mellowing effects of alcohol on his resolve to keep those hopeless yearnings locked away. Best to pay a visit to the refreshment room first and eat something to help clear his fuzzy mind.

Looking up, she spied him watching her. She waved and mouthed something, but he couldn't tell what she said.

Having been spotted, it would be rude of him to slink off in search of food, so he dipped his chin in acknowledgment and loitered in the hall. He'd greet Serena and Lord Huntington first, then he'd excuse himself and they could proceed into the ballroom.

He moved so that he was standing beside the wall, out of the main flow of people, a position impeding his view of Serena and her father but with the advantage that he could lean against the wall. At least it was marginally cooler here than in the ballroom. Maybe if he'd eaten a proper meal before coming, the champagne wouldn't have affected him to the degree it had.

He nodded at a pair of elderly ladies who stationed themselves nearby. Evidently they were waiting for "dear Camilla" and they proceeded to gossip about the new arrivals coming up the stairs as they waited. Charles didn't pay much attention to their conversation, but he did appreciate that one was fanning herself vigorously with a large painted ivory fan.

When Serena and Lord Huntington finally reached the top of the stairs, he left his post and joined them. Serena looked even lovelier up close. Her ball gown made her gray eyes take on a greenish hue, and those gray-greenish eyes were now observing him with some amusement.

"Leaving the dance floor already, Charles?" Serena asked. "How inconsiderate of you when there must be dozens of young ladies in want of a dance partner."

"My absence will make no difference, since I haven't stepped foot on the dance floor yet." He turned to Lord Huntington. "Good evening, sir." Lord Huntington smiled and returned the greeting.

"I vow," Serena said. "I'll never understand why the convention of asking one to dance is the exclusive province of men. I assure you if ladies were in charge of asking there'd be far fewer of those unfortunates stranded on the perimeter of the ballroom in want of a partner."

"Be careful what you wish for. Think of the injuries that might result if every dance resulted in a mad rush to the dance floor," he murmured.

"I doubt it would devolve into total mayhem," she said. "Though it would liven things up if it did."

Charles grinned. "I don't think we'll find out any time

soon. Now if you'll excuse me. I'm in search of something edible."

She tilted her head and gave him an arch look. "In that case, I'll join you. What is there for me in the ballroom if you're not there to ask me to dance?"

"I'm quite unconvinced you're so lacking in dance partners that you must rely on me," he said.

"I rely on you to supply a dance partner with whom I'm interested in dancing. But anyway I did wish to talk to you. Mr. Latimer had some suggestions for my apprenticeship idea, and it will be easier to talk over refreshments than in the ballroom anyway."

At her words, her father shook his head. "Serena, sometimes you need to give yourself and others a rest from work. I imagine Townshend came to relax and enjoy himself tonight, not be roped into working on one of your pet projects."

"Well, all he has to do is say so, of course." She gave him one of those radiant smiles sure to lure him into doing whatever she asked of him. "Nonetheless, I'll keep you company, Charles, even if we talk about nothing more significant that the weather."

"As you wish." Lord Huntington gave Charles a pointed look. "Hold firm, Townshend. Enjoy yourself. The work will keep." With that, her father turned toward the entrance to the ballroom.

Charles offered Serena his arm, and together they set off in the direction of the other set of stairs.

Something was different about Charles tonight and it wasn't just that he looked divinely handsome in his evening clothes—though he did.

He'd stumbled twice coming down the stairs. Just slightly and he'd immediately regained himself, giving her an apologetic smile each time. And now as they walked down the hallway in the direction of the refreshments room, there'd been a definite unsteadiness to his gait. But there were none of the telltale signs that might point to a head cold, with its accompanying stuffiness that might throw off one's equilibrium.

No sniffling or sneezing. No throat clearing or raspy voice or cough.

If anything, he looked more bright-eyed than usual, though perhaps with a touch more color in his cheeks than was normal. But the warmth of the premises could account for that. She herself was wishing she'd brought a fan tonight, but she rarely bothered to carry one, since more often than not she was likely to lay it aside and lose track of it in the course of an evening.

"Are you...are you bosky?" she asked, peering at him. Because as implausible as that seemed, given she'd never known him to overindulge in drink, it seemed a reasonable explanation for the occasional wobble in his walk.

"Bosky? I don't think so. Tipsy maybe, but not bosky." He gave her a lopsided grin. "Definitely not bosky."

"Is there a difference?" she asked skeptically.

"It's a matter of degree." He gave her a haughty look and promptly tripped over his own feet. "I just need some food in my stomach to counteract all the flutes of champagne I drank."

"*All* the flutes?" she teased. "I'm seeing a new side of you tonight, Charles."

"Merely my thirsty side," he countered. "I'm in this

state because there was no other liquid refreshment available and it's devilishly hot in that ballroom."

"You don't have to justify yourself."

"I don't want you to get the wrong idea." His shoulder bumped into hers. Twice.

"Good heavens, Charles. You're the last person about whom I would get the wrong idea."

The only idea presently floating through her mind was that she found a tipsy Charles rather adorable and she wasn't entirely sure she wished him to sober up too quickly. An empty bench sitting on one side of the hallway gave her an idea. Since she had a hand tucked around his elbow, it was a simple matter to lead him over to the velvet-covered bench. "Sit," she said in a preemptory tone.

He studied the bench for a moment, then gave her a quizzical look. "Why?"

"Because you're walking like a sailor who hasn't gained his sea legs. I thought a few minutes of sitting still might be helpful."

"Food would be more helpful," he said.

"We'll get to that," she assured him.

She wasn't sure what she hoped to gain by delaying their arrival in the refreshment room. It wasn't as if this bench offered the same possibilities as a private alcove, which would have been her preference at that moment. But when there wasn't a private alcove at the ready, sitting side by side on this bench in the hallway would have to do. Fortunately, anyone passing by paid them only scant attention.

He sighed and leaned his head back against the wall. "You should have gone into the ballroom with your father."

"Why? I'd rather be here with you."

He made an odd sort of sound, a cross between a snort and chuckle. "Now you're just being nice."

She shook her head. "No. I'm enjoying myself immensely. If I'd known tipsy Charles was going to be here tonight we would have arrived earlier."

His head lolled toward her. "If you'd arrived earlier, I wouldn't be tipsy. I was waiting for you and afraid I'd miss your arrival if I left the ballroom."

A warm, fluttery feeling tickled her stomach. He looked so endearingly boyish and uncertain, and—dare she even think it?—a little bit smitten.

Or if not smitten precisely, not entirely indifferent? She'd seen a similar expression on his face the day they'd gone to Greenwich. Was he experiencing the same tug of attraction for her that she'd lately felt for him?

And if he was…what did that mean for the two of them? Just the other day, he'd said he had no intention of marrying any time soon. As for her, she had no immediate interest in marriage. To be honest, she didn't really have any future interest in marriage either. Given both of their resistance toward wedded bliss, Serena couldn't help but wonder if there could be a middle ground for them. And could she convince Charles to pursue it?

That might present a challenge. He had such deeply ingrained notions of honor. She rather doubted he would be receptive to the idea her mind was toying with, but until she decided whether or not she truly wanted to follow through on it…it was nothing more than idle speculation on her part.

"I'm flattered," she said. "Why were you waiting for me so eagerly? Were you going to ask me to dance?"

"Maybe." His eyes gleamed with mischief and the corners of his mouth quirked up. "You do look awfully pretty tonight."

Was this a flash of flirtatiousness? Was he actually flirting with her? She rather thought he was. Oh, for that private alcove! Because who knew what might happen with this version of Charles in a more private setting.

Her gaze fell to his mouth. It was finely shaped, and she couldn't help wondering what it would feel like pressed against her own. Sadly, that wasn't a question that could be answered right now.

"You couldn't know that before I arrived," she pointed out. "Although I enjoy flattery as much an any other lady."

"Of course I could," he said. "You're always pretty. It's an objective fact."

Well, well, well. *In vino veritas.*

"You've never seen fit to express that thought before," she murmured.

"Not my place to," he said.

"I give you permission to pay me a pretty compliment any time you wish."

"I'll keep that in mind," he said.

Evidently he wasn't in a flirtatious enough mood to pay her a second compliment. Or perhaps the effects of the champagne were starting to wear off.

"I notice you ducked the question of whether or not you intended to ask me to dance," she said.

"Self-preservation on my part," he said.

"Oh now, that is quite the opposite of a compliment," she said, giving him a playful swat on the arm. "Just for that I'm going to ask you to dance."

He blinked and his grin widened. "Why does that not surprise me?"

"Because you know the sort of bossy, managing female I am."

"That I do. Those tendencies might get you some sore toes tonight."

"I'll risk it."

He shrugged. "Do my best not to step on your toes, of course."

"So I should hope," she said. "But just to be on the safe side, let's get some food in you. And don't even *think* about leaving before we've had two dances this evening."

"Two dances now, is it?" he asked, coming to his feet and proffering her his arm.

"Oh, definitely," she said.

Chapter Eight

~

*A*s luck would have it, the first dance upon their return to the ballroom was a waltz.

"Are you familiar with the steps?" she asked. The waltz had originated on the Continent, and while no longer new to England, it wasn't as universally known as, say, a quadrille. If Charles didn't know the steps they'd have to wait for the next set. A disappointing thought, since waltzing with Charles sounded divine.

"I can perform it competently." He gave her a wry smile. "But if you're having second thoughts, I'll step aside and allow you to waltz with another."

"Second thoughts? Hardly. You've never asked me to dance before. I'm not going to let you wiggle your way out of it now."

"As I recall, you asked me to dance with you," he murmured. "Demanded, really." Nonetheless, he reached for her hand and when she took his hand and stepped into position a few inches before him, he placed his other hand on her back.

"*Demand* is such a strong word," she demurred.

He grinned. "Imperious request, then?"

She merely smiled and followed his lead as he began to move in time with the music.

He waltzed more than competently. To her delight, he was an excellent dancer, leading her through the steps effortlessly. Of course, since it was Charles, and he was no longer tipsy, he held her at a perfectly respectable distance. However, the dance floor was crowded with couples, and there were times when they were forced into closer proximity with each other to avoid colliding with the other dancers.

Every time this caused one of them to inadvertently brush against the other, it resulted in a shivery tingling sensation at the point of contact that radiated throughout the rest of her body, leaving her in a state of giddy anticipation for the next touch.

She closed her eyes for a few seconds and let the music—and the return of feelings she hadn't felt in quite some time—wash over her. When she opened her eyes, it was to discover Charles studying her with a quizzical expression.

"What?" she said.

"Just wondering if you'd come to regret your, er, imperious request?"

"Absolutely not. I love waltzing." She wondered what he would think if she confessed it had been an unbearably long time since she'd felt this way while held in the arms of a man.

"My mind is at ease then." His lips twitched and he added, "I suppose that means you wish to hold me to that second dance you requested."

"I'm afraid it does. The next waltz of the evening is mine, Mr. Townshend."

"In that case, I shall be sure to moderate my consumption of champagne so as not to risk injuring your toes," he said gravely.

"See that you do."

All too soon, the musicians began playing the closing strains, and Charles was leading her off the dance floor. She spied Edwina waving them over from where she stood at the perimeter of the ballroom with a group that included Jason Latimer, Lord and Lady Norwood, the Duke and Duchess of Rochester, and young Phoebe Talbot. Serena acknowledged the gesture with a wave of her own before she and Charles made their way over to join them.

Serena watched with amusement as Phoebe plucked a flute of champagne from the tray of a passing footman and took a long sip before her aunt, the duchess, frowningly relieved her of the glass. Catching the girl's eye, Serena gave her a sympathetic smile.

"You're not even officially out, young lady," the duchess said. "Despite that, I'm happy to let you attend select functions, but don't make me regret it."

"It was only champagne," Phoebe protested. "I'd happily drink lemonade, but there's none of that circulating, and it's frightfully hot in here."

"I suppose you have a point," her aunt conceded. Turning to the duke, she said, "Miles, would you mind fetching some lemonade for us?"

"As you wish, my dear," he said.

"William, would you mind fetching some for me as well?" Charlotte asked.

He grinned. "As you wish, darling. Come along, Rochester. Let's get everyone some lemonade."

Jason Latimer turned to Charles. "I've been hoping to run into you, Townshend. I have a business meeting tomorrow evening that might be of interest to you as well. You're welcome to attend if you're free. It's about that shipping venture I mentioned to you."

"I'm definitely interested," Charles replied. "Tell me when and where."

"Meet me at The Swan and Bull at seven o'clock." He pulled a small card from a pocket in his waistcoat. "Here's the address."

Charles glanced at the card. "I know the place. I'll come hungry. They serve some of the best beefsteaks in London."

Serena recognized the name of the tavern. Her father frequently met friends there. It was a popular spot with gentlemen, especially given its proximity to Tattersall's, which held horse auctions once or twice a week throughout the year.

"What sort of shipping venture?" she asked.

"We intend to use steam power to transport goods on the Great Lakes in North America," Latimer replied. "Mark my words. In the future, steam-powered transportation will be the predominant way people and goods get from one place to another."

"The musicians are starting up again," Edwina said, giving Jason an arch smile. "Perhaps we could save talk about business for another time?"

"Why, Lady Beasley, are you asking me to dance?" Jason Latimer drawled.

"You may take it that way if you wish, but I was really hinting that *you* should ask *me* to dance."

Latimer reached for Edwina's hand and bowed over it. "Dance with me?"

"Always," Edwina replied.

Something twisted inside Serena as she watched this exchange. She was truly pleased that her friend had found a man who so obviously made her happy. But there were times it was almost painful to watch the happiness that radiated between those two. It reminded her too keenly of a similar happiness that had been snatched from her six years ago.

"Do you think there's a wedding on the horizon?" Charles murmured, nodding toward the couple as they made their way onto the dance floor.

"I'm not sure," Serena said. "There was a time I'd have sworn Edwina would never give up her status as a widow, but Jason may be the man to persuade her to marry again."

"I hope he does," Charles said.

Phillip Hurst joined them then, pink-cheeked and slightly out of breath.

"Don't tell me *you're* returning from the dance floor," Charles said, placing a hand over his heart as if feigning shock. "Or did you consume enough champagne to bolster your nerve?"

Hurst shot him a pained look. "Charlotte's idea," he said. "And it was only my neighbor, Lady Roxton. If the woman is already married, I can manage to sound coherent."

"It's a pity he can't trick his mind into thinking the unmarried ladies are spoken for when it comes to asking them to dance," Charlotte remarked. "The problem is all in his head."

"Perhaps the underlying reason stems from not being ready to give up his bachelorhood yet, and it manifests as an inability to ask a marriageable girl to dance," Serena suggested. "I'm quite fascinated by what factors cause us to behave as we do."

"Marriageable females make me nervous. It's as simple as that." Hurst gave an emphatic nod to emphasize his point. "I try not to sound like an imbecile in their presence, but invariably I do."

"You're speaking perfectly fine right now," Grace pointed out. "And neither Phoebe nor Serena are married."

Phillip Hurst blinked. "By gad, you're right. But Miss Talbot hasn't made her come out yet, so I suppose I consider her off-limits." He gave Serena a boyish smile. "As for Lady Serena, Charlotte has told me all about the modern notions held by you Wednesday Afternoon Social Club ladies. It takes the pressure off to know you aren't waiting around for some fellow like me to ask you to marry him."

"So I'm considered safe because you know I have no designs on you?" Serena asked.

"Something like that, yes," Hurst said.

"Poppycock," Charlotte muttered under her breath.

Shortly after this exchange, the gentlemen returned with the lemonade, each carrying a tray with several glasses of it.

"We brought plenty for everyone," William said as he offered a glass to his wife.

The duke also passed around glasses before taking one for himself.

"Miles, you would have made a creditable footman," the duchess teased. "As would Norwood."

"More than creditable," the duke said. "On the way back here I was stopped by a trio of thirsty ladies and scolded for hurrying past them too quickly with my tray of drinks, so naturally I stopped to give them each a glass. But then one of them recognized me and apparently was so astonished by the notion of a duke ferrying a tray of drinks that she dropped the lemonade I had just given her."

"But Rochester, ever the gentlemanly footman, helped pick up the broken glass before replacing her spilled drink with another," William said.

"I'm so sorry I missed that," the duchess said. "Though it's probably just as well your mother didn't witness it. She'd have been horrified. She already thinks a hoyden like me with such an undistinguished background has corrupted you."

The duke gave her a roguish wink. "And she'd be right, my love. But I'm not complaining."

The duchess laughed and swatted his arm.

"Come, let's join the dance," the duke said.

"One more sip," the duchess said before setting her glass aside and allowing her husband to lead her off.

"Gad, it's getting sappy around here," Phillip Hurst said. "Norwood, point me in the direction of the refreshments room."

"It's downstairs in what normally serves as the dining room," William replied.

"I wouldn't mind getting a bite to eat," Charlotte said.

"Not to mention I'd like to get off my feet for a while. Would anyone else like to join us in getting some food?"

Phoebe said she would.

"No, thanks," Serena said. "Charles and I recently came from there."

"Now that our group is whittled down to just the two of you, perhaps you should take advantage of the opportunity to dance as well," Charlotte suggested.

"Come along, wife," William said. "I'm sure they can figure out if they wish to dance without our help." He gave Charles and Serena an apologetic look.

"I'll leave it up to you whether or not we follow Lady Norwood's suggestion," Charles said.

Serena shook her head. "I'd prefer to wait for that second waltz I requested."

"As you wish," Charles said.

They sipped their lemonades and watched the dancers moving through the figures.

"How is Jem doing?" Charles asked suddenly. "I feel remiss not to have inquired after him earlier."

"He's doing quite well. I took him shopping and he now has a suitable wardrobe." She glanced at him. "The outfit he wore to Greenwich was supplied by Grace, who sent over a few outfits her sons had outgrown."

"I wondered," Charles said. "Considering that he wore that altered shirt of your father's just the evening before."

"He still insists on sleeping in that, even though I bought him some nightshirts," Serena said with a laugh.

"Any progress in finding him a family?" Charles asked.

"I haven't done much with regard to that," Serena admitted. "But I will. One of the reasons I haven't is that I was waiting for you to take a closer look into his background, just in case there is someone who might have a familial claim on him."

"I apologize for not doing that yet," he said. "Especially after my lecture about placing him somewhere as soon as you can."

"It's fine, Charles. I'm sure you've been busy, and I have as well. It seems small boys don't automatically take care of themselves, and even though I've put one of the housemaids in charge of him, it's largely been up to me to help him settle into the household." She held up a hand. "But not too settled, I know. To the best of my ability I intend to heed your warning about not letting him get too attached to us."

Jem was occupying so much of her attention that, for the time being, she'd abandoned her quest to find a property to house girls dealing with unwed pregnancies. Although she intended to resume work on it as soon as she had Jem settled somewhere.

"Somewhat surprisingly, Sir Roland has kept me busy this week. The Foreign Secretary has been consulting with him on some diplomatic matters. I've done more work in the past two days than I did in the previous two weeks. But the business is concluded and I should have more time to look into it for you. Plus, I haven't forgotten my promise about the apprenticeships."

Edwina and Mr. Latimer returned from the dance floor, and Latimer asked Serena to dance the next set, so Charles offered to partner Edwina. After that various gentlemen requested dances with Serena, so Charles ended up back in the bachelors' corner while he waited for the next waltz.

The next waltz didn't occur for over an hour. Closer to two hours if one were keeping track, and Charles was. He and Serena had drifted apart in the intervening time, but he kept tabs on where she was in the ballroom, anticipating the need to hasten back to her side to claim the waltz he'd promised her.

Serena had danced occasionally, and every time she did, his gut twisted with jealousy. An emotion he had no right to feel, considering he had no claim on her, nor would he ever have one. For the most part, though, she'd mingled with the Duchess of Rochester, the ladies Norwood and Beasley, and a number of other females he didn't recognize. He suspected they were part of the group of ladies who met weekly at Lady Beasley's residence. They looked like the feminine version of the clusters of gentlemen who frequently gathered together at these functions to debate politics.

Charles bided his time back in the bachelor corner. Gilbert Ogilvy, known to all as Gilly, was suffering some good-natured teasing about his latest exploit.

A losing wager had resulted in him being required to smuggle a foul-mouthed parrot into an assembly at Almack's, but the bird, instead of performing as expected and letting loose a string of expletives, had flown to a perch near Lady Jersey and charmed the lady thoroughly by repeating the phrase "Aren't you a lovely sight to behold?" the entire evening.

The consensus was that Gilly had managed to train the bird to say that, but he vigorously denied it.

"'Pon my soul, I didn't. I was as surprised as anyone, and more pleased than most. I bet Micklesby a monkey that it wouldn't utter anything untoward for half an hour, and it didn't. Didn't say one vulgar word the entire time we were there, though it swore a blue streak once I had it back in the carriage. I arrived at Almack's pockets to let, and now I've got five hundred pounds to my name and only a month to go until I receive my allowance next quarter day."

Knowing Gilly, Charles doubted he would manage to hold on to that amount until he received his allowance. He liked Gilly, but the man lived to gamble whether it was at the card tables, the betting book at White's, or anywhere that offered him the opportunity to make a wager.

As Gilly launched into another story, Charles caught the opening strain of the next dance. Recognizing the three-quarter tempo of a waltz, he excused himself from the group and hurried to find Serena.

She smiled as he approached. "Another minute and I would have come in search of you."

"It would have been easy enough to find me. I told you where I'd be," Charles said.

"I was beginning to think you'd forgotten."

"Never," he said. "Gilly Ogilvy had just finished telling his story about taking a parrot into Almack's."

"Papa told me about that. It did sound quite amusing, but..." Serena shook her head. "No matter how amusing Gilly and his antics are, that man is a menace to some poor girl's dowry. If he ever persuades some lady to marry him, I hope her father uses the marriage settlements to keep whatever she brings to the marriage out of his hands."

"One would hope." Charles took her into his arms and they began to dance. "Still, for all his faults, I can't help liking the fellow."

"Oh, I feel the same," Serena admitted. "But that won't prevent me from giving whomever is to become the future Mrs. Ogilvy a little advice about protecting her interests."

She glanced at him through her lashes and his heart did a little jig in his chest. It wasn't a coquettish look precisely, but it was close enough, and once again he was waging an internal battle to keep his emotions in check.

"I don't doubt that for a moment," he murmured.

And then, against his better judgment, he drew her ever-so-slightly closer and let himself enjoy the simple pleasure of waltzing with her.

Chapter Nine

Two days after the Peytons' ball, the Wednesday Afternoon Social Club held its regular meeting at the newest property they'd leased to house war widows. The change of location wasn't the only thing different about today's meeting.

Virtually every woman present wore a mobcap and a large apron over their plainest gown, though the Duchess of Rochester was once again attired in a pair of trousers, as were some of the other ladies present. The sleeves of Grace's linen shirt were streaked with dirt marks, evidence of the dirty cupboards she'd just finished cleaning out.

Serena was sure the sleeves of her own dress would show a similar amount of dirt on them, except the dung brown color hid it quite well.

"Remind me whose idea this was," Julia Keene remarked

as she removed her mobcap in an effort to resecure her long braid, which had worked loose from its pins.

"I suppose it was mine originally," Grace replied. She climbed onto a wooden kitchen chair so she could begin polishing one of the brass lamp fittings that ringed the wall of the room. "It started the other night when my husband was mistaken for a footman at the Peytons' ball. I had a very good time teasing him about it, but then it occurred to me that it could be quite a good thing to fill a role that is different from our usual role in life. And then I thought why not have one of our weekly meetings dedicated to a work day at the new property to help the preparations move along more quickly?"

"Why not indeed?" Julia said as she wound the braid around the crown of her head, pinning it back into place. Or attempting to. But despite her words, she flashed a good-natured grin.

"Here. Let me." Julia's sister, Anna Keene, propped against the wall the broom she was using to sweep the floor and went over to help with the repinning of the hair.

"I don't mind, Aunt Grace," Phoebe Talbot said. She sat at a table, polishing donated silverware. "I mean, I don't *love* this type of work, but I do like the feeling of satisfaction that comes from accomplishing a task that matters. It's a great deal more fulfilling than completing yet another piece of embroidery."

"She has a point, Julia," Anna Keene said. "Embroidery is the bane of your existence."

"True, but waxing woodwork is, in my opinion, only marginally better than needlework. But…" She picked up the rag and wax pot once again. "As Phoebe pointed out, it gives one a great sense of accomplishment. Not to mention a few blisters."

A loud thump from the floor above caused them all to look up. "What on earth...?" Serena began. "Are you all right up there?" she called up in the direction of the ceiling. Edwina was upstairs with about ten other ladies overseeing the arrangement of the bedrooms.

"I'll make sure no one is hurt," Julia offered. She hurried from the room, and they could hear the sound of her footsteps as she ran up the wooden stairs to the floor above. A few minutes later she came clattering back down. "A headboard propped against the wall fell down. The only thing injured was a bucket of soapy water, which was knocked over."

"Thank heavens," Grace said. She climbed down from the chair and moved it beneath the next light fixture, then climbed on the seat again to polish that lamp. "I think we should break for refreshments soon, don't you?"

"You'll get no argument from me," Julia said as she perched her mobcap back onto her head at a jaunty angle. "Physical labor gives me an appetite."

"How about at two o'clock? And let's challenge ourselves to see how much progress we can make in the next half an hour," Serena suggested. "Is that agreeable to everybody?" There was unanimous support for this plan so she added, "Julia, would you mind going back upstairs and let them know to take a break at two?"

Julia gave her a cheeky salute. "Aye, aye, cap'n."

"I don't think I've ever had a more refreshing cup of tea than this one," Julia Keene remarked forty-five minutes later.

They were all gathered in the kitchen, seated around the long worktable in the middle of the room. Charlotte and Winifred Martin, who acted as the club's treasurer, had taken charge of heating the teakettles, since not every lady present had knowledge of how to work the stove. Plates of biscuits and tea sandwiches were placed in the center of the table, although in far fewer quantities than when they'd first sat down for their break.

"Work seems to have given us hearty appetites," Serena said. "For a while there, I feared we would run out of food."

"You've barely touched the food on your plate, Edwina," Grace remarked. "I'm feeling quite gluttonous in comparison. This is my"—she paused for a moment, appearing to consider something—"sixth—or possibly seventh?—biscuit. And don't ask me how many tea sandwiches I had. I can't believe you aren't as ravenous as the rest of us. You worked just as hard."

"I don't know what my problem is," Edwina said. "Initially, I thought I'd caught something from Jason, because he had...well, stomach issues, shall we say. But his went away in a day or two. My stomach has been prone to queasiness for a week and a half now. I'm just going to have to make a trip to the apothecary and get a tonic for indigestion."

"I hope he can give you something to help," Grace said.

"Oh, I expect he will," Edwina replied. "I've put off going because I keep thinking it will go away on its own, but I suppose I need to accept that it is not." She took a sip of her tea. "If anyone would like those lemon tarts on my plate, please feel free to take them since the rest have been eaten already." She didn't have to make the offer twice.

As the ladies continued to munch and sip, Serena stood and walked to the head of the table. "Since we're all in one room, this seems like a good time for this week's business meeting." She waited a moment, then continued. "The first order of business is to hear a report from our exploratory committee. Mrs. Lyndhurst and Anna, since you're both leading this committee, could you tell us what progress you've made toward choosing a charitable entity for us to partner with. And for those of you who missed last week's meeting, we're looking to enhance educational opportunities for children, either through work with a struggling charity school or a charity-run orphanage."

Anna Keene and Mrs. Lyndhurst, the married sister of Winifred Martin, joined Serena at the head of the table.

"I'm sorry to report we haven't made much progress. We've encountered opposition from the institutions we've approached so far. They've all expressed reservations about pairing with a group run by ladies. It's been suggested to us that they would be receptive to a program such as we're proposing, and would be willing to work with us, *if* we had a gentleman to oversee our efforts and to act as our liaison."

"What utter nonsense," Julia Keene said. "They like what we're proposing, but they won't work with us because there isn't a man at the helm? I can't even…" She held up one hand and shook her head. "I can't even express my disgust with that attitude. Honestly. It's 1818, not the middle ages."

"It would be funny if it weren't so tragic," Phoebe Talbot said disgustedly.

"Tragic is perhaps overstating it, dear," the Duchess of Rochester said. "But it's surely infuriating. As well as a completely *unnecessary* obstacle."

"Unnecessary, but not entirely unexpected," Serena said. "In light of this setback, what does the committee suggest as a next step?"

"We still have some institutions that we haven't heard from yet, so we'll contact them again. Hopefully, by next week's meeting we'll have something positive to report. But if they all express similar sentiments, we're not sure how to proceed."

"If that's the case, we could have a gentleman act as a figurehead for us," Serena said. "I don't especially like being forced to do that, but we can hardly wait around for more enlightened attitudes to prevail, so if we must, we must. I doubt they'd say no if a man of stature approached them. I believe we have a few of those among our husbands and male relatives."

"Mr. Townshend might be a good candidate," Charlotte said. "He's already helping with the apprenticeships. I doubt he'd say no."

"True, but I don't want to overburden him with our requests," Serena said. "I'm sure between all of the men in our lives, we can come up with one to be our figurehead, if that's the route we must take to carry out our plans. I think for now, let's table this discussion until the committee has contacted every institution."

There was a chorus of agreement.

"Let's pass around the donation basket, and while we're doing that, Winifred, why don't you update us on the current state of the funds in our treasury." The daughter of a successful merchant, Winifred was the natural person to serve in this position. She was used to helping her father with his business.

Winifred came around to take Serena's place at the head of the table to deliver her report, which, in a nutshell, was that they had sufficient cash for their current operations. When she finished, Serena called Grace up to talk about the upcoming subscription ball they planned to hold.

"Plans are proceeding apace," Grace said. "A date has been set. Mark your calendars for four weeks from tomorrow. We've placed an order with the printer, and we hope to have the printed tickets back in time to hand out at next week's meeting so you can begin persuading your friends and family to buy them. Let's have a repeat of last year, ladies, and sell *every single ticket.*"

As Grace went back to her seat, Serena addressed the group. "Is there any further business or questions?" She waited a moment, but when no one spoke up she said, "All right then. Let's consider this portion of our meeting adjourned. Once we've had our fill of tea and food, we'll get back to work."

Two hours later, everyone had departed except for Serena and Edwina, who'd arrived together and were making one last check to see that all windows had been closed and latched, and that all lamps and candles had been extinguished.

"I'm pleased with what we accomplished today," Edwina said. "But I wouldn't want to do it every week. My back aches, my feet ache, and"—she gave Serena a rueful look—"at the moment I can't ignore how old I am."

"You just turned forty last month. That's hardly old, and you look a good decade younger."

"Even so, I wouldn't want Jason to see me just now. I look like a charwoman and I feel like one too."

"A cup of tea and a bit of time with your feet propped up will revive you, I've no doubt." She gave Edwina a sly smile. "Perhaps Jason could rub your aching feet for you."

"That would be heavenly, but this evening we're supposed to attend a rout at the Denholms. I don't think there's time for a foot rub. I'll have to rush to get ready as it is."

"Afterward then?" Serena said.

"What an impertinent idea." But despite her words, Edwina's eyes glinted with amusement. "What kind of wicked female do you think I am?"

"A very wicked one, now that Jason is your beau." Serena raised a brow suggestively. "And a very well satisfied one too."

"I suppose I am both of those," Edwina admitted. "But above all, Jason makes me happy."

"Has the subject of marriage come up? Or do you intend to remain a merry widow?"

"It's been discussed, but Jason is leaving the decision up to me." She paused, her expression thoughtful. "I have to say that the idea holds a great deal of appeal. I'd be lying if I said it didn't. But I'm not quite sure I'm ready to give up my independence."

"With a forward-thinking man like Jason, do you think things would change all that much if you married him?"

"Probably not," Edwina said. "Which is why I'm seriously thinking of saying yes. Just not yet."

Finished with their task, they returned to the front hall and collected their bonnets. Edwina, standing before the hall mirror, shook her head slightly as she replaced her mobcap with a stylish poke bonnet. "I don't know how presentable I'm going to look tonight. My maid is going to be horrified when she sees my hair."

"You'll look lovely as always," Serena assured her.

They went out the front door, and Serena locked it before they proceeded to Edwina's carriage. Once inside, Edwina picked up the thread of their conversation.

"And what about your future?" Edwina asked gently.

"I trust the future will take care of itself, and in any case, I'm pretty content with the present," Serena said.

Edwina opened her mouth to speak, but then seemed to reconsider, and sighed instead. She studied Serena a long moment, her lips turned up in the hint of a smile. A smile that was a bit too knowing for Serena's comfort.

"Have you considered," Edwina said at last, her words measured and deliberate, "that you're so concerned with the well-being of others that you ignore your own well-being and happiness?"

"I have a very fulfilling life. More than many women I would argue."

"Yes, you do. But fulfilling isn't always the same as happy."

"No, it's not. But I'm not *un*happy. I'm satisfied."

"And I'm glad. But sometimes the key to one's happiness is right in front of you and you don't see it."

"If you're referring to Charles, why the sudden subtlety? You've never made a secret of the fact that you favor a match between us. Why start now?"

Edwina's smile broadened. "Any subtlety was accidental, I assure you. I'd be ecstatic if the two of you made a match."

"Maybe I don't need a man in my life."

"No," Edwina agreed. "But you might want one. They can be...delightfully diverting."

Serena couldn't help smiling at that. Edwina was correct. Men could be very delightfully diverting, to use Edwina's phrase. A vision flashed through her mind—of her and Charles together in a tangle of bed linens and naked limbs, of panting breaths and knowing touches and exquisite pleasure.

"Do you think Charles would..." she blurted out before her mind caught up with her mouth. She hadn't intended to speak the question out loud. But she could hardly retract it now. "Would agree to...an arrangement?"

Edwina contemplated this for a moment. "If by arrangement, you mean would he be willing to indulge in an affair, I'm not sure he would. He's a very honorable man."

"True, but Thomas was an honorable man, and yet we didn't wait for marriage." Edwina was one of only two people who knew the complete truth of her past with Thomas Carlisle, that they'd fallen desperately in love and succumbed to their passions before he'd departed to fight Napoleon's armies on the Peninsula, that they'd planned to marry upon his return from the war. Except he hadn't returned, and the plans they'd made had come to nothing in the end.

But she pushed these memories aside. Now wasn't the time to revisit them.

"Forget I raised the notion," Serena said. "I don't even know why I did."

One of Edwina's delicately shaped brows rose ever so slightly as she gave Serena a knowing look. "To me it's quite obvious why you'd suggest such a thing.

Because you've finally realized it's time for you and Mr. Townshend to quit dancing around your attraction to each other and *do* something about it."

The carriage came to a halt before the Huntington residence, and Edwina leaned forward.

"You're the most fearless person I know. Don't let the fear of getting close to someone again prevent you from finding the happiness you deserve. Whether that person is Mr. Townshend or someone else. Promise me you'll think about that."

Serena just looked at her friend for a long moment and then gave a little nod of acquiescence before stepping from the carriage.

Chapter Ten

~~~

Following through with his promise to probe some more into Jem's background, Charles revisited the neighborhood where they'd found the boy. Completing the task to his satisfaction, he directed the hackney driver to take him to the Huntington residence.

Menken showed him to the sitting room, where he found Serena, kneeling on the carpet, unpacking a wooden crate of books. As he stepped through the doorway, she smiled and dusted off her hands. Books and paper wrapping littered the floor around her.

"I've confined the mess to a smaller area today," she said.

"So I see," he said, drawing closer to take a look. "What have we here?"

"Books for Jem. Storybooks and primers. Colored chalk and drawing paper. Some lined notebooks for him to practice penmanship. And I ordered a few novels for myself," she admitted, looking up at him through her lashes. His heartbeat kicked up a notch.

"As one must." He studied the purchases she'd unpacked so far. It looked as if she expected Jem would be staying here for a while. This didn't necessarily surprise him, but it did make him question her commitment to finding the child a permanent home any time soon.

"I can finish this later. I'm ready for a break. Would you like me to ring for tea?" She stood and flicked her skirts to shake off some small bits of packing material that clung to them.

"No," Charles said. "I don't intend to stay long. I just wanted to pass along what else I've learned about Jem's background."

She gave him a keen look and he could see the concern in her eyes that he might have news that someone else might have a claim on the boy.

"It isn't very much," he said to put her mind at ease. "Details like one's parentage don't mean much in neighborhoods like that one."

"In that case, let's get comfortable and you can share what you do know." She sat on the sofa and he took an armchair opposite from her.

"Where is Jem?" he asked.

"At the park feeding the ducks with his nursemaid, Ellie. They left with a large sack of stale bread and knowing Jem they won't come home until every last crumb has been tossed to the waterfowl."

He nodded. "We can talk freely then."

A gray-striped kitten poked its head out from beneath

the sofa. It rubbed its head against her skirt. "Since when did you get a cat?" he asked.

"Since a few days ago when I took Jem over to visit with the Duke of Rochester's children. We came home with Tabitha, so named because, as you can see, she's a tabby cat."

This was either a brilliant move or a very bad one, and time would tell which. Having a kitten to take to a new home might make the transition easier for Jem, or it might mean that the boy (and his kitten) would become more entrenched in the domesticity of the Huntington household. It was the latter that worried Charles.

He knew it was coincidental that there was a degree of similarity between Jem's and Serena's gray eyes, which were nearly the identical shade of dark bluish-gray. It wasn't an entirely uncommon eye color as far as gray eyes went, but it was a striking one.

If she took Jem in, and raised him as one would raise a ward...he didn't trust that people wouldn't leap to the wrong conclusion. It would be all too easy for the gossips to convince people that Jem was Serena's child, born out of wedlock and kept hidden away for a few years until it seemed safe for him to appear in her life. Gossip could be so vicious. They'd tear her reputation to shreds.

He needed to persuade her that placing Jem elsewhere was the right course of action.

Serena scooped the kitten up and placed it on her lap, where she lazily scratched the top of its head. "I'm waiting for you to reveal your findings," she prompted.

"Yes, of course." He cleared his throat. "Tabitha distracted me for a moment there. First of all, I'm confident that Jem has no one to look after him. I managed to find where Jem lived with Old Mam before she died. No one seems to know where Old Mam found the child originally, but the story I got from her neighbors was she took him in when his mother died. Nor did any of them seem to know anything about his real mother other than she was deceased."

"It's sad that there's no one to claim him, but not entirely surprising."

"So you can move ahead with finding a family for Jem," he said, the words coming out more gruffly than he intended. "Have you been working on that?"

Serena's smile faded and she fidgeted in her chair. Tabitha, perhaps sensing Serena's discomfiture, leaped down and disappeared under the sofa again. "Not really. I've been busy getting Jem settled in."

"I thought we agreed that he shouldn't get too settled here."

"We did, but surely you don't expect me to simply ignore the boy while he's here."

Charles frowned. "No, that's not what I'm saying at all. But looking after his welfare and looking into a permanent home for him aren't mutually exclusive."

She stood up and began to pace about the room. "There are things he needs to learn first."

"I'm sure that's—"

"No, hear me out a minute before you start raising your objections." Her eyes, now the color of gathering storm clouds, flashed angrily at him. "I asked Jem if he knew how old he was."

He waited, giving her the opportunity to have her say, belatedly realizing she wanted a response.

"And? What did he say?" he prompted. He didn't

know what else to say because he wasn't sure where that statement was leading.

"He's not certain. He thinks he might be seven. He heard Old Mam talking to a clothes peddler when she was buying clothes to replace those he'd outgrown and she told the man she needed shoes to fit a seven-year-old boy. So I asked Jem if he remembered how long ago this was and he said it was after the snows were gone, that the yellow flowers were getting ready to bloom. I presume the yellow flowers were daffodils. At any rate, I said 'That sounds like it must have been last March' and that's when I discovered he doesn't even know the names of the months of the year. Or that the year is even divided into months."

She stopped pacing and turned toward him with her hands on her hips. Serena the crusader.

"Well, that means he probably turned eight recently," Charles said. "In a way, that's good news because he's around the size an eight-year-old boy should be, albeit a thin one. So he's probably not suffering from stunted growth due to malnutrition as we suspected he might be."

"Well, yes, but that's not the point, Charles. I'm only coming to realize how much he doesn't know for a child that age." She resumed her pacing. It did show her figure off to great advantage, though he was sure she wouldn't appreciate that observation.

"He doesn't know the months, he doesn't know his ABCs, he doesn't know how to count. He couldn't tell me what number came before seven or after it, although when I named six and eight, he knew that they *were* numbers, but he has no conception of how they're ordered."

"He's a bright child. I'm sure he'll catch up quickly."

This response did not have the soothing effect he might have hoped.

"Yes, but it will still take quite some time because he has so much to catch up on. Even things like saying 'please' and 'thank you' are foreign concepts to him. And simple things like correctly using a knife and fork to eat. Taking baths when needed rather than just once in a great while and combing his hair each morning and washing his hands before meals, or even simply when they're dirty. Don't you think he ought to learn those things before we attempt to place him somewhere?"

"I'll concede learning basic manners would ease his transition into someone's home, but surely the rest could wait until he's settled somewhere."

"Oh for the love..." She threw her hands in the air. Her cheeks were flushed, her eyes snapping with hot, gray sparks of exasperation, and to Charles, she looked absolutely beautiful, despite his being the reason for her ire.

"...of all that's holy," she finished. "Sometimes you resemble nothing so much as a dog with a bone he refuses to set down."

Ouch. Charles bit back the retort that rose to his lips, the one where he pointed out he could say the same about her. He did, however, express the thought with one scathingly lofted brow. When it came to contests of which of them was the most stubborn, he would lose. Every time.

After a moment of trading glares (during which he still couldn't help but admire her beautiful face), she let out a huff of air, and the tension between them began to give way, as if vanquished by her exhale.

"For the moment, can we agree to disagree on the timing? I don't want to argue anymore. In the end, we share the same goal for him, we just disagree on the path to arrive at that goal."

He hoped she was right, and that he was wrong to suspect that their goal for Jem diverged in one significant way. Namely, that Serena wouldn't be able to bring herself to send the boy to live with someone else.

"Very well, though I reserve the right to nag you if I feel things are dragging out to the detriment of Jem's interests."

Her lovely mouth curved into a wry smile. "What if I win you over to my way of thinking?"

"You can try."

Something shifted in her gaze and he had the oddest sense of imminent danger, which was ridiculous he knew. Nonetheless, his heart thudded harder and faster in his chest and a new kind of tension crackled in the air between them.

He came to his feet. "Let's call a temporary truce. I've delivered the message I came to convey, so I'll forgo any further nagging for the time being and bid you good day."

She took a step toward him. And then another. "As long as you understand, *I'm* not encouraging you to rush off."

No, rushing off was his own idea, borne of a need to flee what he heard in her voice…*I'm not encouraging you to rush off.*

And what he thought he saw in her gaze.

Curiosity. Invitation. Yearning.

They added up to temptations he ought to resist.

"Not encouraging my departure perhaps, but probably glad of it all the same," he said, trying to diffuse the atmosphere with levity.

She closed the distance between them. "Not glad at all, Charles. Not even a little bit." She lifted her chin and studied his face, and because it was Serena, she wasn't trying to hide it behind flirtatious glances or lowered lashes. She was bold. Unabashed. Confident.

She reached out, caught his hand in hers. Again, that zing of awareness flashed through him at her touch. "The other night when you helped me put Jem to bed, and then the next day in Greenwich...was it just me or did you feel there have been moments of connection between us?"

He struggled to keep his expression neutral. "I don't think..." But he couldn't bring himself to lie to her, and besides she could probably see the truth in his eyes. "If there was, I think it's best we ignore them."

"I don't think I can any longer," she said. "Or, at least, I don't want to."

"Serena, we can't..."

She placed one finger against his lips, silencing him. "Why can't we see where our feelings take us?"

"Because it's not a good idea." His words had a hoarse, almost strangled quality, but dammit how could he speak normally with her finger pressing lightly, warmly against his mouth.

"But *why*?" she asked.

"You know why. There are numerous reasons."

"I don't know what you know. Or think you know." She lightly traced his bottom lip with one finger. "I do know I'm curious about what your lips would feel like on mine. And I think you're just as curious, but that your notions of chivalry...propriety...social prohibitions...all prevent you from acting on that curiosity. But I don't let myself be bound by those considerations." Her eyes followed the track of her finger as it continued to trace a path to and fro along his lip. "Well, perhaps sometimes I do, but not always. Let's not be bound by them right now. What do you say, Charles?"

He didn't say anything. He couldn't. It was as if his breath had left his lungs, making speech impossible. And even if the ability to speak hadn't deserted him, he didn't wish to interrupt the way she softly caressed his mouth. His will had crumpled before it.

She cupped his chin lightly, her thumb now simply resting against his mouth. "Shall I kiss you then?" She paused, and as the question hung in the silence, a hint of a smile tipped up the corners of her mouth. "You're not protesting, which isn't quite the same as permission. But does it imply permission?" Her other hand curled around his neck as she raised herself up onto her toes to bring her mouth level with his. "Let's make it clear. Meet me halfway, Charles," she whispered. "Please. Meet me halfway."

His heart felt like it would beat right out of his chest as wild feelings of desire coursed inside him, overwhelming his good sense. Surrender was inevitable. He knew it and he was quite sure she did too. Her finger slipped away from his lips as he moved to close the gap between them.

Petal soft he thought when their mouths met, and then sensations replaced thinking. Warm lips opening, a moist tongue seeking, a kiss no longer tame sending heat flooding through him. Serena's body pressed into his, but through whose effort...his?...hers?...he didn't know.

One part of his mind registered the contours of her breasts, womanly and wanton against his chest. A soft groan escaped him, and his arms tightened around her. She clung to him as well. Her fingers, threaded in his hair, pressed into the back of his head, making demands of their own.

Even if he'd had the wherewithal to call a halt to the proceedings, it was clear from the way she held on to him that she wasn't ready to stop.

Thank God.

They kissed and clung and caressed until, breathless and mussed, reality began to intrude upon them once again.

Serena was the first to remember that they might be alone, but that didn't mean they had more than a modicum of privacy. The door to the sitting room was wide open. Hence, it was possible to hear anyone in the hallway. Or even in the foyer, if a person was speaking loudly enough.

As an excited eight-year-old returning from the park might do. Was, in fact, doing. She could hear Jem's voice shrill with childish excitement and Menken's voice replying, deep and measured.

The sitting room was toward the back of the house, but if Menken directed Jem and Ellie there, as well he might, knowing that she and Charles were here, they had only a few minutes to set themselves aright. She didn't disregard propriety to the extent that she wanted to have the two of them caught in a passionate embrace by the boy and his maid.

She slid her hands to cradle his cheeks and broke the kiss. "Charles." His name came out in a breathy whisper. "I think we're about to have company."

His eyes, hazy with passion, widened as the implications of her remark sank into his consciousness. His arms abruptly dropped away and he stepped back, before sweeping a hand through his hair as a look of utter chagrin crossed his features. She could see the apology forming in his mind before he even spoke the words.

"Don't," she said. "I know what you're about to say and it's unnecessary."

"Hardly," he objected. "I forgot myself and I'm not proud of that. And whether you want to hear my apology or not, I feel I owe you one."

The voices of Jem and Ellie were becoming clearer. They'd be in the sitting room at any moment now.

"Don't be an idiot. I started that and we both know it." She reached out and adjusted his cravat, which had gone slightly askew.

Before either could say another word, Jem rushed into the room. To no one's surprise, he made a beeline for Charles, impetuously clasping him about the legs in a tight hug.

Charles ruffled the boy's hair. "And who do we have here?" he said.

"It's me. Jem," the boy replied, looking up at Charles.

"No, you're bamming me," Charles said, shaking his head. "Jem has shaggy curls that spill over his collar and hide his eyes. Now you must tell me what you've done with him for he's a great favorite of mine." He narrowed his eyes and gave Jem a mock glare.

The boy giggled. "Mr. Towns. It *is* me. Jem. I got my hair cut."

"Aha. Now I recognize you. I was fooled for a minute."

Jem unwound his arms from about Charles's legs and skipped over to a sofa. He was about to climb up and take a seat when Charles cleared his throat. The boy turned about and gave him a questioning glance.

"It's not polite for us fellows to take a seat before a lady. We must wait until Lady Serena has taken her seat."

"Oh," Jem said, appearing to contemplate this tidbit of etiquette. He turned his gaze to Serena, then he put his hands on the sofa cushion, prepared to boost himself back onto the sofa, but obviously waiting to do so after she'd taken a seat. She pressed her lips together, fighting a smile. He looked so determined to take this rule seriously.

"Ellie, I'll keep Jem occupied for a while. You may go have some tea, if you wish," Serena said. "I'll ring when I need you to take charge of him again."

"Very good, ma'am," the maid replied with a little curtsey. She slipped out the door.

Serena chose to settle in one of the armchairs flanking the sofa. As soon as she sat, Jem's head pivoted to Charles, who gave him a slight nod. With a bit of a backward hop, Jem slid onto his chosen seat. Charles sat in the armchair at the opposite end of the sofa, as far away from her as the seating arrangement allowed. She had no doubt this was deliberate on his part. Jem looked as if he shared her disappointment, probably hoping his favorite would choose to sit next to him.

Jem began telling Charles of his visit to the park to feed the ducks, animatedly describing the "giant duck with the black eye mask" that tried to bite him. A swan probably, she thought, only half-listening to Jem's account of his park adventure.

In her mind, she was replaying that kiss and wondering what she could do to bring about another. Unfortunately, she'd be up against his rigid notions of right and wrong. Among them was undoubtedly the idea that a gentleman didn't trifle with a lady's affections by kissing her capriciously. And what's more she was quite sure he blamed himself for the incident, and therefore was probably steeling himself to not let it happen again. *But...*

That kiss was worth repeating.

For her, long dead emotions had started to reanimate, and clearly Charles wasn't immune to this attraction between them either.

The man, however, was too honorable for his own good. But as maddening as that was, she couldn't help admiring him for it too. Not that she intended to let his penchant for all things noble get in the way of exploring a mutually satisfying dalliance, if that's what they both wanted.

She tried to suppress the gleeful smile that threatened to form on her lips. Charles could try to deny there'd been an attraction between them all he wanted, but they both knew he'd been unable to hide that he desired her. She could use that knowledge to her advantage. Both of their advantages, really. She just had to convince him to take a chance.

Besides, if it came down to a battle of wills, she intended to emerge the victor.

Chapter Eleven

⌇

The following afternoon, Sir Roland decided to pay a visit to sick friend and told Charles to consider himself free for the rest of the day once he finished copying the three letters that he'd taken in dictation that morning. He completed the task by half past one.

This had become more and more common as of late—Charles easily finishing the day's work by noon, or by early afternoon at the latest. Charles appreciated his employer's generosity, but he still felt guilty being paid for hours in which he did no work.

The last thing he wished to do was sit at his desk twiddling his thumbs and dwelling on yesterday's kiss.

That kiss.

That kiss had been many things…magical, bold, enchanting, fiery, revelatory, complicated. There were any number of adjectives that could describe it. Any number of emotions he felt in the wake of it.

But hanging over all that was one truth that couldn't be ignored. It had been a mistake. A lapse in judgment. A one-time happening they mustn't repeat.

Ever.

He didn't have vast experience with women. At Cambridge, funds had been too tight for him to afford even the modest baubles a man usually gave to a woman with whom he dallied. During the final year of his studies, he'd had a brief liaison with a widow. Since then, there'd been no other female in his bed. Nor did he have any plans that there would be.

He straightened the papers on his desk, took the finished letters and placed them on Sir Roland's desk to await his signature, and contemplated what he wished to do. Something to keep his mind from dwelling on how Serena's lips felt pressed to his, the sweet taste of her mouth, the way his body roared to life when he held her in his arms.

Hunger pangs reminded him it was time for a bite to eat, and with no work requiring his presence here, he rather fancied eating elsewhere, among people rather than alone. So the question was...his club or a tavern? White's seemed the obvious choice since he'd almost certainly run into acquaintances there. He wouldn't mind a bit of company to keep him from thinking about Serena.

Decision made, he retrieved a leather portfolio from a large cabinet. The portfolio held papers related to his meeting at the Swan and Bull tavern yesterday. He'd peruse them after he ate, preferably while seated in one of the club's comfortable leather armchairs with his feet propped on an ottoman and a glass of ale at the ready.

However, his visions of a leisurely afternoon at the club were dispelled immediately upon entering White's. Loud voices from a rowdy group in the billiards room assailed his ears as soon as he walked in the door. This was not typical for a midday during the week, but neither was it unheard of. A highly anticipated curricle race or boxing match often prompted rowdy celebrations after the fact and Charles assumed that something of that sort was at play here.

He proceeded to make his way upstairs to the dining room, and by the time he reached it, he'd heard enough chatter to know that an unsanctioned boxing match had taken place earlier that morning on the outskirts of London. There were no empty tables in the dining room, but Ambrose-Stone, who was with two other gentlemen, waved him over to his table, which currently sported one vacant seat.

"Brosey, Farrars, Plumley," Charles greeted them. He seated himself in the remaining chair, setting the leather portfolio on the floor so that it leaned against the chair's legs. "I didn't anticipate this crush at the club. I thought I'd pop in for a quick bite to eat. Glad I can share in your spot."

"I take it you weren't at the fight then," Lord Farrars remarked.

"Didn't even hear a whisper about it until just now," Charles said.

"Unfortunately, the authorities did. The match wasn't supposed to take place until the day after tomorrow, but it was moved up to evade the magistrates," Plumley drawled. He and Farrars were close friends. "Impressive fight, even if it only lasted seven rounds."

"Who won?" Charles asked.

"A giant of a fellow originally from the West Indies. Apparently, Borland discovered him working the docks here in London and had him trained in the art of boxing."

"Borland?" Charles asked. "I've never heard of him."

"Neither had I until today," Ambrose-Stone said. "He's the grandson of a baronet from somewhere in Yorkshire. Rumor has it, he's been living on the Continent, avoiding his creditors. Likely spotted his protégé when he was returning home for a visit." Ambrose-Stone tilted his head to the side, as if motioning in that direction of the room. "Borland's the tall fellow with dark blond hair at the head of the long table in the back corner."

Charles turned to get a look at the man. Borland was standing at one end of the table, holding a glass aloft as if making a toast. The man's cheeks were flushed and he looked slightly unsteady on his feet, as if he'd already imbibed a great deal of spirits. Indeed, as he swept the glass through the air, he accidentally tipped it causing some of the contents to spill out, and eliciting raucous laughter and guffaws from his similarly inebriated companions.

But what struck Charles most forcefully about the man's appearance was that Charles might have been looking in a mirror. Or almost. A closer inspection revealed there were some differences in their features—Borland's jaw was rounder, his ears were overly large and stuck out from his head. His hair, slightly lighter than Charles's shade of medium brown, was beginning to recede, giving his forehead a greater prominence.

But for all these differences, the similarities were striking. Uncanny even. A cold sense of foreboding gripped Charles. He swallowed hard and, with difficulty, tried to assume an expression of detached amusement.

"Does this fellow Borland have a first name?" he asked.

As it turned out, Charles didn't linger once he finished his food. He excused himself, citing a pressing engagement, and since there was nothing requiring him to return to work, he went back to his rented rooms. Once there he holed up in the main room, which functioned as both a study and a drawing room on the rare occasions he entertained guests there.

If he'd been craving company when he chose to lunch at his club, once he spotted Borland, he'd wanted nothing so much as a quiet place to think. His resemblance to the man had shaken him, and frankly, he was surprised that none of those with whom he'd dined had remarked upon it. To him, the similarities had been obvious, but apparently no one else had noticed despite the fact Borland, his fighter protégé, and that morning's mill had figured prominently in their conversation during lunch.

He went over to the bookshelf and after a few minutes of searching through the titles found what he was looking for: *DeBrett's Peerage*. He flipped through the pages until he found the entry that interested him. Edgar Borland, oldest son of Casper Borland, who was in turn the third son of Sir Walter Borland, baronet.

Edgar was the man from White's, a man with a strong enough resemblance to Charles that they might have been brothers. Or if Charles's suspicions were correct, they *were* brothers. Half-brothers.

The Borland family hailed from Yorkshire, and four years ago Charles had inherited a modest house and acreage *located in Yorkshire* from his maternal grandmother, a woman he'd never met and whose existence his mother had kept from him. Instead, she'd supplied him with a fictional maternal grandmother, one he'd been told had died before his birth.

That had been just one in a string of lies it turned

out. Including the cruelest lie of all—namely that John Townshend, the father who'd supposedly died prior to his birth, had never been more than a figment of his mother's imagination, created to conceal that Charles was born out of wedlock. Illegitimate. A bastard in the most literal sense of the word.

He'd only discovered part of the truth when his stepfather, a solicitor, had handled the legalities of his grandmother's will. It was at that time his stepfather had revealed what he knew of Charles's past, but that hadn't been much. And his mother seemed determined to carry the whole truth to her grave.

So until today, he'd had no clue as to the identity of his real father. But his resemblance to Edgar Borland, coupled with the family's roots in Yorkshire, left little doubt in his mind that Casper Borland had more than likely sired him.

The question now was...what the hell was he going to do with the information? It wasn't as if he'd be welcomed into the family bosom if he were to show up on their doorstep. Very few people were willing to acknowledge a bastard in the family tree.

It was his illegitimacy, even more than the gap in their social standing, that prevented the possibility of any romantic entanglement between Serena and himself. But he poured himself a whisky, settled into his most comfortable armchair, and spent the rest of the afternoon drinking and pondering what the knowledge meant for him.

Chapter Twelve

*S*erena had made no progress on finding a home for Jem in the two days since Charles had followed up on the boy's family background and confirmed that there were no known relatives to claim him. She'd meant to, but the following day there'd been a small kitchen fire at the Red Lion Square property, which belonged to Edwina and was the original site they'd converted to house war widows. The damage hadn't been too serious, but she'd spent the day helping Edwina oversee the clean-up.

She'd spent this morning with Jem, helping him learn his numbers and teaching him a few easy sums. The boy had a quick mind and a natural affinity for maths. She knew it was much too early to consider a future vocation for him, but she couldn't help wondering, with an aptitude for mathematics, if perhaps he'd like to study architecture someday. He loved building with his wooden blocks, which didn't necessarily mean much, given that he was still a child, but then again a person's natural interests often appeared during childhood. She couldn't help filing the idea away in her mind as a possibility.

Probably best not to mention to Charles that she was already taking a maternal interest in the child's future. He already worried about bonds forming between her and Jem. But really, was that so unusual? She'd also formed a bond with the widows the Wednesday Afternoon Social Club supported. She couldn't help but take an interest in the welfare of others. Particularly those who didn't have someone to champion their cause.

She drummed her fingers on the desktop. There was only an hour before she needed to leave for today's meeting of the Wednesday Afternoon Social Club. She supposed she could use that time to begin making a list of potential families from among those who worked the land for the Huntington estates. When she saw Charles tonight at Edwina's soirée, if he questioned her about it (and knowing Charles he would), she could honestly say she'd started work on finding a home for Jem.

Although... *would* Charles attend tonight? They hadn't communicated since their kiss. Serena had half expected Charles to send a note of apology, since he hadn't really had the opportunity to voice one the other day. Maybe he'd come to see there was nothing to apologize for.

Or maybe he was warming to the idea there was nothing that prohibited them from kissing, or from doing anything else with each other that they deemed pleasurable.

The thought drew a wry chuckle from her; that last seemed about as likely as the prospect of seeing pigs flying past the window. He'd liked kissing her, and more than that she hadn't been oblivious to the signs of his "male ardor" as her governess used to delicately phrase it.

She planned to keep up her campaign of persuasion though, and she looked forward to seeing him this evening. However, thoughts of Charles must wait if she hoped to get started on her list of families. She reached for her pen, dipped it in ink, and began listing names of her father's tenants. After a few minutes of relying on her memory to supply names, she realized she'd need to retrieve the estate ledger from her father's study to make a full and comprehensive list. She worked on it until it was time to leave for her club meeting, satisfied that she'd at least made a start.

When she arrived at Upper Grosvenor Street, she saw that Edwina's sitting room was already crowded with clusters of ladies mingling before the start of the meeting.

"The footmen are bringing in some more chairs from the dining room," a smiling Edwina informed her. "We have quite a crowd this week."

"I wonder why," Serena said. "Not that I'm complaining. I love seeing our numbers grow. But if we keep this up, we'll outgrow this room."

Edwina nodded. "I know. I think we may have to start holding our meetings in the music room. It's nearly three times the size of this room, large enough that we used to host balls there. The downside is that it's largely unfurnished, but that's not an unsurmountable problem. It wouldn't be as comfortable as the seating in this room, but I can rent chairs if necessary."

"We'll worry about that when the time comes. Which may be the week after next, if word continues to spread," she said.

"I think I can explain why we have so many here today," Grace said. She and Charlotte had come over and heard their discussion. "Julia and Phoebe will announce the schedule of topics for our speakers' series. Apparently they've been hinting that members won't want to miss obtaining a schedule, although they've been coy about what is to be covered in the coming weeks."

"Didn't you say Phoebe is keen to learn the details about what happens on the wedding night?" Serena asked.

"I expect that will be one of the first topics covered," Grace said dryly. "I've explained the basics of the marital act..." She gave them all a pointed look. "But in light of the fact that she's only seventeen, I didn't cover every aspect of conjugal love. I mean, she's never even been kissed. It seemed best to remain silent on some of the more shocking aspects of what can pass between a couple in the bedroom. But leave it to my niece to find a way to acquire the knowledge anyway."

"I wish I could have known more about what to expect beforehand," Edwina said. "My mother was regrettably vague about the details."

"I was only fifteen when I read a racy French guide to lovemaking which I stumbled across at my favorite book-seller's," Serena said. "I don't believe the shopkeeper could read French or else he wouldn't have agreed to sell it to me. Nor allowed it to be displayed so openly on the shelf. Needless to say, I found it quite enlightening."

Charlotte's brows rose in amusement. "No doubt."

The grandfather clock in the corner chimed twice, signaling it was time to start the meeting. Nearly every seat was already occupied, although some ladies were still helping themselves to refreshments before the start of the meeting. Serena waited a few more minutes before she headed to the front of the room. For the first time, she noticed a tall, marble-topped stand had been placed there. Atop it lay a wooden gavel.

She picked it up and rapped smartly on the marble surface, quickly gaining the attention of every lady in the room. She smiled at the sea of faces turned in her direction. "This is a much better way to call our meetings to order. Was this your idea, Edwina?"

"I wish I could take credit, but that honor goes to Julia Keene," Edwina replied.

"This is brilliant, Julia." Serena held up the gavel for all to see. "It's so efficient...and official."

Julia grinned. "My thought was that the ladies of the Wednesday Afternoon Social Club are not a quiet bunch."

"That we are not," Serena agreed.

"The *unconventional* ladies of the Wednesday Afternoon Social Club," someone called out.

Serena laughed. "I like that. We *are* a bunch of unconventional ladies."

She proceeded to call Mrs. Lyndhurst and Anna Keene to the front to update them on whether or not they'd found an organization willing to partner with them.

"Thanks to Mr. Latimer," Mrs. Lyndhurst said with a nod in Edwina's direction, "we've found a small orphanage run by a widow in Bloomsbury. Mrs. Bakersfield currently cares for ten children of various ages from three to eleven. However, she can't afford to do more than feed, clothe, and shelter them. We could hire a tutor and a governess for the children old enough to be schooled. It would be more limited in scope than we envisioned, but it would be a start."

After Anna and Mrs. Lyndhurst filled in some more details, Serena opened the floor for discussion after which a vote would be taken to decide if they wished to partner with Mrs. Bakersfield. After nearly half an hour, it appeared that the membership had no more questions and Serena called for a vote.

"By a show of hands, how many are in favor of supporting Mrs. Bakersfield by providing the funds to hire either a tutor, or governess, or both, and all necessary materials to allow for the education of those in her care. And further, to provide financial assistance that would allow her to take in more children."

Every hand in the room went up.

"Let the record show the vote was unanimous," Serena said. "If the committee could relay the news to Mrs. Bakersfield, and then work on coming up with an initial amount of the funds necessary to accomplish these goals, and report back next week."

The next order of business was the treasurer's report. Winifred Martin came to the front of the room and reported their bank balance now stood at £493.

Winifred's report was followed by Grace announcing that the tickets for their subscription ball had arrived from the printer and therefore members would be able to take some with them today and begin selling them.

"Now that we've expanded our charitable efforts, we need to fatten our bank account, and this ball is our best means of raising funds," Grace said. "So let's go forth and sell to friends, family, and strangers, if we must. We set the bar high last year by selling every ticket and I'm confident we can accomplish that again this year."

Finally, Serena called Phoebe and Julia forward to

announce the upcoming topics for the informational series they were starting up.

"Here is a card with the schedule of speakers printed out." Phoebe's smile turned impish as she held up a palm-size card for all to see. "If you could please take one, and then pass them to a person seated next to you." As she spoke, Julia handed out stacks of cards to a few ladies seated in the front.

"Our first topic, as you can see, is a discussion of a lady's finances. My aunt Grace will be speaking about wise management of such funds as we have control over, which regrettably, is usually limited to pin money or allowances. Before she married, my aunt, with the help of an older brother, began investing her own pin money in the exchange, and it's grown into quite a tidy nest egg." A few people started to clap at this, prompting the duchess to stand and give the room an impish smile before taking a bow.

Once it quieted down again, Phoebe continued, "She'll also speak about marriage settlements and why a lady should be well versed in how to protect her financial interests through them. Ideally, whoever negotiates them on our behalf is doing their best to protect us, but how can we be sure they are? Knowledge is power, is it not? Our goal with this monthly speakers series is to empower ourselves through knowledge."

Receiving her schedule, Serena scanned the list of topics, grinning when she saw that the second month's topic was entitled Secrets of the Wedding Night—what you may not know about achieving feminine pleasure in the marital act. She doubted Grace had covered that in her explanation to Phoebe of marital relations.

After Phoebe and Julia finished, Serena thanked them for their efforts. "I'm sure the rest of you will agree they've compiled an intriguing list of topics. Education of our members is certainly one of the goals of our group."

She then opened the floor to new business. No one came forward with any, so she adjourned the business portion of the meeting. She liked to run the meetings efficiently so that there was plenty of time for socializing.

Ladies got up from their seats to mingle and help themselves to the refreshments. Her throat dry from talking, Serena strolled to the table holding a pair of crystal punch bowls, some teapots, as well as a silver tray upon which were several bottles of strong spirits.

Grace was ladling some of the rum punch into a china cup. "Would you like some?" she asked Serena.

"Yes, please," Serena said. She turned to Phoebe, who stood by her aunt with a glass of lemonade in one hand. "I'm glad you and Julia took the initiative to get our speakers' series started. It's been my intention to get something like that going, but I hadn't gotten around to it."

"Trust Phoebe to step forward if there's an opportunity to learn about something she's been discouraged from learning," Grace said dryly. Despite her words, the smile she directed at her niece was indulgent.

Phoebe assumed a primly virtuous expression. "It's for the benefit of *all* the ladies," she replied. "Besides you're the one who always tells me an educated mind is an empowered mind."

"That I do," the duchess said. "But when the day comes for your mother to give you the wedding night talk, for my sake, please feign ignorance." She turned to Serena. "While I wholeheartedly agree a girl should know what to expect, if my sister ever got wind of Phoebe learning the unvarnished truth before she's even received a proposal of marriage, Anne would be livid. She might not wish to let me sponsor Phoebe's younger sisters for their debuts."

Grace turned back to Phoebe with a little frown. "Nor does that mean I'm encouraging sneakiness as a rule. But I do think your mother is wrong to keep you cloistered in ignorance, so there are times I'm willing to go against her wishes, and this is one of them."

"I understand, Aunt Grace. I appreciate that you don't brush off my questions like Mama always does." Impulsively Phoebe gave her aunt a quick kiss on the cheek. "Julia's waving me over. If you'll all excuse me, I'm going to join her."

After Phoebe left, Grace turned to Serena. "I do suffer twinges of conscience when it comes to what I allow Phoebe to be exposed to, but only because I know Anne would consider it scandalous. Not because I do. Still, I don't want Phoebe to get the idea she can overstep every boundary."

"From what I've seen, Phoebe has a great deal of good sense. Besides your sister knows you've always pushed against the boundaries of correct behavior, and she still sent Phoebe to live with you."

"I know, but I think she's old-fashioned enough to believe Miles, by virtue of being my husband, has reigned in my penchant for doing so."

"A misguided belief if I ever heard one." Serena gave her friend a reassuring smile. "I suspect she knows in her heart of hearts how unlikely that is."

"I hope so," Grace said. "By the way, how's Jem doing? The children asked if he could come over to play again some time."

"He's doing quite well. There've been no more tears since that first morning. He still frequently asks when he can see Charles though." She laughed. "The man is a great favorite of his. Too bad Charles is a bachelor, or he might make the perfect guardian for the boy."

One of Grace's brows rose slightly, and she murmured, "I'd say it's about time for someone to lead Charles to the altar."

Serena chose to ignore this comment. "I'm sure Jem would enjoy seeing your brood again. When Papa visited him in the nursery after our last visit, Jem told him all about his new friends. The child can be quite a chatterbox. Papa was late getting to the parliamentary session that night."

"It sounds as if he has both of you wrapped around his finger."

"He does rather." Serena let out a faint sigh. "Charles is urging me to place him somewhere before he gets too attached to us, and us to him."

"Must you place him elsewhere?" Grace asked.

Serena blinked. Of course, the notion of keeping Jem had occurred to her, but she hadn't let herself seriously consider the possibility. She was hardly in a position to raise a child. Her work to advance the causes of others took up a great deal of her time. Besides, unmarried as she was, she couldn't offer him the benefits of a family.

"It's what I intended from the moment I found him," Serena said slowly. "I still lean toward that being the best course of action, although I confess he's wormed his way into my affections."

"Children have a way of doing that," Grace agreed.

"I can't let my decision be based upon my emotions though. That wouldn't be fair to Jem."

Grace reached out and patted her arm. "I've known you too long to doubt that you'll do the right thing. But I would caution you against ignoring your feelings entirely." She paused, and gazed directly into Serena's eyes, seeming to read the thoughts that she wasn't voicing. Thoughts she was hardly able to acknowledge to herself. "Perhaps it's time for your life to take a different direction."

Serena glanced around the room, letting her friend's words—so remarkably similar to sentiments Edwina had voiced the other day—sink in. Edwina's life had taken a turn when she'd met Jason. As had Charlotte's when her pretend engagement to the Earl of Norwood had led to marriage.

"Perhaps it is," Serena said. "But I wouldn't be willing to abandon the work we do here either."

"No one who knows you would expect that," Grace said. "Now I must collect Phoebe. We have an appointment with a representative from Gunter's to finalize the list of refreshments they're providing for the subscription ball."

Later, on the carriage ride home after the meeting, Serena considered her friend's advice. The more she turned it over in her mind, the more she was willing to consider possibilities she wouldn't have dreamed of considering in the not-so-distant past.

She arrived home in an optimistic frame of mind, eager to hear what Jem and Ellie had been doing this afternoon during her absence.

Menken met her as she divested herself of her bonnet and gloves in the foyer. "This arrived for you this afternoon." He handed her a sealed note, the thickness indicating it contained multiple pages. She didn't recognize the design on the seal, and her name had been written in a bold scrawl that looked as if it had been written by a masculine hand.

Her curiosity was piqued, but then the sudden thought that it might concern Jem caused her to draw in a sharp breath. Was there a relative to claim him after all? Perhaps one who'd somehow heard about Charles making inquiries on her behalf...though the possibility seemed remote.

Nonetheless, a cold foreboding built within her and her hand shook slightly.

"Thank you, Menken," she managed. But her voice sounded hollow, even to her own ears.

Menken gave her an odd look, but he only said, "Will you be in the sitting room? I'll have tea sent in."

"Yes. Lovely." But her response was rote as her mind contemplated the potential contents of the note. She hoped she was jumping to a wrong conclusion. She probably *was* jumping to the wrong conclusion.

Jem's origins didn't seem to indicate a connection with a personage able to send a note on expensive paper. But what if Jem had been stolen from his rightful family? To be sure, the notion was the stuff of novels, but it had been known to happen.

No, she was being silly leaping to such a fanciful conclusion. Nonetheless, part of her was tempted to burn the note in the fire and simply ignore whatever message it held. But, of course, she wouldn't do that, much as she might want to.

Hadn't she told Grace less than an hour ago that any decision she made regarding Jem must be in his best interest? She couldn't shirk her duty to him.

Once in the privacy of the sitting room she turned the

note over a few times in her hands, stiffening her resolve to read its contents.

Finally, she slid a finger beneath the folded flap and ruthlessly broke through the wax seal. There was another note within, accounting for the thickness of it. Oddly, the second note was wrapped in plain brown paper, folded, but not sealed. She set this aside on a nearby table and began to read.

Dome Hill, Hampshire

Dear Lady Serena,

We've never met, but I found the enclosed note addressed to you in my late brother's personal effects. It was among a box of items that came home with him from the Peninsula where he fought with the 43rd Light Infantry. He was wounded at the Siege of Badajoz...

A sense of dread washed over her. The young man she'd loved and intended to marry had been killed following the Siege of Badajoz.

...wounded at the Siege of Badajoz badly enough to warrant that he be sent home, but not so badly that it would prevent him from making the trip. However, despite his injury being considered survivable, on the journey home he developed an infection at the site of his wound, and succumbed to it a mere three weeks after being joyously returned to the

*bosom of his family. His effects stayed with my
mother, and it wasn't until her recent passing
that this letter was discovered among them.*

*I apologize for the delay in getting it to you.
I don't know for sure why it was among his
possessions, but I would guess it was given to
him to bring back as a more secure alternative
to the usual channels by which messages were
sent home from the war. Whatever the reason,
I'm forwarding it on to you now. Hopefully,
this long delay in receiving it has caused no
great inconvenience to you.*

*Your obedient servant,
Sir William Highsmith, Esq.*

For a long moment, Serena just stared at the second
note resting on the table where she'd set it. If Highsmith's
brother had been entrusted to bring a letter back from the
battlefield, then surely it meant...She could hardly comprehend the possibility, but there could only have been
one person who would have asked a returning soldier to
carry a message to her from the Peninsula. Finally, with
trembling fingers she picked up the other note and freed it
from its wrapping paper.

One glance at the handwriting on the front of it caused
the room to start spinning, and black dots began to dance
before her eyes. She was vaguely aware of dropping Sir
William's note as she somehow stumbled over to a chair,
gripping the other one, still-sealed, tightly in one hand.

Her vision blurred as tears filled her eyes. It wasn't
possible. It *couldn't* be possible. Every fiber of her being

screamed at the impossibility of receiving anything from this particular sender.

But there was her name...Lady Serena Wynter.

Written by one whose handwriting she knew as well as her own.

It couldn't be from him.

And yet it clearly was.

Thomas.

Her beloved Thomas.

Chapter Thirteen

⌒

The maid bringing in the tea discovered Serena collapsed in a chair. She hadn't fainted precisely. It was more that a wave of overwhelming emotion had rendered her momentarily insensible, but regardless, her state frightened the maid who screamed and dropped the tea tray. This roused Serena out of her shocked stupor and she realized with growing dismay that the maid's response would bring the household staff running to see what was the matter. The last thing she wanted was the glare of everyone's attention.

Or sympathy.

Or pity.

All she wanted was to hide away and read the letter from Thomas. Alone. She preferred privacy to deal with the myriad of feelings this long-lost communication had unleashed.

Seeing her name written by Thomas so long ago had brought the heartbreak rushing back. Not as raw or as intense as it had been six years ago. Nonetheless, a sense of loss, however muted, had returned, demanding release. She really didn't want to fall to pieces in front of the servants.

She slipped the unopened note from Thomas into her pocket, swiped at her wet cheeks, and sternly commanded that the maid "hush."

It was too late, of course.

Two footmen rushed into the room, followed by Menken, who hastened to her side.

"My lady, what is the matter? What has happened?" Gone was the butler's facade of imperturbability, replaced by sincere concern for her welfare.

He pulled out a snowy linen handkerchief and gently wiped her cheeks. She hadn't wanted comfort, and yet, the man's tender gesture was a balm of sorts. Still, she didn't want anyone to make a fuss over her.

"Shall I have your father summoned?" the butler asked. "Tell me what has distressed you."

"No, don't fetch Papa." She grasped Menken's hand pleadingly, and he nodded. "'Twas just..." She drew in a deep breath. "Just a bit of...surprising news. I was taken aback for a moment, and when Mollie came in, I was upset and not myself." She took another deep breath. "It's no small wonder that I startled her."

Menken glanced at Mollie, who'd drawn close and was now standing by Serena's chair.

"I...I thought she was having a fit or something. She looked so stricken and unlike herself, staring off at nothing like she was. M-my grandmother experienced something like that once and she was never the quite the same after it." Tears welled in the girl's eyes. "I...I'm sorry I panicked and spilled the tea."

"There's nothing to be sorry about, Mollie," Menken assured the girl. "Go down to the kitchen and have a fresh tea tray prepared. Have it sent to Lady Serena's room. And then get another maid to help you clean this up." He turned back to Serena. "I think it's best if you lie down." His eyes were kind as he studied her face. "I'll summon the doctor. He can give you something to ease your nerves."

"Tea will be sufficient for that, Menken," Serena said. "I'm feeling better already."

This was only marginally true. But the alternative was to admit that she needed nothing less than a good cry to wash away the ghosts of the past.

Menken looked unconvinced, but he didn't argue. He picked up Sir William's note from where it had fallen, folded it, and handed it to her. She tucked it into her pocket, alongside the other one, and then accepted the hand he'd extended to help her out of the chair.

"Really, Menken. I had a moment, but I'm not an invalid." She came to her feet only to have her knees buckle, requiring a steadying hand from a frowning Menken.

"You've clearly had a shock, my lady. I don't think it's wise to even try to get you upstairs until you've had more time to recover. Let me help you to the sofa."

"No, Menken. I prefer to go to my room." Above all, she needed privacy, *complete* privacy, to finally read the message from Thomas, to cry, to storm about and rail against fate if that's what made her feel better. "Please," she added, the plea soft and for his ears alone.

"Very well," he agreed, but she could tell that he didn't

think this the best course of action. "But I will assist you. You can't just will away the lingering effects of a shock to the system, and I don't want you falling on the stairs."

"If you insist on mollycoddling me, then so be it." She attempted a smile, but the effort was too much and she felt her lips begin to wobble as tears threatened to overcome her. She gave him a nod to indicate she was ready to accept his assistance.

Once upstairs, Menken informed Giselle, her lady's maid, that she was unwell. He instructed the maid to put her in her nightclothes, and then stay to watch over her should she need anything, and to let him know if her mistress took a turn for the worse.

Serena countermanded this as soon as the door closed behind the butler's back. Menken meant well, but she couldn't bear the thought of lying in bed, stuck with her own thoughts. And she didn't want to read the note from Thomas with Giselle looking on.

She needed a good cry, but just as much as that she needed to pace about her room, to sit, to stand, to curl in a tight ball on the floor if that made her feel better.

She told Giselle to help her change to a simple day dress and put her hair in a braid, then she tucked both notes into the bottom drawer of her dressing table.

Later.

While she was changing, Mollie brought in a fresh tea tray, placing it on the corner table, which Serena sometimes used as a writing desk. Serena thanked her and then took a seat at her dressing table so Giselle could braid her hair as she'd requested.

Once Giselle had finished, she went over to a mending basket kept in the corner of the room opposite the table-cum-writing desk, clearly intending to do some mending while she kept an eye on her mistress.

Serena remained seated at her dressing table. "I'd like to be alone, Giselle. I'll ring for you if I need anything."

Giselle's expression seemed to question Serena's directions. "I think perhaps I should stay," the maid said. "I'll just sit quietly, catching up on my mending, but I'd be here should you needed anything."

"Thank you, but I won't need anything so urgently that you must be here in the room with me," Serena said, kindly, but firmly. *Please*, she thought. *Don't argue. I don't know how much longer I can keep this appearance of calm from crumbling.*

Giselle looked uncertain, obviously waging an internal battle between obeying the butler's instructions and the dictates of her mistress. Finally, she said, "Very well."

Serena heard the note of unhappy resignation in the maid's voice. "Thank you, Giselle. I promise to ring if I need you."

Alone at last, she eyed the tea service, thinking she ought to have had Giselle pour her a cup before sending her away. Not that she wasn't perfectly capable of doing it herself under normal circumstances. But receiving a long-lost letter from Thomas could hardly be considered normal circumstances, and since her maid's departure meant she no longer had to act as if she weren't in danger of falling to pieces, a bone-deep weariness had come over her. Fixing herself a cup of tea would require an act of more willpower than she could muster at the moment.

She lost track of time as she continued to sit beside her dressing table. Memories flitted through her mind, and she was vaguely aware of the tears flowing down her cheeks. Finally, with an unsteady hand, she opened the drawer where she'd tucked the notes and withdrew the message from Thomas. She studied her name written on the front, imagining his pen scratching across the paper as he addressed it. Had it been written by candlelight late one night in the privacy of his camp tent? Or during a free moment one afternoon?

She turned it over and studied the wax seal with its imprint of his initials: a *T* and an *F*, flanking a larger *C*. Thomas Fitzgerald Carlisle, the youngest son of Viscount Baddesley. The boy she'd fallen desperately in love with when she was seventeen, and he one-and-twenty, fresh out of Oxford and destined for a life in the military. If she could have known what the future held for them, would she have snuck into his room at the house party they'd both attended?

Yes, she would have. And she would never regret what came from that night.

Of that she had no doubt. Did this note hold a clue to his response to the baby? Once there had been no question that she was pregnant, she'd written to him, delivering the news that she was expecting his child, but she'd never received a response. Never knew if the news had ever reached him, because within a few weeks of dispatching that note, she'd gotten word of his death in battle. And a few weeks after that the tragic details of how he'd died at the hands of British troops.

Maybe now she'd have an answer to the question that had nagged at her all this time. Had Thomas known about the baby before he died?

She drew in a long breath, and aware that the seal had remained in place since his own hand had put it there, gently broke it, leaving it as intact as possible while still being able to open the note. She opened it slowly, almost as afraid to read the contents as she was eager to read them. It was her last chance to receive a message from him.

All of his other letters had been read and reread so much, especially in those first years after he was gone, before the healing hand of time had softened the blow, that the creases had become increasingly frail and the pages were in danger of falling apart entirely. She'd finally forced herself to pull them out only on rare occasions, lest she destroy them.

The words on the page blurred as fresh tears formed. She held the paper away so they wouldn't fall on it and cause the ink to run. She blinked several times to clear her vision and began to read.

2 April 1812
Badajoz, Spain

My dearest love,

You can hardly imagine the joy I felt upon receiving your last letter. A baby! Of course, I'm delighted. Set your mind at ease on that account. I've already put in for a leave to come back to England. My commanding officer was not pleased to hear that I would be going home after being here so short a time, but officers may take leave at their own discretion, so while he may not like it, there's nothing he can do to prevent it, either.

As soon as I get home, we'll be married by

special license. As you said, people will know the reason behind our hasty marriage soon enough, but does that bother me? Not one whit! I love you. And I already love this child. We planned to marry after my service anyway. This merely moves that event forward by a year or so. And I'm not sorry about that, darling.

I can't even begin to express how much I miss you. This time apart from you has been wretched for me. I played down how desperately I miss you because I didn't want to cause you any unhappiness, or give you reason to worry about me...any more than I know you already do. But now that I'll be heading home, I can confess it's been hellish being so far from you.

As soon as I can, I'll make my way to Lisbon, and from there, catch a ship bound for England. In the meantime, I will arrange for this letter to go back with a transport of wounded men. Their passage has already been secured on a ship sailing next week. Hopefully, you'll see me only a week or two after you receive this.

Just know, darling, that I will be by your side as soon as possible and we'll be married with all haste. I can't wait for that day to come.

Until then, my love, know that my heart beats for you, and now, for our little one as well.

Take care of yourself and the babe,

all my love,
Thomas

She read the lines over and over, absorbing the bitter-sweet pain of each word. Mourning again their plans that were never fulfilled, grieving the baby she didn't carry to term.

Her breathing, uneven and labored, sounded harsh in the silent room. It was as if a band was being drawn ever more tightly around her chest, and the harder she tried to catch her breath, the more starved for air she felt, until at last a large sob burst out of her and a torrent of tears began to flow again.

Eventually, the tears ran out, and her spent emotions gave way to an exhaustion. She folded the note from Thomas, brought it to her lips, kissed it, then walked over to the bedside table and gently tucked it in a delicately carved rosewood box where she kept the rest of his letters.

As she closed the drawer, it was as if a weight lifted from her shoulders, and she felt a lightness of being she hadn't experienced in a very long time. The sadness was still there, and she imagined always would be to some degree. But this note, she realized, had given her the ability to say a final "good-bye" to her past with Thomas.

She climbed in bed and within a short time had fallen asleep.

When she awoke, she'd no idea how long she'd slept, but a glance at the clock on her bedside table showed that it was nearly half-past eight. She wondered if Giselle had come in to check on her. Probably.

She'd planned to attend the soirée at Edwina's tonight, but despite the nap, she still felt tired. Tired, but at the same time strangely refreshed. She wasn't a woman prone to tears, but crying had been the best remedy for all the feelings resurrected by reading Thomas's letter.

To be sure, she still felt a lingering sense of sadness, but she also felt a measure of peace. She hadn't realized how badly she'd needed to know what Thomas had thought about the baby—that he'd been overjoyed as she had been, that if fate hadn't intervened he would have come home and married her.

She rose from the bed and went over to her dressing table. Her reflection showed eyes still red and the lids puffy from crying. Even if she'd felt like going out, there was no way she could put in an appearance looking as she did.

She'd just have to make her apologies next time she saw Edwina. Her friend would understand. But if she were staying in for the evening, what did she want to do?

She didn't want Jem to see her in this condition, and anyway he'd expected her to be gone all evening, so she needn't visit the nursery tonight. She felt too restless to read, and despite her tiredness, it was much too early to go to bed. She supposed she could get some work done.

She could resume work on the list of potential families for Jem. Her earlier conversation with Grace had her reconsidering the option of keeping him, but in fairness, and to ensure that this decision was truly based on exploring the alternatives, she still needed to do this.

"No time like the present," she muttered.

Even though, deep down, she was becoming more and more reluctant to follow through with that plan. She had an idea of what Charles would think of this reluctance, could just picture his extreme disapproval if he found out she was considering keeping Jem.

Not that she had any intention of telling him the

direction of her thoughts, not unless and not until she decided to follow that course of action.

Resolutely, she splashed some water on her face, patted it dry with a towel, and smoothed back a few hairs that had worked loose as she slept. Feeling slightly more presentable, she opened her door and turned toward the stairs, determined to go down and stop avoiding the task she'd put off for too long already.

Chapter Fourteen

～

*P*rickles of unease ran along the back of Charles's neck as he checked his pocket watch for roughly the dozenth time that evening.

"Where *is* she?" he muttered under his breath. He'd circled through the rooms of Lady Beasley's residence for the past two hours, mingling among the various guests as he waited for Serena's arrival. But the truth was, there was only one guest who interested him, and she wasn't here yet.

He hadn't seen her since that afternoon when they'd kissed and things had suddenly gotten complicated between them.

Or so it seemed to him. Serena appeared to have no reservations about turning their at-times-prickly friendship into one that included kissing. But kissing a female implied a certain level of commitment. Or it should, and

Charles could offer nothing of the sort. Not to someone like Serena.

But clearly, even with the best of intentions, his self-control had failed him. And now here he was, hoping to see her in the type of environment—a crowded soirée—that would prevent any repeat of the weakness he'd shown the other evening. So much for that plan since she hadn't shown up yet.

He was probably overreacting, but he couldn't shake his uneasiness. He felt a bit less idiotic knowing that even Lady Beasley shared his concern because they'd spoken of it earlier this evening. Perhaps it was time to seek her out again and see if she'd received any message from Serena explaining her absence.

"No, I haven't heard anything from her," Lady Beasley said in response to his query once he finally located her. Thanks to her small stature it hadn't been an easy task, given the crush of people attending her soirée this evening. "It's unlike her to fail to appear and not send her regrets, but I have to believe there's a good reason for it." Despite her words, Lady Beasley frowned. "Still, like you, I'm a bit anxious. It could be because of something to do with Jem, or…"

She gave him a pointed look and he knew what she wasn't saying. They both knew Serena's propensity to shrug off caution at times.

"I don't think it would be a bad idea if you paid her a visit to discover what's kept her away tonight," Lady Beasley suggested. She laid a hand on his arm. "In fact, I wish you would."

Charles had needed no other urging. Five minutes later, he was outside, hailing a hackney cab.

He was glad to have the excuse of Lady Beasley's concern to offer once he arrived. Serena was likely to accuse him of being overbearing and annoyingly *male* if he appeared on her doorstep simply because of his own concern for her welfare.

If she was even at home when he got there.

Surely she would be. But if she weren't, then what?

Although maybe he was the reason she hadn't put in an appearance at Lady Beasley's tonight. What if *she* wanted to avoid *him*? If that was the case, then things were about to become awkward.

Right now, he didn't care about that. He just wanted to find her safe at home. Even if she instructed Menken to turn him away, at least he'd know his concerns were for naught.

At last the cab pulled up in front of the Huntington residence with Charles out the door as soon as it drew to a halt. He handed some money up to the driver, who dipped the brim of his hat and asked, "Would the gentleman like me to wait?"

Charles hesitated, then handed up some additional coins. "If I'm not back out here in twenty minutes, consider yourself dismissed."

"Right enough, guv'nor."

Twenty minutes should be sufficient to ascertain the reasons behind Serena's absence from Lady Beasley's soirée, and whether or not he needed to be concerned about those reasons.

A footman, rather than Menken, answered the door. His alarm ticked up a notch. Why wasn't Menken at his usual post?

"I'm here to see Lady Serena," he said.

A fleeting expression of...surprise?...alarm?...
dismay?...flitted over the footman's features. Charles
wasn't sure how to interpret the look, but it didn't allay
his anxieties.

"I will see, sir, if she's receiving visitors."

Oh, she's going to be, Charles thought. If he had to
wrestle his way past this footman to make it happen.

"No need. She's expecting me. The sitting room, I
presume?" He brushed past the servant, who ceded to the
authority in Charles's manner and voice.

Since the footman hadn't challenged him or indicated
she was anywhere other than the sitting room, Charles
proceeded down the hall in that direction. He halted
when he reached the doorway. Relief flooded through him
because the sight that greeted him was far from the dire
scenarios his mind had imagined.

Seated at her desk, Serena was bent over a large book,
probably a ledger from the size of it. And yet the ordinari-
ness of the scene before him didn't completely allay his
concerns. Wasn't it odd that she would choose to miss the
soirée at Lady Beasley's to stay in to look through a ledger?
Surely that was something she could do any time.

Aware that his stealthy observance of her was bordering
on a rude invasion of her privacy, he opened his mouth
to announce his presence, but then she sighed and looked
up, her gaze apparently drawn to something on the back
of her desk.

He watched as she reached for the object. He couldn't
see what it was, only that she cradled it in her hand,
studying it intently before letting out a long, shuddering
breath.

Finally goaded into action, he stepped through the

doorway. "Serena, what is it?" he said, his voice loud and harsh with concern.

His thoughtless utterance startled her. He should have knocked or cleared his throat or chosen some less abrupt way to announce himself rather than practically shouting at her.

She came to her feet so quickly she knocked over her chair and dropped the item she'd been holding. Whirling around, her hand flew to her throat, and she regarded him, her eyes wide with shock. Their red, puffy state told him she'd been crying earlier.

"Serena," he said, as he drew closer her. "My God, I'm sorry I frightened you, but what has upset you? Is Jem all right?"

Her lips pressed together, but instead of replying she knelt and retrieved the item she'd dropped, closing her hand around it and obscuring it from his view, but from the glimpse he'd gotten, it appeared to be a miniature.

Straightening, she gave him a guarded look. "No, it's nothing to do with Jem. Hopefully he's sound asleep by now, though he is a master at the art of bedtime procrastination. I received some upsetting news. But then I expect you could tell that already."

Very upsetting from the look of it.

"I'm sorry," he said. Not sure what else to say, since he didn't know exactly what troubled her. "I don't suppose you wish to discuss it?"

A sad smile, small and fleeting, appeared. She shook her head.

Of course, she didn't. He wasn't her confidant, and nothing about her posture or her manner indicated his presence was anything but a nuisance. Or if not a nuisance precisely, not something she welcomed, either.

"In that case, let me also apologize for invading your privacy this evening. It's clear you felt the need to be alone. I only came here because... well, Lady Beasley and I both became concerned when you didn't appear at her soirée..." His voice trailed off as her face crumpled and tears brimmed in her eyes.

Without even thinking he gathered her into his arms and held her, one hand cradling her head, the other stroking her back as, lips pressed against her hair, he murmured soft words of comfort mixed with inarticulate sounds meant to sooth her distress.

She nestled into his embrace for several minutes, crying quietly, almost tiredly, as if her emotions were leaking out of her in a gentle trickle rather than an unstoppable torrent. And yet he couldn't help but suspect that it had been a torrent earlier—the evidence still showed in her eyes.

His heart gave a painful twist in his chest and his arms reflexively tightened around her.

"Serena," he murmured. "My dear, dear girl."

The words were ill-considered, spoken without thought. He tried to never reveal his true feelings to her. Tried only to offer her a steady friendship. But sometimes his heart's truth insisted on showing itself in spite of those intentions.

She stilled against him, then raised her head to gaze at his face. He struggled to keep his expression from betraying him, but it was a difficult task with her eyes, sad and vulnerable, studying him with such perceptive intensity.

"I'm sorry. I don't know why I did that. I thought I was past the tears." Her gaze shifted downward, her lashes concealing her expression. "It concerned someone I held very dear at one time."

The miniature.

He wished he'd gotten a better look at it. He tried to recall his brief impression of it, tried to remember if that fleeting glimpse had been of a man or a woman. A man, he thought, but his conviction in the accuracy of this recollection was shaky at best.

"Then your tears are entirely understandable," he said. "If there's anything I can do to...help."

"You already have by letting me cry on the front of your jacket," she said.

"That's a start, I suppose, but I'm here if you need anything else."

"Coming from you, Charles, that goes without saying." She placed a hand against his cheek, her palm a warm caress on his skin. "You're a good friend."

It took every ounce of effort he could muster not to turn his mouth into that soft palm and place a lingering kiss there. But he wouldn't. Nor was he proud of himself, that in her moment of need, his thoughts so easily focused on his desires rather than on her turmoil.

She withdrew her hand and studied him thoughtfully for a moment. "I think it's time I told you about someone."

She looked down at the miniature she held. "His name was Thomas Carlisle. Few people know that we intended to marry because there was never a formal engagement. He was killed in battle during the Siege of Badajoz." Her mouth twisted into a grimace. "Or more accurately, after the siege, trying to prevent the looting and violence some of the English soldiers visited upon the inhabitants of the town."

"My God, Serena. I can't even imagine..."

Words failed him. She'd loved and lost. His heart ached for her, and in a small way, he could relate to her pain. He'd never lost someone he loved, but he loved someone he could never have. It wasn't quite the same, but still, it gave him some measure of understanding for what she must have felt, must have suffered when the news of his death reached her.

She held up the miniature so he could see it.

He stared at it. Thomas Carlisle had possessed reddish hair and strikingly blue eyes. A slight smile curved his lips as if he knew a good joke he could be persuaded to share. He looked like someone Charles would have liked had their paths ever crossed.

He was also jealous as hell that Serena had loved this man. Well aware this was petty of him, he was glad she couldn't read his thoughts. The man had died serving his country—Carlisle should be the recipient of his gratitude and appreciation.

He swallowed and returned his gaze to her face. "I'd no idea. I'm...I'm so sorry. I know words are hardly sufficient..." Again his voice trailed off.

Who was he to try to offer her comfort? He'd barged in here and intruded on her grief—for reasons that had seemed legitimate at the time, it was true. But there was no excusing that the sympathy he held for her was tainted by his jealousy for a dead man. He despised himself for feeling that way, and yet he couldn't seem to help it.

"I only came to see that you were safe. If you wish me to go, simply say the word and I'll be gone this instant. But if it would help you...that is, if you would prefer that I stay because...because it's easier than being alone, I can stay."

An odd expression flickered across her features. "Now that you're here, I don't want you to go." She spoke the words slowly, but not, he rather thought, due to hesitancy on her part since her eyes looked into his with forthright conviction.

It seemed to him that this *deliberateness* of manner was meant to convey some unspoken message, one that he didn't trust he was understanding correctly. Because the message he *thought* he saw in her eyes, and heard in her words, set his heart beating at a harder, faster clip and made his lungs feel as if he'd just had the air knocked out of them from a punch to his gut. He must be mistaken. Surely he was misinterpreting her intent.

Good God, what sort of selfish, deluded monster was he to believe she was signaling a desire for him that went beyond his mere company. And yet, that was precisely what he did think, despite her reddened eyes, her faintly splotchy skin...despite the miniature she held of a man she'd obviously loved very much.

He cleared his throat. "Very well, then. I will stay and keep you company until you wish me to leave." The words sounded stiff and formal, though he hadn't intended them to.

Ah, well. Better she think him an insufferable prig than a man struggling with inappropriate desires at what was surely the most inappropriate moment to do so.

Her mouth twitched into a fleeting hint of a smile. "I think it's time for me to tell you everything about Thomas. It's only fair you understand my past so you can understand what I wish for my future."

What the hell did she mean by that?

He had no idea. But then again his interactions with the

fairer sex had never been all that plentiful. He envied men who had a better grasp of how the female mind worked.

"In that case, perhaps we should sit down," he suggested.

"Yes, I suppose we should." But then she surprised him by grabbing his hand and leading him to one of the armchairs. She sat at one end of the sofa, immediately to his left, so close that her skirt actually brushed against his legs.

And then she told all about falling in love with Thomas Carlisle when she was seventeen, only a few months before he was to head to the Spanish Peninsula to fight under Wellington against Napoleon's forces. She recounted the unvarnished truth, frankly admitting they'd had a physical union and not glossing over the fact that she'd become pregnant just before he shipped out. Unfortunately, she didn't become aware of that fact until after Carlisle was gone and it was too late for a hasty marriage.

She told him of writing to Thomas with the news, of her worries that he would be upset about the pregnancy, of never receiving a reply to her letters, and then finally receiving the news of his death without any confirmation that he knew of their child's existence before his own was snuffed out.

Charles felt his own throat clog up as he imagined her at seventeen facing all of that. He wasn't surprised she'd prevailed. He didn't know anyone stronger or more determined that Serena.

"Besides Edwina and one of my aunts, no one knows all of these details," she said. "Not even my parents. My aunt Josephine lived with us at that time. Her bedroom was next to mine, and she figured out my condition about the time I did. I was wretchedly sick, *literally* wretchedly sick.

"I'd retreat to my room to retch in the chamber pot several times a day, and Aunt Josephine, hearing me through the wall, suspected what ailed me. She arranged for the two of us to spend the next several months at a small seaside town where it would be unlikely we'd encounter anyone we knew. Ostensibly, I was to be her companion, but, of course, the truth was she was looking after me. News of Thomas's death reached us there, and a month later I miscarried the baby. So now you know all about my secret past. I'd insist you reveal some deep, dark secret in yours to make us even, but naturally someone like you doesn't have deep, dark secrets."

And yet he did, didn't he? Why else had Borland's arrival in London upset him so? Because it threatened to expose his family secret if people questioned the strong resemblance between them.

But now, in the face of her unflinching honesty, would be the perfect time to confess, but something held him back. Confessing the truth about himself would mean revealing his mother's missteps, and surely, he didn't have the right to do that. Or was that merely a convenient rationalization? Was the real reason he remained silent because he couldn't bear to risk being seen as tainted and less than worthy because he'd been born on the wrong side of the blanket?

Of course, if anyone would be willing to overlook his illegitimacy, it would be Serena. But what if even she couldn't help judging him for his parents' actions? Or if not judging him, then pitying him?

"I'm honored that you trust me enough to share your secret, Serena," he said quietly. "It couldn't have been easy to go through what you went through."

She sighed. "It's not an uncommon tale, sadly. But as long as I haven't shocked you to such a degree that you want nothing more to do with me, I'm glad you know." Her gaze dropped to her left hand where she followed the fabric's pattern of a flowering vine along the sofa's arm. "I feel it's something you *should* know about me, because there's something I wish to discuss with you..."

To his surprise, her glance was uncertain, hesitant. Serena was rarely either of those things, which made him very curious about what she wished to discuss. Especially, if it was somehow connected with her past. He waited for her to continue.

"I loved Thomas," she said. "I'll always love him, but that past is irretrievable. The news I received today was a letter from him, sent back with a wounded soldier who died soon after reaching England, and so it remained undelivered until it was recently discovered and forwarded to me. Receiving it was a gift—a painful one—but a gift that answered some lingering questions."

She leaned forward, her expression earnest now. "Since I lost him, I've filled my life with many good things...meaningful projects that keep me busy, my friends who keep me sane, who've supported me when despair threatened to overtake me. But those things, important as they are to me...I see now that they will never fill the void left by Thomas's death."

Her words were coming faster now.

"What I'm about to propose is something I've considered for a while, but something held me back from acting on it. That letter today..." She paused and caught one side of her lower lip in her teeth. "That letter today," she repeated, "was like a release, and I knew I was ready to say something."

She stopped, and he waited for her to go on, waited for her to reveal...what? It felt as if every nerve in his body was tingling with anticipation. Was she going to propose to him? Is that what this was about? Was this part of a plan to give Jem a family? Was she hoping that Jem could somehow replace the child she'd lost? That he would be some sort of stand-in for the man she'd loved? Because why else had she shared the truth about her past?

She could have simply stuck with the vague explanation of having received bad news as a reason for her tears, and he wouldn't have pressed.

"I'm not sure—" he began, just as she said, "How would you—"

They both stopped speaking, and after a moment in which each waited for the other to continue, he said, "Ladies first."

"No," she said. "You've been listening to me speak at length, so you go first. What I have to say can wait."

"You paused and I thought you were waiting for me to respond. I was just going to say I didn't know what you wanted me to say because, well, I'm a bit confused."

She gave a short laugh. "I paused because I'm not at all sure how you're going to receive what I wish to say."

He was glad to see some of her sadness had receded. "In that case," he prompted, "perhaps it's best to simply say it."

"No doubt you're right." She bit her bottom lip, and he sensed she was searching for the right words. "Here goes then. Since Thomas's death, I've missed him, of course. Terribly at first, and then less intensely as time passed.

But apart from missing him, I've missed having a man in my life. The company of a man, the scent of a man, the touch of a man. I don't know how to say this delicately, but I'm propositioning you, Charles."

He sat frozen, his mind trying to comprehend her words. Propositioning him? Did she want him to court her? Marry her? Or something that fell somewhere between those two?

"I'm still not sure what your proposition is exactly," he said slowly.

"I wish us to become lovers." She didn't flinch when she said this, although he felt his own face warm because the image of bedding Serena had tortured him on more than one sleepless night. His imaginings, however, had included the bond of marriage being a precursor to that event.

"That would be a very bad idea." One he didn't dare entertain. He knew his weakness where she was concerned.

She sighed. "I expected you might say that, but honestly, Charles, we're both adults. It's not as if you'd be ruining me. If society had been privy to what occurred between Thomas and myself, I'd already be ruined."

"Maybe I wouldn't be ruining you, but I'd be dishonoring you, Serena. I couldn't do that."

"I respect your sense of honor, Charles. I truly do, but in this case it's misplaced, I promise you."

He shook his head. "What you ask is out of the question."

"Why?" She leaned forward and placed a hand on his knee, the shock of her touch, warm and intimate, sent a wave of heat cascading through him. "Why is it out of the question? It's something that's been very much on my mind since I kissed you the other day. Are you going to deny that you enjoyed it? Or tell me that you didn't feel that spark of attraction between us...the heat of desire?"

"What I felt or didn't feel is immaterial," he began. She could never know that he burned for her like he had for no one else.

"So immaterial you avoided answering directly. Is that because of what you *did* feel?" She came forward until she was perched on the edge of the sofa cushion, and as she did her hand slid up his thigh a few inches.

He should move, get out of the chair, put some distance between them.

He should...

He really, *really* should...

And yet his willpower had abandoned him. Only Serena could affect him this way.

He sat unmoving, his feet not responding to the urging of his mind to step away. His heart had entered this internal battle and his emotions refused to be tamped down and tucked away. The scent of the jasmine cologne she wore was beguiling him, her rosy mouth beckoning him, her intense gray eyes radiating an unmistakable invitation.

He recognized what the smoldering fire in her gaze promised. And just like a moth can't resist the flames even though it ultimately leads to its destruction, Charles found himself drawn to that fire in her gaze.

"You're thinking about this much too hard," Serena whispered.

But he wasn't so sure. Under any circumstances this would fall under *A Very Bad Idea*, but now? Her eyes might be sending him a message of invitation, but they still bore the remnants of her recent tears. Tonight she might wish to pursue this, but in the light of tomorrow's dawn, would she?

Her lips quirked up in a knowing little smile and, still keeping her hand on his thigh, with her other hand she reached for one of his. "You probably don't believe I know my own mind, seeing as though I've just been weeping for another man."

This was an eerily accurate guess of his thoughts, and indicated a failure on his part to mask his feelings. An all-too-common failure of late.

"So," she continued, "I wouldn't entirely blame you if that's what you're thinking. But the fact that I will always miss Thomas doesn't negate what I want right now."

Her fingers pressed warmly against his, her thumb stroking the back of his hand, the movement setting off sparks of electricity that ran up his arm.

"I want you, Charles. I hope you want me too."

Well, she'd lain her cards on the table. The next move was his. She could feel his resistance in the stiffness of his thigh muscle beneath her hand, could hear it in the harsh, ragged rhythm of his breath, but he hadn't moved away, hadn't protested her touch.

Perhaps she needed to bolster her argument a bit and take advantage of his proximity before his damnably strong sense of honor compelled him to move out of her reach. She wasn't sure what was keeping him in place now, but she didn't trust that it would do so much longer.

She came to her feet and pulled Charles to his, clinging to his hand with a firm hold lest he decide to take the opportunity to put some distance between them.

Distance *would not* be conducive for what she had in mind.

To her surprise, he didn't try to resist or pull away, but a wariness had crept into his gaze, and she knew she wouldn't have much time until he put some distance between them. So she'd better make her case quickly.

She closed the gap between them, entwining her fingers with his as her other hand slid over his shoulder to wrap around his neck. She raised herself up onto her toes and brought her lips to his. Gently at first, a soft, tentative brush of her mouth against his, before increasing the pressure of her kiss, seeking a response to her kiss... to the question of pursuing a relationship...

Because accepting one was tantamount to accepting the other. At least she hoped he saw it that way.

His lips were warm and pliant against hers, and yet for the first few seconds, it was only her kissing him. But she could sense his resistance ebbing with each kiss she bestowed, until finally, with a sound that was part sigh, part moan, he began kissing her back with a sweet fierceness as he wrapped his arms around her and drew her into his embrace.

His surrender unleashed her own desire. She grasped his bottom lip between her own, and when his mouth opened slightly in response, her tongue ventured in. This seemed to take him by surprise because he froze for an instant, but then his tongue tangled with hers and a wave of heated pleasure roared through her.

She twined her hands in his hair, clutching sections of it between her fingers, feeling its texture, its thickness, tugging it gently, just because she could.

His lips began to trail kisses along her cheek, reaching

her hairline, he lifted his mouth and lightly nipped her earlobe with his teeth. His breath was hot against her skin and sounded ragged, harsh. She tilted her head, and one of his hands came up to cradle her cheek as his mouth moved to kiss her jaw, her neck, the base of her throat, along her collarbone. Hot, desperate kisses that turned her insides into liquid warmth.

Serena had missed this so much—the shared passion with a man. But not just any man. She wanted Charles. Tension built in her body and she wanted more. So much more.

She reached for his hand, drawing it downward before turning his palm and pressing it against her breast in a silent plea.

Touch me. Knead me. Satisfy this hunger building inside me.

He lifted his head so that he could look into her eyes, his own gaze dark and hungry with a need that mirrored her own. "My God, Serena. I'm only capable of so much restraint."

"I don't want restraint, Charles. I've been clear about this. I want *you*."

He stared at her a long moment and she could see the internal battle waging inside him. His gentlemanly instincts at odds with his carnal desires.

At last he said, "You deserve someone far better than I. And you deserve marriage. Whatever happened between you and...and Mr. Carlisle, in the end, you were to marry. I can't marry you, and because I can't, we can't do this. I'm sorry."

She heard the regret in his voice, but also the resolve. For now, the gentleman inside him had prevailed. He removed his hand from her breast and reluctantly she accepted his refusal. If she hoped to win him over to the idea of a physical relationship between them, she'd have to temper her own eagerness. Charles wouldn't be rushed into it, but she might succeed with slow persuasion.

What she didn't intend to do was abandon the notion entirely. Her body was still on fire for him, and if anything his refusal only strengthened her conviction that if she took a lover, she wished it to be him.

She leaned back enough to meet his gaze. "I'm not asking you to marry me, Charles, though if that's what we wanted, there's nothing to prohibit it. Just because my father is an earl it doesn't mean I care that your father isn't of the peerage."

His eyes went wide, and for a second she thought she caught a glimpse of panic in his gaze. Or was it guilt? It almost seemed to be both, but it was quickly replaced with a guarded look that told her nothing.

"That's not the way the world works, Serena."

"It ought to be," she shot back. "And between us, it absolutely should work that way."

His lips twisted into a mirthless smile. "Even between us, those lines must be observed, I'm far beneath your touch and we both know it."

"If you're trying to make me mad, Charles, you just might succeed, but even if you do, it won't change my attitude one whit. So your father isn't a peer...*I'm* a fallen woman. If you're going to insist on measuring these things, I'd say we're about even."

He shook his head. "Hardly. You'll always be too good for me. We can be friends. Nothing more. We must stop this madness."

And yet for all his protestations, he hadn't yet put more distance between them. She wasn't sure why. Perhaps those gentlemanly instincts of his weren't invulnerable after all. She still had a hand curled around his neck, but he could easily step away from the embrace if he wished. That he didn't gave her hope.

She leaned in and, placing her cheek against his chest, rested against him. He felt deliciously male—firm and solid, all angled planes in contrast to her curves. She could picture the muscles in his chest, honed and sculpted from physical exercise. His chest rose and fell as he breathed and she could hear the beat of his heart beneath her ear, a steady rapid beat.

Why, oh, why must he be one of the few men who would hesitate to say yes? He wasn't indifferent to her. If he were she could accept that. And why did his principled attitude make her want him that much more? Although really, the answer to that was easy. She admired men of strong principles, was drawn to them, found their character a potent attraction. First Thomas, and now Charles.

"So you don't hold my past against me?" she asked at last.

"Serena, I'm hardly the person who should be holding anyone's past against them." His voice was weary, resigned even.

That drew her curiosity.

She looked up at him again. "And why is that? Does Saint Charles have a past?"

She hadn't meant the saint reference as anything but a joke, yet a pained look flashed across his face.

"I'm sorry. That sounded horrid and I didn't mean anything by it."

"You needn't apologize, Serena. I know you didn't. And I can be a prig, at times. A nag." A ghost of a smile appeared. "Why you tolerate my company is a mystery to me."

It wasn't a mystery to her. Not any longer. She very much wanted to explore her newly acknowledged attraction to him, to satisfy her lust with him. She would even miss the more aggravating aspects of his personality if he weren't in her life.

"I don't merely tolerate your company and you know it," she said, offering her own smile in return. "You're good for me, Charles."

"Then perhaps I should go before you revise that opinion," he said, gently disentangling them from each other.

Serena didn't protest. She'd pushed him too far already, and she didn't want to scare him off. They were friends, after all. She hoped she hadn't given him cause to reconsider that.

"As if I would. You're one of the finest men I know." She paused before adding, "While I don't make a habit of revealing such personal details, I'm glad you know the truth."

He didn't say anything for a moment, just studied her with a grave look on his face and inscrutable eyes. "I'm glad too," he said at last. "I hope you know that your secret is safe with me..." He hesitated and his brows drew together. "And that you also know I understand that love can lead people to, well, make the decision you did, and that I have no contempt for your actions. Only sympathy for what you must have suffered after his death. After your baby's death. I'm so sorry, Serena."

She nodded. His understanding meant more to her

than he probably realized. Something welled up inside her, a tenderness toward him. If she hadn't made her earlier brazen proposition, she might have reached out and touched him, perhaps cradled his cheek with her hand. But she feared he might mistake what she meant by the gesture, and so she didn't.

"I hope nothing I said tonight will change our friendship."

"It won't," he assured her. "But that's all we can be... friends. Now I should be going."

Once he departed, she stood and stared at the empty doorway for a few minutes. Had she ruined things between them? To be honest, she couldn't tell.

In any case, she finally felt a lightness in her soul that she hadn't felt in a long time. The letter from Thomas had released her from the past and her confession to Charles had freed her from the burden of her secret.

But would it free Charles from his notions of propriety enough that he would entertain the type of relationship she'd proposed?

Most men would have shown no reluctance to accept what she had freely offered. Particularly, with no expectations on her part.

But Charles wasn't most men.

And perhaps that's why she wanted him with such intensity.

Chapter Fifteen

Charles was awakened the next morning by an insistent knocking on the door of the suite of rooms that he rented from a pair of spinster sisters. The Misses Abbott owned the house on Nassau Street, a quiet thoroughfare near Leicester Square, and they rented out two of the upper stories. A pair of bachelor brothers shared space in the rooms on the second floor and Charles rented the entire third floor.

"One moment," he called.

He threw back the covers and slid out of bed. A stripe of bright sunshine spilled through a crack in the drapes. What time was it? Before he'd fallen asleep this morning, he'd heard the clock strike four and now he feared he'd slept far past his usual rising time.

Fortunately the clock resting on the top of a tall chest of drawers showed the time as a quarter to nine, later than he normally awoke, but still early enough he could get to work at a reasonable time if he hurried.

Quickly he ran his hands through his hair to bring it into some semblance of order and grabbed his dressing gown from a hook near the bed and hastily drew it over his rumpled clothes. Consumed by thoughts of Serena's proposition, he'd spent much of the night restlessly pacing until exhaustion finally overtook him and he'd simply crawled between the blankets fully dressed.

He opened the door, expecting to see one of the house-maids, however, he was met with Miss Minerva, the younger of his landladies. She blinked as she took in his appearance. Apparently his efforts at achieving a measure of presentability had fallen short of the mark, but then she smiled and said, "Good morning, Mr. Townshend. I'm so sorry to disturb you. When you didn't appear at breakfast this morning, Leticia and I assumed that either you were feeling not quite the thing, or that Sir Roland had given you the day off, and you'd decided to catch up on your rest."

He smiled and gave a slight nod of his head, a tactic meant to avoid answering the question implicit in her last statement—was he sick, or had he merely been sleeping in?—since neither option explained the true reason he hadn't been up at his usual time.

However, the Abbott sisters were far from indifferent landlords, instead taking a friendly interest in the welfare of their boarders. So when Miss Minerva tilted her head and studied him with an expectant look, he knew she wasn't satisfied with his vague response. Normally, Charles found this maternal attitude endearing, but this morning it was merely inconvenient.

"Um, yes, well, I intend to go into work this morning, but I appreciate your concern. Thank you for checking on me." He gave a politely dismissive nod and began to shut the door.

Miss Minerva took a step forward, insinuating herself into the doorway to prevent him from shutting her out. "Yes, but I didn't come up to check on you, although I'm glad to see you don't appear to be...unwell." That little pause seemed to imply that whatever she thought of his appearance, she didn't quite approve of it.

"I came," she continued, "because you have some visitors."

"Oh?" he said, not feigning his surprise. He rarely had anyone call on him here, and even more rarely unexpected callers. He usually met with friends elsewhere...at his club, social events, Gentleman Jackson's, even a tavern now and again. "That's odd. I'm not expecting anyone. Who, um, who are these visitors, may I ask? It's awfully early in the morning."

Had Serena brought Jem to see him? As improbable as that seemed, he couldn't think of a likelier possibility.

"As to that, I'm afraid I can't enlighten you." A mischievous little smile appeared. "It's meant to be a surprise. But I'm sure you'll be glad to see them. They're waiting in the parlor for you. And don't feel you must rush through your toilette." She hesitated a moment. "You'll want to look your best. Leticia and I will entertain them until you're ready." She smiled sweetly at him. "You're going to be delighted," she said again.

"Thank you, Miss Minerva," Charles replied. "I'll finish dressing." More like finish undressing, since he'd done no more than remove his jacket and his shoes last evening. "I'll be down there as soon as I can. I don't suppose you can give me a *little* hint as to the identity of my visitors?"

She shook her head. "I promised," she said in a singsong tone. "But you're going to be delighted. I just know it."

He wasn't delighted. Far from it. Nonetheless, he managed to place a broad smile on his face as he greeted his mother, two younger half-brothers, and a shyly-smiling Miss Lewis, all the while wondering why his family had shown up out of the blue like this. And with Miss Lewis in tow, yet.

As if he needed his life knotted into any more tangles than it was already.

The Abbott sisters, appearing as excited by this surprise reunion as anyone (save for himself), made a discreet exit as his family milled around him.

"I can't believe you're actually here," he said after greetings had been exchanged all around. His mother settled herself on the sofa as did Miss Lewis and his youngest half-brother, David. Stuart ambled over to the window and stood looking out at the street below. Charles preferred to remain standing.

"You didn't breathe a word of these plans to me," he added. The cynical side of him suspected this had been done deliberately, since the inclusion of Miss Lewis implied this visit was to be a continuation of his recent trip home complete with a repeat of his mother's matchmaking efforts.

Miss Lewis had warned him back in Frome that her mother had expressed a wish to come to London during the Season. He'd been mentally prepared had those plans come to fruition. He'd have called upon the Lewis ladies once and been content that would have fulfilled the social obligation. What he hadn't anticipated was the possibility of Miss Lewis accompanying his family on a surprise visit.

Points to the gamesmanship of his matchmaking mother. As if anticipating his plan to merely pay a cursory call on the Lewis ladies should they show up in London, Mama had now made it impossible for him to ignore Miss Lewis without ignoring his family as well. And she knew him well enough to know he'd never do that.

He did hold a great deal of affection for them all, despite the times they tried his patience.

Times like this very moment when he felt cornered.

"So we managed to surprise you?" Charles's mother asked, gleefully clasping her hands before her. "Did you suspect it was us when you heard you had callers?"

"When Miss Minerva told me I had visitors, you were the last people I expected to see here." This at least was the unvarnished truth, even if he spoke it through gritted teeth.

"I thought you might guess the truth since it's unfashionably early to call, but we wanted to catch you before you left for work." His mother's eyes narrowed slightly before she added, "Who, then, did you think had come to visit?"

"I had no idea, Mama." Charles didn't like the speculative gleam in his mother's eye, nor the faintly suspicious tone of her voice. It wasn't hard to deduce what direction her thoughts had taken. Because Serena was the only female with whom he associated with any regularity, his mother had long harbored the erroneous notion that

Serena had some romantic designs on him. Even if he hadn't already known how Serena felt, her businesslike suggestion that they enter into a physical relationship had made it clear her feelings for him were lustful rather than romantic.

He'd never understand why Mama had jumped to the wrong conclusion instead of the more logical (and closer to being correct) one—namely that it was Charles who yearned for Serena. But she steadfastly maintained her belief despite his repeated protestations to the contrary.

Nor was she shy about expressing her disapproval for Serena, whom she judged by what she'd read in the gossip pages and whom she considered far too outspoken and unladylike for her own good.

"When did you arrive in London?" he asked, attempting to stir the conversation in a different direction.

"Yesterday afternoon. We rented a private coach, and between that and the fine weather, we had a most pleasant journey."

He glanced toward Miss Lewis, who, aside from her initial greeting to him, had remained silent so far. She sat with an arm around David's shoulders. It was a very sisterly gesture and it made him curious about the evolution of her relationship with his family. After all, it had been less than a month since his brief trip to Frome, and she hadn't displayed any particular closeness to his brothers at that time.

Had Miss Lewis joined the conspiracy to get the two of them wed? During his recent visit home, she'd expressed only amused exasperation with their mothers' obvious attempts at pushing a match between them. But now, seeing her on such cozy terms with his family, he couldn't help feeling that she'd undergone a significant change in attitude. He felt a faint sense of betrayal, followed by a tinge of guilt in the event he was judging her actions unfairly.

"And how long do you plan to stay?" Charles asked.

"Oh, that depends on your step-papa and how long his business takes," Mama said, giving a careless shrug. "A week, at least, and quite likely longer. Miss Lewis and I hope to have some new clothes made while we're here, and that will take some time, what with the fittings and such. Really, there's no reason we must rush back home."

Charles could think of a very good one. His life was complicated enough without his mother making further attempts to meddle in his love life. On the other hand, he was pleased to hear that his stepfather, Roger Avery, had made the trip to London as well. And not just because Roger's presence might help quell his mother's intrigues.

"He came to town with you then? I wasn't sure, since he didn't accompany you this morning."

"Why, his business here in London is half the reason we decided to come, since I'd be loath to make the trip without him," his mother replied. "Besides it was fortuitous timing, since we were able to secure housing for practically a song thanks to poor Sir George Biggs. He took an unfortunate tumble down the stairs." She glanced uncertainly at Stuart and David before adding in a voice dripping with disapproval, "Too much to drink one evening. Anyway, the upshot is that he and Lady Biggs are unable to make use of the lodgings they'd secured for the Season until he recovers from his broken leg. In the meantime, they offered to sublet to us for a fraction of what they paid for it."

"Well, you must take advantage of your time here

and plan some outings," Charles said. "The boys would enjoy a trip to see the Royal Menagerie. And the British Museum shouldn't be missed."

"I'd like to go to Astley's," David spoke up. "And the Egyptian Hall."

"Those are both excellent choices," Charles said. "London is full of things to do. Far more than you can possibly get to in a short visit."

"Perhaps you could give us a list of suggestions," Miss Lewis said. "Places we really shouldn't miss seeing while we're here. We must make the most of our opportunities."

"I could do that," Charles agreed.

"And don't forget Almack's," his mother said. "You can get vouchers for all of us, can't you? Miss Lewis and I were especially hoping to gain entry, since we've heard so much about it."

"I'm afraid vouchers to Almack's are out of the question, since I don't have the necessary connections to obtain them for you," Charles said. And a good thing that he didn't as he had no wish to get pressed into attending an assembly at Almack's with his mother and Miss Lewis.

"Oh, that's disappointing," his mother said. "I was sure you'd be able to. Well, there are other assemblies in London. I suppose we could attend some of those even if they won't have the same prestige as dancing at Almack's."

"I'm afraid attending any assemblies is out of the question for me," Charles said hastily. "What with parliamentary sessions most evenings of the week and Sir Roland frequently requiring my presence at social events. I can still see about obtaining tickets for the rest of you, if you like."

"I suppose you could do that," Mama said, but without

any real enthusiasm in her voice. "I hope you'll be able to join us on *some* of our outings, at least. You must know London so well by now, it would be like having our own tour guide."

"I'll see if I can carve out an afternoon or two," Charles hedged.

"Well, I suppose that will have to do," his mother said.

"I hate to rush you out, but I really must be going now," Charles said. "Where are you staying? I'll call on you there after work today, and we can talk some more then."

"We're staying at 27 Bird Street, just off Oxford Street. It's an ideal location. Miss Lewis and I can walk to the shops so conveniently."

"How handy for you," Charles remarked.

"It's all worked out so beautifully." She came to her feet and the others did likewise. "But we won't keep you any longer. I'd feel dreadful if our call got you in trouble for being late, but we just couldn't wait to see you."

"I'll hail you a cab, and then I'll see you this evening."

"That would be lovely, dear." His mother came over and gave him a quick kiss on the cheek. "Plan on dining with us. The cook Lady Biggs engaged is quite competent, and I've requested roast pheasant for this evening. I chose it with you in mind since you like it so well." She smiled and tucked her arm in his so that they might walk out together.

After he'd seen them off, he hailed a hackney for himself, rattling off Sir Roland's address before climbing in. As he settled back into the cracked leather seat cushion, it occurred to him that his family's presence could provide a convenient excuse for avoiding Serena for a little while.

At least until he was confident he could comport himself

in a more gentlemanly manner. Because as tempting as her suggestion was, his answer must be no. To say yes would be to choose a course that went against his principles, and even if his notions of honor and proper behavior could be set aside, what would happen when the arrangement no longer appealed to her?

It didn't bear contemplating. It would break him. He knew that. He'd given her the right answer last night. Of that, there was no doubt. Even so, he'd spent most of the night grappling with the temptation to tell her yes.

A little more time to shore up his emotional defenses wouldn't be a bad thing. Looking at it that way, he supposed the timing of his family's visit couldn't have been better.

She was beginning to wonder if he was avoiding her. What else was she to think when she'd received only a brief note four days ago telling her his family was in London for a visit, and then nothing but silence. She didn't begrudge him time with his family, but at the very least, she'd expected to hear something about the list of London tradesmen he'd promised to get for her. Or that he would inquire if she'd found a family for Jem yet. (She hadn't, but she had settled on a half dozen families who looked promising.)

She missed him and somehow she'd thought she'd have heard from him by now, even if it was another brief note about being too busy to call.

Jem continued to ask after him, and she'd used the boy as an excuse to contact Charles again and see if he'd like to accompany them on an outing to the Pantheon Bazaar this afternoon, but if he'd gotten her note, he'd yet to reply.

She still held out hope that Charles might join them right up until their one o'clock departure time. Fortunately, she'd been wise enough that she hadn't mentioned the invitation to Jem, so that only one of them was burdened with a sense of disappointment.

Ironically, it was during the ride to the Pantheon Bazaar that Jem brought up Charles yet again.

"When will we see Mr. Towns again? I want to show him Tabitha's new trick." Jem was very proud of his pet's accomplishment. With the help of her father's groom, Jem had taught Tabitha to fetch, an unusual feat for a cat.

"That is a very good question," she said. "I've been wondering that myself." Wondering. Obsessing. Fixating. "Remember, I told you that his family is in London, and spending time with them must still be keeping him quite busy."

She gave Jem a reassuring smile. However, the more time went on, the more she feared it probably resulted from the circumstances of their last meeting.

Maybe she shouldn't have confessed everything about her relationship with Thomas. At the time, she'd wished that Charles know the truth—the complete truth—but perhaps she oughtn't to have revealed it all in one fell swoop. Or perhaps she oughtn't to have suggested they become lovers on the heels of telling him about Thomas.

In hindsight, she'd dumped rather a lot on him that night.

"And I want him to see that I've learned to do a somersault like a performer in the circus," Jem said. This had also been learned from the groom, and Jem had been somersaulting about the house ever since.

Serena reached over and brushed back an unruly lock

of hair. Jem's curls still displayed a mind of their own despite having been trimmed to a considerably shorter length since he'd first joined the Huntington household.

"He might also enjoy seeing the other tricks you've learned recently."

Jem tilted his head and gave her a puzzled frown. "What new tricks? I haven't learned any others."

"Writing your letters. Writing your name. He's going to be very pleased with your progress."

"Oh, that," Jem said. "That's just schoolwork." His tone left little doubt that learning one's letters did not fall in the same category as Tabitha's cunning trick or somersaulting.

"Nonetheless, he's going to be proud of all you're learning."

"I suppose," Jem said. "But when will we see him again?" He wriggled across the seat and snuggled against her side, tilting his head to give her a cajoling smile.

"Soon I hope," she said. "But I don't know when."

His smile dimmed.

"How about if we invite him to accompany us to the British Museum? Would you like that?" In lieu of doing his usual lessons, she and Jem were planning to visit this august institution the day after tomorrow. He'd been quite excited about the prospect of going when he'd learned there were stuffed animals, a very much alive tortoise, and antique coins, some of which had been donated by her father. The latter had sparked Jem's interest because it was believed some of the coins had once been part of a pirate's booty.

"That would be most capital," he said, using a phrase he'd learned from Peregrine. To Serena's amusement, he unconsciously mimicked Peregrine's rather posh inflection whenever he said it. So quite frequently, since Jem used it any time he was excited by something.

"Very well. I will extend the invitation to him."

"Tell him about the pirate's treasure at the museum," Jem urged. "And the tortoise."

Serena laughed. "I certainly will."

This time, she'd try to extend the invitation in person. She and her father were attending a gathering at Lord Castlereagh's tonight. She knew from past experience that Sir Roland rarely missed these informal events at the Foreign Secretary's residence, and that Charles often accompanied him.

Although, he might not if he were dancing attendance on his family, but it seemed worth a try to catch him there, rather than leave the matter to a note that could go unanswered. If he weren't there tonight, then a note would have to do. Perhaps she could enlist Sir Roland to deliver the message if she didn't see Charles at Lord Castlereagh's.

She slipped her arm around Jem's shoulders and gave him a hug. "Let's hope he can join us, but try not to be disappointed if he can't. All right?"

Jem nodded, unaware that her statement was meant just as much for herself as it was for him.

Charles arrived at work by quarter past eight, much earlier than he typically did, but it was a sop to his conscience since he'd cited work as an excuse to cut short his time with his family and Miss Lewis last night. He simply hadn't been able to endure another long evening of expectant looks from Mama and blushing glances from

Miss Lewis, who was proving much less indifferent than he'd believed her to be when he was in Frome. So he'd announced an unusually early work morning prevented him from lingering after dinner. Even though he'd already had the perfect excuse—an invitation to accompany Sir Roland to a gathering at the Foreign Secretary's residence.

He often tagged along with his employer to these events. It was a good chance to mingle with "the right people" as his mother was so fond of saying. Not to mention, the added attraction that he frequently ran into Serena at these gatherings. Which was precisely the reason he'd declined to go last night. His emotions were still so torn between what he believed he must do, and what he so badly wanted to do, that he kept putting off a face-to-face meeting with her.

He'd barely gotten seated at his desk, however, when a footman informed him that Sir Roland wished to see him in his study.

Odd.

His employer rarely started his work day so early anymore, and Charles found it particularly surprising, given that Sir Roland had surely stayed out late last night. A social function hosted by the Foreign Secretary was sure to lean heavily toward a guest list drawn mainly from the diplomatic corps. In other words, the very people who were Sir Roland's closest cronies, and therefore precisely the sort of event to keep Sir Roland out late.

"Yes, sir?" Charles said, standing in the doorway of Sir Roland's study. The older gentleman looked up from the newspaper he was reading. A tray of food and a steaming teapot sat off to one side of the massive walnut desk.

Apparently his employer was so eager to get to work this morning, he'd had breakfast served to him here rather than in the dining room.

Sir Roland studied Charles with a keenly assessing eye long enough that it made Charles recall his school days when a teacher would stare down his pupils, trying to ascertain the perpetrator of some boyish mischief. No doubt Sir Roland was curious about Charles's early arrival, and this close appraisal was his employer's way of trying to divine the answer without having to ask the question.

Finally, he motioned for Charles to enter. "Come in, come in. I have a few things to discuss with you this morning."

Charles came over and stood before the desk, awaiting further instruction, since it wasn't clear if Sir Roland had called him in to take dictation, or just because he wished to pass along a snippet of information.

"Go on. Have a seat. Make yourself comfortable. This is not a matter of only a moment." He glanced at the paper, quill, and pot of ink Charles held. "I have something to discuss before we get to today's dictation."

Charles took a seat, setting the writing supplies he'd brought on the desk.

"It's a shame you weren't at Castlereagh's last night. Lots of talk about the upcoming diplomatic gathering in Aix-la-Chapelle this fall. Attending as part of the diplomatic staff could bump up a man's career prospects. There are many who recognize this and are circling around trying to get appointed to these posts." Sir Roland paused and his eyes narrowed slightly as he studied Charles. "I know that so far, you've shown little interest in a diplomatic career, but this event could lead to opportunities beyond the diplomatic circles, provided you come to the attention of those in power. I can pull the necessary strings, if you like."

"You're the second person to make such an offer to me in as many weeks," Charles said.

Sir Roland's brows rose in surprise. "I am, am I? And who, pray tell, was the first?"

"The Earl of Norwood."

Sir Roland leaned back in his chair and studied him. "He's a man who's about as well-connected as anybody in London. My advice, which you're free to ignore, is to take one of us up on it."

Charles let out a long breath. He found Jason Latimer's proposed business venture far more interesting than a diplomatic posting. However, investing in steamships was highly speculative in nature. Probably more speculative than a man of relatively limited means ought to consider.

Would it be foolish to ignore what Norwood and now Sir Roland were offering to secure for him? Most probably, even if the prospect failed to ignite the slightest enthusiasm in him.

"From your silence, I can only conclude either you're giving this serious consideration, or you're trying to come up with a way to turn me down gently," Sir Roland remarked.

"I'm going to give it serious thought," Charles said. "It may, in fact, be the best step for me to take."

"It could be," Sir Roland agreed. "But I don't want you to feel pressured into it. I sense some reluctance on your part, and I understand." He smiled wryly. "Not everyone feels the lure of a career in diplomacy."

There was another reason to consider it. A diplomatic

posting would remove him from the temptation Serena presented. He didn't trust that his resolve to refuse her would be able to withstand repeated requests to become her lover.

Pulling his thoughts back to his conversation with his employer, he said, "I admit it isn't something I ever seriously considered, but I think now I must."

"Give it some thought. If you conclude it's not for you, you have a spot here for as long as you wish."

"Thank you, sir. Is there anything else? Or was this the sole reason you called me in here?"

"There's one more thing," Sir Roland said. "At last night's gathering I ran into Lord Huntington and his daughter. She's a lovely girl. Told me more about that group of ladies she's involved in and the good works they do."

"Yes, sir. Lady Serena stays quite busy with her projects."

"I asked Lady Serena about the child the two of you discovered sleeping in the yard of an abandoned house."

"Not abandoned, merely empty until someone wishes to rent it," Charles said.

"Ah, my mistake." He chuckled. "It sounds as if he's doing well. According to Huntington the boy has livened up their household quite a bit."

Charles nodded. "I don't doubt that."

"I understand he's quite fond of you," Sir Roland said.

"I suppose so, sir. It's only natural, I guess, since I helped remove him from a tenuous living situation."

"Perhaps so," Sir Roland agreed. "Lady Serena is taking him to the British Museum this afternoon."

"Jem will enjoy that," Charles said.

"I hope that you will as well."

"Sir?"

The older gentleman cleared his throat. "I offered that you would accompany them today." He held up a hand. "I know. It was presumptuous of me, but capable as Lady Serena is, I'm old-fashioned enough to prefer that a lady have a male escort when she's out and about."

"Did you voice that thought to her?" Charles asked in some amusement. He could imagine Serena's reaction.

"Good gad, no. I'm not such a fool as that. I couched it in terms that implied you could use an afternoon off."

"Thank you, sir. Perhaps you would like to accompany us as well?"

"I think not," Sir Roland said with a knowing smile. "Three is company, four's a crowd."

"That's not quite how the saying goes," Charles said with a wry smile.

"No, but it serves my purposes, and a slight misquote still makes the point."

"Yes, sir. What time are they expecting me?"

"A quarter past noon, my boy, so let's make haste. I wish you to take down a letter for me."

Chapter Sixteen

~~~

They set out for the British Museum at half past twelve. Jem was a far cry from the scruffy little fellow they'd first brought back to the Huntington household. His cheeks were rosy and slightly rounder, a testament to the regular meals he now enjoyed. His hair had been brushed into some semblance of order, but the springy curls defied taming even though they'd been cropped to a shorter length.

Today he wore a handsome suit of clothes, the navy color chosen, according to Jem, "to hide the dirt that I invariably attract," clearly a phrase he'd picked up from Serena or his nursemaid. He looked quite the little gentlemen, and if he'd gotten any dirt on his clothes this morning, the navy color hid it admirably.

Upon their arrival at the museum, they'd run into a

brief snag when a supercilious doorman informed them that children under ten were not to be admitted.

Serena had raised one imperious brow and said, "Really? That's quite unfortunate, since I promised my father, Lord Huntington, that I would bring his young friend here to see the display of ancient coins that he donated to the museum last year."

At this display of aristocratic hauteur, the doorman's attitude underwent a rapid transformation. He offered a few stammered words about that particular collection being displayed in the gallery rooms and asked if they would like him to summon a guide for them.

"No need for that," Serena assured him. "We prefer to tour as our whims guide us. I'm quite familiar with the museum's layout."

Serena took one of Jem's hands in her own and turning to Charles said, "Shall we visit the live tortoise first? I think Jem will find it most diverting."

As predicted, Jem was quite taken with the tortoise. A plate of lettuce leaves had been set out for any museum visitors who wished to feed the animal. Serena and Charles demurred, but Jem eagerly fed the phlegmatic reptile half a dozen leaves before agreeing to move on. From there, they went to the room that housed a display of stuffed animals, including a particularly winsome monkey. As they continued to make their way from room to room, they viewed seashells, the Egyptian antiquities before reaching the area where ancient coins were displayed, including a few dozen donated by Lord Huntington.

"Papa's father was the coin collector," Serena said. "This represents only about half of the coin collection

Papa inherited from him. I expect he'll end up donating the rest eventually."

"Does your father collect anything?" Charles asked.

"Old books," she replied. "He has some particularly fine folios of Shakespeare, a very early edition of *The Canterbury Tales*, and some beautiful psalters that date back to the 1300s. He has more, of course, but those are the gems of the collection."

Charles nodded, impressed. "My stepfather owns a great many books, but for the most part, they're dog-eared from frequent readings."

"As books should be," Serena said. "On the other hand, I'm glad some were tucked away through the years so that we can see books from a bygone era. I especially like the Psalters with their beautiful illustrations so painstakingly drawn those many years ago. I can just picture the monks bending over their work, a candle sputtering nearby to give them light." A smile softened her face, and he couldn't look away, captivated by watching her indulge in this bit of romantic whimsy.

Jem stirred relentlessly beside them, breaking the spell, and Charles wondered if the boy's interest was beginning to wane. They'd been touring the museum for nearly two hours now.

"Shall we continue touring or have we seen enough?" he asked Serena, but he cast a significant look in Jem's direction.

"If he's not weary of it, I'm not either. What do you think, Jem?" she asked the boy. "There are still rooms we haven't seen, but if you're getting tired, we can head home."

"I'm not tired," Jem said stoutly. "This place has

practically the whole world in it. I want to see everything."

Serena laughed. "Then so you shall. Or as much as we
can manage before the museum closes for the day." She
took Jem's hand in her own and they proceeded to the
next room, which housed an exhibit of terra-cotta pottery
and statuary.

However, after only a few minutes, Jem tapped Charles
on the arm. Turning to the boy, Charles was mildly
surprised at the boy's strained face. "Yes, Jem?"

Jem made an urgent motion with his hand indicating that
he wished Charles to bend down. When he complied, Jem
drew close and whispered in his ear, "I've got to piss."

Charles told Serena that he was taking the boy to attend
to his private needs.

"I'll just wait here for you then," she said.

Not able to remember where the facilities were located,
Charles had to ask one of the museum guides where to
find them.

"Ground floor, back corner, north end of the building"
was the reply. Sensing that the boy's need to go was
urgent, he led Jem as swiftly as he could through the
maze of rooms and Jem's overburdened bladder was soon
relieved.

After Charles tipped the attendant whose job it was to
empty the chamber pot, he and Jem retraced their steps
back to the room where Serena had promised to wait for
them. She wasn't there, but Charles could hear voices
coming from an adjacent room, and assuming that's where
she'd gone, he led Jem into it. However, he drew to a swift
halt when he saw with whom she was speaking. He didn't
recognize the two ladies, but the gentleman accompanying

them was another matter. The last thing he wanted today (or any day, for that matter) was a face-to-face meeting with Edgar Borland.

Serena stood with her back toward them, still unaware of their return, so Charles quickly dragged Jem back through the doorway before they caught the attention of her companions.

His heart raced in his chest, even though no one seemed to have paid the slightest attention to him and Jem. If any of the trio mentioned their presence to Serena, she would know they were back and wonder what kept them from joining her. She might even bring everyone trooping in here with her. Wouldn't that be a spectacularly awkward moment?

"But Lady Serena is in there," Jem objected, obviously confused by Charles's actions.

"Yes, but she's met with some friends, so we'll let her have her visit with them while we look at the displays some more. We barely saw anything in this room earlier. It would be a shame not to do it justice."

Jem's brow wrinkled and he glanced back through the doorway. "Who are they?"

Good question. One of the ladies, a petite blonde, expensively dressed, had clung to Borland's arm in a possessive manner. The second lady was perhaps ten years older, more plainly dressed, and, Charles presumed, a companion meant to act as the chaperone for the other two.

"I'm not acquainted with them," Charles replied.

A half-truth. The females were strangers to him, and since he'd never been introduced to Borland, it wasn't quite lying on his part to deny an acquaintanceship with him, even if it was thoroughly misleading. His conscience was uncomfortable with this half-truth (or half lie, depending on how you wished to view it), but the reality was too complicated to try to explain to a child.

Charles wondered if Jem had noticed the physical resemblance between himself and Borland. But even if the child hadn't, he had no such hope that Serena wouldn't. Nor did he want to give those with whom she'd been speaking an opportunity to note the similarity in their features. He could only hope that they didn't all come in here together.

He ought to have a plan in case they did. If someone commented on how much he and Borland looked alike, could he laugh it off with a flippant remark?

He didn't feel particularly jolly with a cold lump of dread lodged in his chest. He suspected any attempt at humor would likely sound forced, insincere, a flailing effort that would drop into the conversation with a resounding thud.

Nonetheless, it was the best idea he had at the moment.

Jem tugged on his hand.

Charles turned his attention to the boy who was pointing at a large, painted terra-cotta vase depicting a lion biting the throat of a gazelle. It was a rather gruesome depiction with blood droplets spouting out of the gazelle's neck in several directions.

"Look at that giant kitty," Jem said.

"That's actually a lion. He's a type of cat, one that lives far away from here. He's much, much bigger than a cat like Tabitha. She's a pet who's meant to live with people. Lions are wild. They don't live in people's homes."

Jem nodded solemnly. "A lion must be a very scary cat."

"Yes," Charles agreed. "I expect most people when they

come across one in the wild would find them terrifying. Did you know that there's a lion that lives in London?"

Jem's eyes grew round. "Where? 'Cause I would stay away from there."

"This lion belongs to the king and he lives at the Royal Menagerie in an enclosed space. Visitors can see him, but he can't hurt them because he can't get near them. Would you like to go see him sometime?"

Jem thought about this for a moment before nodding slowly.

"Very well. I'll talk to Lady Serena and we'll arrange a time to take you. There are plenty of other animals there that you will enjoy seeing."

They moved on and soon the scene on another of the terra-cotta urns captured Jem's attention.

"They aren't wearing any clothes," he remarked with a trace of envy in his voice. The painted urn he referred to showed a group of spear-holding hunters circling what appeared to be a horned cow, or perhaps it was an African buffalo.

"No. Apparently, ancient hunters didn't always wear clothes."

"But wouldn't they get cold?" Jem asked.

"Not if they lived where the weather is always warm," Charles replied.

"There are places like that?" Jem asked, clearly incredulous at the thought.

"There are, but not in England."

Jem made a face before shrugging and turning his attention back to the exhibits.

They continued to drift past the displays, Jem happily chattering, Charles answering the questions that cropped up while keeping an eye on the doorway that led to the room where the hum of conversation was still audible. He was feeling slightly less on edge now.

After fifteen minutes or so of this, Serena stepped through the doorway alone. She caught his eye, and he could tell that she had questions.

Chapter Seventeen

~

Charles looked...apprehensive, heightening Serena's suspicion that there was a connection between Charles and Edgar Borland. A connection that, for some reason yet unknown to her, prompted Charles to avoid coming into the same room with the man.

She'd been shocked to discover a man who looked so remarkably like Charles they could be brothers. Yet when she'd gently probed about a connection between them, Borland had claimed ignorance of any relatives by the name of Townshend.

Borland had seemed sincere in his denial of any Townshend relations, and yet Charles appeared to be avoiding the man.

Why?

If not for this avoidance on Charles's part, she might

have thought it only an extraordinary coincidence that he and Edgar Borland looked so much alike. It did happen on occasion that one ran into a person whose features closely matched another's without there being any family relationship.

But because of Charles's obvious attempt to avoid Borland, she didn't believe this to be the case. She was consumed with curiosity and yet Jem's presence prevented the possibility of a frank discussion.

"Can we go see the tortoise again?" Jem asked as she rejoined them.

"Of course, if that's what you would like," she said.

Slipping a hand through Charles's arm, she could feel the tension in his muscles. "Let's go this way, shall we?" She turned in the direction opposite to the room where she'd run into Borland. "I'd like to walk past the exhibit of armor on our way to see Theodore."

"Theodore?" Jem asked with a puzzled look.

She reached for his hand. "That tortoise needs a name and I think Theodore suits him."

Jem's eyes widened. "Can we do that?"

"I don't see why not," she replied.

As they left the room with the terra-cotta artwork, a look passed between herself and Charles, one that was a silent acknowledgment they would table any discussion of Edgar Borland until later.

However, once they returned to the Huntington residence, Serena sent Jem off with Ellie, his nursemaid.

"*Who* is Edgar Borland?" she asked now that she and Charles were alone in the sitting room. He'd taken up a position near the window, standing with his hands clasped behind him. "And what does he have to do with you?"

"First of all, I know very little about Edgar Borland. I wasn't even aware of his existence until I spotted him at White's a few days ago, and was struck by the uncanny physical resemblance between us. I don't believe he noticed my presence that day. He was in a celebratory mood and well into his cups."

"Is that why you stayed back in the terra-cotta room? So he wouldn't see you? I knew there must have been some reason because you're too much of a gentleman to leave me on my own for far longer than it would take to locate the water closet and let Jem take care of his business."

Charles let out a long sigh and ran a hand through his hair. "It's true, I didn't want to meet Borland today, and frankly, I'd be perfectly happy if I never came across him again. As far as I know, Borland remains ignorant of my existence. I'd like to keep it that way."

"He denied knowing anyone by the name of Townshend," Serena said.

Charles gaped at her in dismay. "You asked him?"

"Well, yes. It seemed a reasonable question, given that the two of you look similar enough to be closely related. I presumed you were cousins, so I was, well, shocked to hear otherwise."

Rather than answering, he turned toward the window, his shoulders set in a rigid line, his hands clasped in a tight knot. She went to stand beside him and laid a hand on his arm.

"It's all right," she said gently. "You don't have to explain anything to me. But if you ever feel the need to confide in someone, you'll find me a sympathetic listener."

He nodded and continued to stare out the window for several moments before drawing in a long breath.

"If we're related," he began in a flat voice, "and I don't *know* that we are, although the evidence seems to argue that chances are good we share a common ancestry somehow—but *if* we're related," he repeated, "I'm guessing that…" He bowed his head for a moment, then turned so that his gaze met hers, and she could see the pained expression in their depths. "That is to say, I believe there's a very good chance I'm his illegitimate half-brother."

Illegitimate? Charles? She stared at him for a long moment, trying to wrap her mind around this idea.

"But how can that be? Your father died before you were born…" Her voice trailed off as she realized what a convenient story that made to explain the absence of a father in a baby's life, leaving the mother a sympathetic widow rather than a fallen woman. It wouldn't be the first time such a tale had been concocted to cover up an out-of-wedlock pregnancy.

"I see you comprehend how it could be."

"But why…? I mean, I don't understand why you've continued to conceal the truth from me. Especially in light of my own recent confession. Did you think I would judge you harshly for something that you had no control over? I may have shamed myself—in society's eyes, even if I've never regretted my actions—but you? You were an innocent baby."

"I'm a bastard, Serena. I don't have an illustrious family name to help overcome people's censure. Is it any wonder that I don't want to speak of it? So far, it's been a well-kept secret and now Borland threatens that."

He gave a humorless laugh. "A secret even I knew

nothing about until my maternal grandmother bequeathed me a modest property in Yorkshire. My stepfather, Roger Avery, handled the legalities. He's the one who told me that John Townshend was a figment of my mother's imagination rather than the man who sired me. But even Roger doesn't know the true identity of my father."

He turned and looked out the window once more, but not before Serena saw the torment in his eyes, the stark, bleak, weary resignation that he couldn't quite hide. She gently stroked his arm, trying to offer what solace she could.

"For the last four years, I'd no clue as to who my real father might be," he continued. "But when I saw Borland at White's... Well, it seemed to answer the question I never wanted to have to ask." Another humorless chuckle. "Never suspected I'd need to ask for the first twenty-two years of my life. The Borland family is from Yorkshire. I looked them up in *DeBrett's*. Their home is near the property I inherited, which just seems to confirm my suspicions. Wouldn't it have been ironic if I'd taken up residence in my grandmother's house instead of living in London? I might have stumbled across my paternal relatives before now."

Realizing that anyone could look up from the street and see them standing together, Serena gently tugged on his arm and led him to the other side of the room. His anguish deserved a measure of privacy.

"Once you knew you'd been lied to, did your mother never tell you the truth of your parentage?"

His jaw tightened and he shook his head. When he spoke, it was in a voice so low she could barely hear his reply. "No. I confronted her, even though Avery argued against it. He said Mama would be crushed to find I knew her shameful secret and asked me what would be served by digging it up. But I was hurt and angry and I believed she owed me the truth."

"And she refused to tell you?" Serena asked.

"The answer to that is both yes and no." He massaged the back of his neck and blew out a long breath. "I began by telling her that Mary Bartles, my grandmother—her mother—had bequeathed me a house and a modest acreage. I knew that as soon as she heard that, she'd realize that I didn't believe the family history I'd been told, since supposedly my maternal grandmother had died before I was born."

He paused, his gaze fixed on a spot on the wall, as if he were lost in thought. Serena wondered if he was replaying in his mind the memory of that confrontation with his mother. After a long moment of silence, he turned his attention back to her, his mouth drawn into a tight line, his expression one of both frustration and, somewhat to her surprise, regret.

"I got no further in the little speech I'd prepared. Mama gasped and put her hand to her heart, saying her chest hurt. I thought she was simply putting it on for show as a way of avoiding the discussion, but then she began struggling to breathe and the doctor was called."

"Oh my God, Charles," Serena said.

He nodded. "I felt wretched for bringing on her attack."

"Had she had similar episodes before?" Serena asked.

"Nothing like that," Charles replied. "I thought she was dying. That by not heeding my stepfather's request to say nothing, I had sent my mother into a fatal decline." He gave her a humorless smile. "Fortunately, I didn't."

"You can't blame yourself for that," Serena said. "How could you have known?"

"That's just it. I do blame myself." He closed his eyes, his face twisted into a grimace as if he were in pain. He reached up and rubbed his forehead with his hand before opening his eyes again. "We'd been warned by the doctors years ago after she suffered a serious illness that she had a weak heart. She was to avoid strenuous activity and we were to avoid bringing on a state of mental excitability. The thing is she routinely ignored the doctor's orders about avoiding activity and never appeared to suffer any problems. There were a few times she received distressing news and suffered mild heart palpitations, but nothing worse than that. For heaven's sake, my step-aunt Delia frequently suffers from similar symptoms, and she has no health conditions that we're aware of. Still I should have known better. I should have heeded Avery's warning."

"Oh, Charles, it wasn't your fault. If she hadn't hidden it from you all those years, you wouldn't have felt compelled to demand the truth."

"Well, in the end I didn't find out the truth," he said. "I never broached the subject again, nor do I ever intend to. I'm not going to be the one to leave Avery a widower or my stepbrothers motherless. Besides, Borland's appearance seems to supply the answer I was looking for anyway."

Serena frowned. "Not entirely. You still don't know..." She hesitated, trying to think of a delicate way to say what she was thinking. "Well, you don't know how your conception came about. Whether your father abandoned your mother once she became pregnant, or whether he forced himself on her and a pregnancy resulted. Either way I suppose, it leaves your mother a sympathetic figure, although withholding the truth of your parentage was wrong of her."

"I received a letter from my grandmother, one she'd written that was to be given to me after her death. In it she refers to her wayward daughter and says something about how she—my mother—rejected every precept her parents had taught her. I don't know precisely what my grandmother meant by that, but it did lead me to conclude that my father did not force himself on her. Because I did wonder, of course."

"Naturally. Anyone would," she said.

"And now you know my deep, dark secret." His mouth twisted into a sardonic smile. "The truth is I wish I could go back to being the man I thought I was before I knew any of this."

She reached up and took his face in her hands, forcing him to look at her. "You are still that man, Charles Townshend. None of this changes that."

"It changes everything, Serena. Can't you see that?" he asked sadly. "You saw Borland today. This secret has been buried a long time, but how much longer? Not much, I fear."

Of course, a man like Charles would agonize over something like this. Bastardy was a mark of shame, and she was sure he felt that keenly. And then there was his mother's concealment of the truth *even from him*.

Serena understood concealing it from the world at large, but for a mother to conceal that from her son...To Serena that seemed a sort of betrayal, and if she were Charles, one she wouldn't be able to forgive easily.

Slipping her hands from his cheeks, she slid them over

his shoulders, embracing him, pressing herself against him, as if somehow by doing so she could absorb some of his pain.

He stirred within her embrace. "Serena."

"No," she said, refusing to let him go. "The truth of your birth doesn't make a bit of difference to me."

"But it will to others if it ever becomes common knowledge, and I fear that with Borland in London, it's only a matter of time before people start...wondering."

She tightened her arms around him. "Let them wonder."

He shook his head and gently loosened her hands from around his neck. They fell to her sides and he took a step back. "I can't do that. I have my mother to consider. And my half-brothers. Gossip can be cruel. I don't want them subjected to the misery of whispers and speculation."

"Brazen it out. Deny it. Laugh it off as a fantastic coincidence. I've heard Lord Byron say many a time the truth is often far stranger than fiction. Seize upon that idea, and let people dare to contradict you."

One corner of his mouth quirked up in a rueful smile. "Unlike you, I'm not the kind of person who could pull that off."

She reached for his hands and held them tightly in her own. "Then let me help you do it, if anyone dares question your legitimacy."

"I love your boldness, Serena. Your defiance. That fierce light that comes into your eyes when you're passionate about something."

"I'm passionate about you, Charles."

"Don't say that," he protested. But his eyes contradicted the words. She saw the hunger in them, the yearning he wasn't able to hide. His confession appeared to have left him vulnerable, unable to fully put his guard up. He could make himself *say* the words, but he couldn't make himself *feel* them.

"Why not? We may have our secrets that we hide from the world, but at least let's be frank with each other. I want you, Charles. *You.* I don't give a fig about the rest of it."

With that, she flung herself into his arms, which obligingly encased her in a tight embrace. Delighted by this, because she'd expected resistance, she pressed into him, reveling in the feel of his body against hers, and even more delighted when his mouth swooped down and took hers in a searingly hot kiss.

This...*this* was the side of Charles she'd been hoping to coax out from the staid and proper side of him. Hungry, wanting, *taking*.

Uninhibited, thank God.

She moaned as his hand found her breast, molding it in his lean, capable fingers.

Yes. Yes! *Yes!*

Heated desire spiraled through her, making her knees weak as a heavy throbbing built in parts of her body hungry for this man's touch.

His hand slipped inside the edge of her bodice, his nimble fingers caressing her bare breast, teasing her tightly peaked nipple.

She bracketed his face with her hands and drew it downward to her throat. His lips began to kiss and nibble the sensitive skin there. She tilted her head back to give him better access to her neck...to her bosom, if he wished to explore there.

She desperately hoped he would, even though the sitting room was far from ideal for what was happening between them. At least the door was closed. She'd made sure of that when they'd come in here, not wanting the servants to overhear their discussion concerning Edgar Borland.

Even so, she longed for a more private location where she could push his jacket off his shoulders, unwind his neckcloth, unbutton waistcoat buttons, draw his shirt over his head, before finally undoing the buttons of his trousers. Her mouth watered at just the thought of undressing him.

She didn't even yearn for a bed, though that would be ideal. No, she'd be satisfied to simply have the privacy to be able to discard their clothing and come together in a wildly frantic, gloriously naked coupling.

Unfortunately, this was a sitting room, not a bedroom. Even a closed door couldn't promise a sufficient level of privacy.

Instead, she settled on the next best thing possible. With a strategic wiggle and a firm yank, her bodice rode down, exposing one breast to his dark, hungry gaze.

"This is madness," he muttered. And yet he wasn't able to draw his eyes away from her naked breast, the rosy brown nipple puckered into a hard knob.

She slipped a hand beneath her breast, raised it toward him, a carnal offering. A silent plea. A promise of all she yearned to give him. And what she wished to receive in return.

However, a more complete intimacy would have to wait until another time and a more propitious place.

His breath came in hard pants as he stared at the breast she held up to him, but after only a moment of hesitation, his mouth came down, covering her nipple, drawing it into his hot, hungry mouth, his tongue swirling around the tip, before he began suckling on her, sending waves of pleasure cascading through her. She bit back a groan.

For a few seconds, she watched his dark head bent over her, pleasuring her just as she'd been craving. Then she closed her eyes and with her hands tightly gripping his shoulders, surrendered herself to the keen pleasure of a man's lovemaking.

Something snapped within him. There could be no other explanation.

The tight rein he kept wrapped around his emotions had unraveled, and like a dam giving way to torrential rains, the feelings he'd kept hidden away spilled forth in a rushing current, all rational thought swept away in its wake.

Even now, with his mind fuddled by a sensual haze, he wasn't entirely sure how they'd gotten to this point— Serena in his arms, bodice down, hair awry, her breasts thrust toward him, inviting him to feast.

And feast he had.

But he must put an end to this madness.

He pulled back, his mouth reluctantly releasing its grip on her hardened nipple. His loins throbbed at the sight of her bare breasts, the skin rosy from his attentions to them.

His attentions, *his* plundering mouth on *her* breasts.

To his dismay, he felt no regret for his actions, only a primal male satisfaction as Serena panted in his arms. But despite her acquiescence, he'd had no right to behave as her lover, to be granted liberties that should belong to a husband. He ought to be ashamed of himself, but more than anything he felt as if he'd claimed her for his own.

She'd offered herself up to him, and he'd accepted,

without a fight, his sense of honor disappearing as soon as temptation reared its head. However, he was not Thomas Carlisle, with a titled father and all the benefits that went along with that. Serena and Carlisle could have made a future together. He and Serena could not.

His conscience urged him to avert his gaze from the sight of her nakedness, and yet, it was beyond his power to do so. To be fair, she didn't seem to wish him to, as she made no effort to cover herself.

No, she stood before him without shame. Unabashed. She'd made her desires clear, and she wasn't shying away from them. Or him.

His secret had made no difference to her. She hadn't been repulsed by it. Not that it changed anything because she deserved far more than he could ever give her, but if he weren't already in love, her acceptance would have won his heart.

But while she hadn't condemned him when he'd confessed his illegitimacy, he had plenty of self-recrimination for what he'd just done. By heavens, they were in the sitting room of her father's house. He deserved to be horsewhipped. Or worse. He had no more chance of marrying her than he did of flapping his arms and being able to fly.

After a few moments of standing there, each silently studying the other, she finally drew up her bodice.

"Don't do it," she said quietly. "Don't flay yourself with the martyr's whip. What just passed between us doesn't make you a rake of the worst order any more than it makes me a harlot. We're two adults who can determine the course of our relationship without need for recrimination or regret."

"Serena, I, of all people, should know better than to allow myself to indulge in... in any type of dalliance." He blew out a long inhale and pinched the bridge of his nose. He needed to say this. "I don't know the circumstances that led to my conception, but I do know my mother was forced to shoulder a heavy burden, while my father did not. He got to take his pleasure, she had to concoct a story to explain the presence of a baby in her life. I will never put a lady—or a child—in the same position. I can't do this. It's clear I can't be trusted to behave myself with you, and equally clear you don't want me to."

"And I admire your attitude. But surely you know there are ways to prevent pregnancy, Charles. Thomas and I weren't canny enough—or prepared enough—to employ them, but you and I can."

He shook his head. "Those means still fail at times. Nothing is guaranteed to prevent pregnancy, except abstinence."

"Well, yes, but..." She stopped abruptly, her gaze sharpening as she studied him closely. "Does that mean you're currently celibate?"

He felt his cheeks grow hot. "Yes, I am," he said shortly.

One of her brows rose and she smiled slightly. She appeared to find this tidbit of information interesting. "Really. How long has it been? Or have you never? Now *that* would be... interesting."

Were they really going to discuss this? Apparently the answer was yes, because Serena was looking at him expectantly.

"I have," he said, the blush still warming his face. "But it's been a few years, and to be perfectly honest, my experience isn't vast." Now what had compelled him to share that? Oh, well. It wasn't the most embarrassing piece of information he'd shared with her today.

"'Not vast' is such a relative term," she said thoughtfully. "I confess, I'm curious about how limited your experience is."

"One woman, Serena. I've only been with one woman. A widow. And even then, our liaison was fairly brief. Once I discovered I was illegitimate, it drove home what I risked by being with her. I didn't love her. I certainly didn't want to marry her, any more than she wished to marry me. Our arrangement was merely a convenience for both of us."

"And you received your inheritance from your grandmother how long ago?" she asked.

"Four years ago. Nearly five now."

"Goodness, Charles. That means you were with her shortly after you finished at Cambridge. I thought most men started well before that."

"I'm sure many do." He was beginning to blush again. Unlike Serena, he wasn't able to remain coolly poised while discussing such personal details. "But I wasn't exactly plump in the pockets during my Cambridge years. My money had to go toward living expenses, not women."

She laughed. "What a pair we are, Charles. It seems as if both of us have endured a very long time without physical intimacy." She licked her lips and eyed him as if he were a tasty morsel. She reached out and brushed back an errant lock of hair. "I do wish you'd change your mind about...the nature of our relationship."

Before he could reply, she laughed again, and said, "Don't worry, you needn't look so alarmed. We're done with any such activities tonight. It was torturous enough just now to stop what we started."

"We can't keep crossing these lines," he said.

She tilted her head. "I can tell you that once crossed, it's nearly impossible to go back."

He groaned. "Don't say that. It's clear I have... wretched self-control where you're concerned, but we must observe the proper boundaries."

"I'd say a lack of self-control rather argues the opposite. Why fight the attraction between us if we don't want to?" She reached for his hands, holding them loosely in her own. "We have a choice," she said earnestly. "We can do precisely as we like."

He studied their joined hands. "Serena..." he began.

"You don't have to say yes," she interrupted him. "Just don't say no yet. Think about it. I know what I want, Charles, and I think you do too. You're just letting the opinions of others get in the way."

She gave his hands a squeeze before stepping away from him. She walked over to the sideboard and looked at him over her shoulder. "Let's have a drink while we discuss what to do about Borland."

Her complete aplomb was... impressive. *He* was still keyed up with heightened emotion—and more than a little thwarted sexual gratification.

"Well, what will it be?" She asked. "Whisky? A brandy? I can call for tea, if you'd prefer that."

"Whisky," he said. He rarely drank spirits before dinner, but whisky might be just the thing to mellow his riotous emotions.

She lifted the decanter of whisky and poured a generous splash into a glass and held it out to him. He took it and then she poured herself a small glass of sherry. "Let's sit, shall we?"

The utter normality of her suggestion was a bit disconcerting, but if they could command themselves with such decorum, perhaps they could return to some semblance of their usual friendship.

The image of her lovely breasts flashed through his mind. He could see the truth in her words that it could be impossible to go back once certain lines were crossed, but he was determined to try.

He took a seat across from her.

"We need a plan in place in the event his resemblance to you...complicates things for you."

"I have a plan. It's to avoid the man. The less we're seen together, the less likely that people will make connections."

"And you know his habits so well that you can do that?" she asked, sounding more than a little skeptical.

"I know mine," he retorted. "However, I think it's largely a matter of avoiding places where people congregate."

"So your plan is to become a hermit," she said. She took a sip of her sherry. "That sounds quite dull and highly impractical, in my opinion."

It did when she put it that way.

"Do you have a better one?" he asked.

She nodded. "I still like brushing it off as coincidence. As long as there's nothing to prove that it's more than a remarkable resemblance between the two of you."

"That's part of the problem. Perhaps there is proof, people who know the truth and would speak of it. Borland's father for one, assuming the man is my father too."

"That is not *proof*, and if no one's spoken up in all these years, I doubt they'd start talking now. So tell me, what do you know about the family? You said you looked them up in *Debrett's*." She took another sip of sherry.

Realizing that he'd had none of his whisky, and feeling the need for its mellowing effect, he took a long swallow before he answered.

"Casper Borland, the man who may have sired me, is the third son of a baronet." It was hard to think of him as his father. For much of his life, that role had been filled by his stepfather, Roger Avery, and to a lesser extent, the vague mental image of John Townshend, the conveniently deceased fictional father his mother had invented for him.

"From Yorkshire, you said."

"Yes."

"So gentry with origins well away from London." She drummed her fingertips on the arm of her chair. She had a habit of doing that when she was thinking. "I suppose that explains why I've never heard of the family. Which is good for us, because I doubt they have many social connections here in town. When you saw this Edgar Borland at White's, who was he with?"

"To be honest, I was so shocked to see the man, I don't really remember."

"Well, think," she insisted.

He cast his mind back to that day. "I was at a table with Farrars, Plumley, and Ambrose-Stone, and none of them seemed to know much about him. Just that he was new to town, and was rumored to have spent time on the Continent in a bid to dodge his creditors. He was at White's with a table of rowdies, celebrating the victory of a boxer Borland had discovered. Or so Ambrose-Stone informed me."

"Can you remember the identities of any of the men at his table? Close your eyes and try to picture what you saw that day." She leaned forward a bit, as if willing his memory to cooperate.

He didn't close his eyes, preferring instead to look back into hers, but he did try to conjure a mental image of the men he'd seen with Borland.

"Ogilvy was there," he said at last.

"Of course, he was," Serena replied. "He's never far from the betting action. Who else?"

"Mobley, I think. Bunbury, definitely. Leggins. Simon Trentwell." He shook his head. "I can't remember anyone else, though there were certainly more at the table. Sorry."

"Well, this is still helpful. Sounds like the usual sporting set, and with the exception of Trentwell, no one of particular significance."

"To be honest, I was a bit surprised Trentwell was there. His grandfather, the Duke of Penwarren, is a friend of Sir Roland's. The duke has been trying to get his grandson to give up his profligate ways."

"Poor Simon has been a lost soul since his brother died in that accident a few years ago. Nonetheless, I can see why a man like Borland would desire an acquaintance with a duke's heir. At any rate, I'd venture to guess your connections are far loftier than your maybe-or-maybe-not half-brother."

"My connections? Are you joking? The bastard stepson of a solicitor? My loftiest connections *are* the Borlands, and you just dismissed them as of little importance."

"Pfff," she said with a careless wave of her hand. "I'm not just talking blood relations. You, my dear, Charles, have important friends. Myself, of course, although I'm not sure friend is precisely the correct term for us anymore."

Ahh, this was quintessential Serena, boldly proclaiming a spade a spade. She wasn't going to let him ignore what they'd done this afternoon, or bury it with silence as others might.

She continued, "The Norwoods, the Rochesters, my father, Edwina and Mr. Latimer, Lord Ambrose-Stone, Sir Roland...shall I go on naming people who will rally to your defense should the need arise?"

"Or," he said. "I can try to get a posting with the English delegation to France. That would eliminate the need of dragging all those people into my problems, and then I could parlay it into a career with the diplomatic corps."

"No," she said.

"No?"

"No," she repeated. "I put my foot down. You're not a coward and neither am I. So let's just set aside the idea of swanning off to France, and deal with Borland right here on English soil."

It occurred to him then that men who preferred their females biddable and compliant were fools. He far preferred a lady unafraid to speak her own mind, to stand up to him. Hell, to stand before him half-naked without an ounce of shame. By god, she was magnificent.

"Borland aside, accepting a diplomatic posting would be a prudent move. I was already considering it, since my time in the House of Commons is coming to an end. Borland simply makes the decision easier."

"And yet we both know you aren't terribly interested in becoming a diplomat, or you'd have already pursued that avenue."

She was right, of course. The diplomatic corps didn't have any special appeal for him. On the other hand, it could lead to a successful career, and there would be nothing to keep him in London once his term in the House of Commons was over.

Nothing except the woman he'd secretly loved for some time now. Who was offering him more than he'd ever dared to hope for—her body, if not her heart.

"It's true. Accompanying the English delegation to Aix-la-Chapelle wouldn't be my first choice."

"Are you sure you're not running away from me as well? From us? Because that's what I think."

"We both know there can be no 'us.' I'm not in a position to offer marriage, and despite my earlier actions, which displayed a regrettable lapse of restraint, I refuse to enter into a mere dalliance with you. In the end, I have to do what I believe is right." To his surprise, she didn't argue. Instead, a wistful smile played upon her lips.

"Oh, but you've delivered the one argument capable of silencing me. I can't argue with doing what one believes is right, because that, above anything else, is what I measure my own actions by." She reached for his hand and cradled it in her own. "But that doesn't mean I won't try to convince you there can be another right way, an equally right way. Consider this your fair warning."

Chapter Eighteen

Charles woke to a splitting headache, a dry mouth, and a lingering sense of sexual frustration because, well, because he was a man, not a monk. Remaining celibate was challenging enough, but these recent encounters with Serena were pushing him to the breaking point.

Which was quite likely the reason why last night he'd thought it would be a good idea to pull out the bottle of whisky he kept for medicinal purposes and drink nearly half of it. He was paying the price for that poor decision this morning.

He only vaguely remembered the series of erotic dreams that had plagued him in between bouts of sleep-lessness. Finally, he'd awakened from one in such a state that he'd been forced to take matters into his own hands, so to speak, but bringing about his own release was a far less satisfactory solution than finding it with the woman he loved.

He raised his head and squinted at the clock perched atop the chest of drawers. A quarter to ten. *Hell and damnation.* He'd have to rush if he didn't want to arrive late at Sir Roland's for the second time in little more than a week. Although, admittedly it would bother Sir Roland less than it would Charles.

Still, it was the principle of the thing, and Charles liked to think he was a man of principles, even if some of his recent actions didn't fully reflect that.

With a groan, and no small amount of willpower, he scooted to the edge of his bed and gingerly brought himself into an upright position. He gave himself a few seconds to adjust to a vertical posture, then walked over to the washstand and poured some of the water in the pitcher next to the basin into a glass, downing it in one gulp. His stomach briefly rebelled, but the water didn't come back up.

So far, so good. He rummaged around in a drawer until he found a packet of headache powders, which he mixed with the last of the water in the pitcher. Normally, he would turn his nose up at drinking water intended for washing, but beggars couldn't be choosers. And if it stopped the incessant pounding in his head, he'd consider it all to the good.

He reached for his dressing gown and pulled it on as he walked out of his bedroom and through the room that served as his main living area. Opening the door that led out into the hall, he bent down and retrieved a fresh pitcher of water for washing. A housemaid delivered a new pitcher of hot water every morning by eight o'clock.

Since it was nearly ten, the contents had cooled to a merely warmish temperature, but it would have to do.

Returning to his bedroom, he poured some water into the washbasin. Once he was clean and had shaved, he went over to the wardrobe and pulled out a fresh set of clothes and got dressed for the day.

He'd missed breakfast, the one meal of the day provided to those who boarded with the Abbott sisters. The dishes were cleared away every morning at precisely half past nine. It hardly mattered; his stomach didn't feel ready for food yet. He did, however, head down to the kitchen, hoping to get a cup of black coffee. Cook made a pot every morning for the younger Mr. Longhugh, one of the brothers who shared the suite of rooms on the floor below his.

His appearance in the kitchen caused Miss Minerva to purse her lips and raise a questioning brow, but all she said was, "Good morning, Mr. Townshend. We missed you at breakfast."

"Yes. I overslept," he replied. "I'm in search of a cup of coffee, if there's any left."

"I believe there's some," Miss Minerva replied. "That is if Cook hasn't disposed of it yet."

The cook turned from the pot she was tending on the stove. "Sure enough, I was just about to pour it out, Mr. Townshend." She wiped her hands on her apron front, poured him a cup, and handed it to him.

He murmured his thanks and drank it as quickly as he could without burning his mouth and bid the ladies adieu.

By the time he arrived at his employer's residence, his headache had lessened to a dull throb.

Gad, what had happened to him? Arriving at work suffering the ill effects of too much drink. After a long period of abstinence, throwing aside his gentlemanly principles and cavorting with Serena. And craving to do so again…and again and again.

And again.

He closed his eyes and massaged his temples. He didn't know who he was anymore. But he'd better figure it out and fast. He had decisions to make about his future.

Today he'd inform Sir Roland he'd decided to accept his help with securing a post to accompany the mission to Aix-la-Chapelle. He could alert Norwood, as well. Between the two of them, he ought to land a plum assignment.

He didn't feel any excitement at the prospect, however. Quite the opposite. A heavy feeling of dread had settled in his chest and a sour taste rose in his throat. But as he'd told Serena, it was the right choice for a myriad of reasons. That he didn't particularly want to choose it was of little consequence.

Ah, well. He wouldn't be the first person to rely on a stiff upper lip to carry on with an unpalatable task. And there were far worse things than temporarily exiling himself to France.

Maybe it didn't feel that way right now. And maybe he wouldn't feel that way any time soon.

Until it did—and even if it didn't—he'd put his head down, grit his teeth, and move forward. It was his only option.

Chapter Nineteen

By the next morning, Serena had reached a few conclusions about her future. She'd had happiness snatched from her before and there'd been nothing she could do about it. But she wasn't going to let happiness slip through her fingers this time without a fight. She didn't know what the future held for her and Charles, but she did know that he made her happy. Which meant the biggest impediment to her happiness currently seemed to be Edgar Borland, since Charles was convinced the two of them couldn't coexist in London without endangering his family secret.

The obvious solution to the Borland problem, or so it seemed to Serena, was to permanently remove him from London. The best way to accomplish that was less clear to her, but she was used to solving problems and she was confident she'd find a solution to this one. She simply needed to figure out what the options were and then pick the one with the best chance of success.

The Duke of Rochester owned a large estate in Yorkshire and Serena knew he'd spent many summers there in his youth. She'd dashed off a note to him earlier requesting a meeting as soon as was convenient. She'd see what insights into the family she might glean from him (if any), and hope they'd help decide her next move.

Her impression of Edgar Borland had been of a man on the lookout for any advantageous opportunity, given the way he'd plied Louise Mitchum with flattering comments at the British Museum. So what would prompt an opportunist like Borland to abandon London permanently? That was the question she hoped to know how to answer soon.

The next afternoon, Serena joined some of the ladies from the Wednesday Afternoon Social Club at Edwina's residence. Mrs. Lyndhurst and some of the other members of the education committee had been busy shopping for the items that were to go toward the care and education of the children in Mrs. Bakersfield's charge.

Naturally the larger items such as school desks and chairs were being delivered directly to the property where the children were housed. But in a flash of inspiration, the committee members had decided to present each child with a bundle of items meant specifically for them.

Which was why those who were free had agreed to meet at Edwina's to sort and gather the items together. Each child was to receive two school uniforms plus one everyday outfit and a nicer set of clothing for Sunday. In addition, every child would be supplied with new shoes, a winter coat, hat, mittens, scarf, sleeping attire and undergarments, plus an assortment of personal items: comb, toothbrush, tin of tooth powder, a small hand mirror, hair ribbons for the girls, a penknife for each boy, and wooden boxes meant to hold each child's possessions.

By the time Serena arrived, Phoebe and the Keene girls were already busy painting each of the boxes with a child's name on the front. Charlotte and Edwina were cutting lengths of colorful ribbon off the spools the committee had purchased. The rest were busily sorting items and grouping them into a series of piles—each pile containing the purchases meant for a particular child. Once everything had been sorted, the large items would be wrapped in lengths of fabric and tied with twine. A pile of name tags was waiting to be affixed to the finished packages.

With so many hands, it only took a little over two hours and the job was done. The packages were set against a wall, the wooden boxes stacked beside them. Tomorrow the members of the education committee would deliver them to the children.

"Thank you all for your help," Mrs. Lyndhurst said. "I don't know the last time I had so much satisfaction in doing a task. I can't wait to see the children's faces tomorrow when we give them their things."

"You'll have to tell us all about it at the meeting this week," Grace said.

"When will the rest of the items be delivered?" Charlotte asked. She looked more rotund than ever, and Serena had noticed she frequently adjusted her position in her chair, as if searching for a comfortable position and failing to find one.

"We should have everything by this time next week," Mrs. Lyndhurst replied. "The crate of books arrived yesterday. The art supplies should have been delivered this morning and we'll unpack them tomorrow while we're there. Once the big items for the schoolroom are delivered we'll need a group of ladies, and probably a few footmen, to help us set up the schoolroom. Hopefully by then, we'll have found a governess and a tutor."

"It's all coming together quite nicely," Edwina said.

"It certainly is," Serena agreed. "The next phase will be providing what Mrs. Bakersfield needs to take in additional children. She has enough room to double the number in her care, but she'll need more of everything, from household furnishings to linens to dishes, not to mention more school supplies."

"If any group is good at collecting those items, it's the Wednesday Afternoon Social Club," Julia Keene observed with a wry grin.

"Let's hope our subscription ball fills the club's coffers," Grace said. "I brought some tickets with me today in case anyone needs more to sell."

"I've sold all of mine," Charlotte said. "Thanks in large part to my husband having four sisters." She turned to Edwina. "I must get the recipe for this pear tart. It is divine." She made a face and laughed. "Oh, for heaven's sake, this pregnancy is making me sound like my brother, raving over a tasty dish."

"I'll have Cook write it out for you."

"I can't believe you're only having a slice of buttered bread when you could be having something as scrumptious as this." Charlotte lifted her fork, on which rested a bite of the tart. She popped it into her mouth. Serena half-expected her to roll her eyes as she chewed, but she didn't.

Edwina's nose wrinkled into a little frown. "My stomach still can't tolerate anything but the plainest food. It's quite annoying actually."

"Did you never get that tonic for indigestion?" Charlotte asked. "You look a little peaked, but I suppose that's understandable if you're living on bread and butter."

"The apothecary recommended a tonic. It's helped some, but what seems to help the most is a dreadfully plain diet," Edwina replied. "You, by the way, look radiant."

"It's kind of you to say so, but I think it would be more accurate to say I look big. I can't even buckle my own shoes anymore."

"I remember that stage," Grace said as she joined them. "I couldn't sleep well either at that point."

"I'm just so ready to have this baby, but I have almost two more months to go." Charlotte groaned.

"This too shall pass, my dear." Grace gave her a comforting pat on the shoulder.

"I would have liked children," Edwina said. "My marriage was rather…empty without them. However, it failed to happen for Beasley and me, and once he focused all his attentions elsewhere…" She shrugged. "Well, I knew it never would."

"You've got Jason's sons in your life now," Serena said.

Edwina nodded. "Very true. I enjoy fussing over them immensely, although I'm not sure they enjoy it quite as much as I do." She turned to Charlotte. "Did Serena see the print you brought?"

"Not yet," Charlotte said. "I laid it on the half-cabinet over there." She gestured vaguely in the direction of a walnut cabinet with an ornate inlay pattern across its front. "Let me waddle over and get it."

"I'll get it," Grace offered. She retrieved the print and handed it to Serena. "We're not sure what to make of this. Do you think it's referring to us?"

Serena studied the picture, a satirical caricature such as were sold in print shops all over London. It showed a group of ladies, some in trousers, some smoking cigars, and one pouring liquid from what was clearly a bottle of spirits into a teacup. The caption read *The Scandals of Mayfair*.

"Do you think they're referring to us?" Charlotte asked. "I mean, these things are usually based upon *something*, even if they exaggerate or twist the truth."

"Well, if it doesn't, I'd like to meet this other group of ladies who are defying convention," Serena murmured. "If it *is* about us, I'd be curious to know how the artist learned enough about our meetings to depict them accurately." She sent a wry look in Edwina's direction. "Although he evidently didn't know our hostess has prohibited smoking at our meetings."

"So I have," Edwina said briskly. "It's a nasty habit and it makes the draperies smell."

Grace frowned. "If it is referring to us, how did he learn these details? As a membership, we agreed not to disclose any of this because we don't wish to attract undesirable notoriety to our group."

"That was my concern," Charlotte said. "If our group caught the attention of the gossip mill, our ability to carry on with our work might be compromised."

"We'll reiterate to all the members the reasons for discretion. For now, let's hope that's enough and we won't see any similar prints in the future."

"If it's any comfort, Jason hasn't heard any rumors

circulating about us," Edwina said. "With his newspaper work, he has his finger on the pulse of London."

"That's somewhat comforting, I suppose," Charlotte said. "There's a reason we chose an innocuous-sounding name like the Wednesday Afternoon Social Club."

"We still don't know this print is about us. And while I love the irony of our name, The Scandals of Mayfair does have a certain flair," Grace observed. "Still, it's precisely the type of soubriquet that would put my sister Anne in an uproar and have her forbidding Phoebe from participating. She'd completely ignore that our group has given Phoebe a real desire to serve others in need and not just worry about wearing pretty frocks and attracting the attention of bachelors."

"And yet no one bats an eye if a gentleman is considered a rake or a libertine," Serena said with a rueful shake of her head. "It's supremely unfair, but it's the world we live in." She passed the print to Edwina, who handed it to Charlotte, who set it on her lap.

"William mentioned that Mr. Townshend requested he help him find a posting with the delegation going to France later this year," Charlotte said, directing this statement at Serena.

"I knew he was seriously considering it," Serena said.

Charlotte frowned. "I suggested that perhaps William could fail to find him something, but his conscience refuses to do that. And besides, he thinks Mr. Townshend's employer is also assisting in the search for a position."

"I appreciate your attempt to sway William," Serena said. "But if Charles is bent on going to France with that delegation, he'll find a way to do it."

Though not if she could help it.

Charlotte's frown deepened. "And that's it? You're fine with him leaving for heaven knows how long? Serena, I was fool enough to think letting William go was a wise decision, and I couldn't have been more wrong. Don't make the mistake I almost made. Did make, really, but thank goodness William refused to take no for an answer."

"As a matter of fact, I'm not fine with it. I've voiced my objections to Charles."

"Well, hallelujah!" Charlotte said, throwing her hands up in the air. "It's about time."

"Excuse me," Edwina said abruptly. She bolted out of her chair and fled the room.

"What on earth...?" Charlotte began, staring at the now-empty doorway. "Maybe she needs a different kind of tonic."

"I'm inclined to wonder if she shouldn't be examined by a doctor in case it's something other than indigestion," Grace said. An odd, almost speculative look came over the duchess's face. "I hope whatever it is, she feels better soon," she said slowly.

Something in Grace's manner struck Serena as odd. Grace knew something. Or thought she did. And then, in a moment of lightning-bolt clarity, Serena realized what her friend might be thinking, leaving her to wonder why the explanation hadn't occurred to her earlier.

And if she and Grace were correct, Edwina's stomach distress had nothing to do with indigestion.

Her meeting with the duke the next day proved fruitful. Rochester knew the Borland family well, although he hadn't heard that Borland was currently in London.

"Last I'd heard, the creditors were breathing down his

neck, and he'd taken off for the Continent," he'd said. "Even if he's managed to sort things out for the present. I doubt it's long before he lands himself back in the suds and has to go to ground again."

That was all well and good, but Serena didn't have the luxury of time. She was unwilling to simply wait for Borland to rack up gambling debts large enough to force him to leave London of his own volition.

Describing Edgar Borland's character, the duke had said, "A wastrel, like his father. No concept of spending their money wisely, and, from what I've heard, quick to chase after questionable schemes if they think there's money to be made from them."

From that statement, Serena felt the kernel of an idea spring up, but she'd need the help of Jason Latimer. Canada was conveniently far away for her purposes, and since Latimer had lived there for a number of years, he ought to know how to counsel her as to opportunities that might lure Edgar Borland to those far shores.

Or, perhaps, France would do. Not so far away as Canada, but she rather liked the irony of Edgar going to France while Charles stayed put in England. Italy. Greece. Australia, even. She didn't really care where he went, as long as it was far away from England.

For now, though, Canada was at the top of her list of *Potential Places for Edgar Borland to Live That Aren't Here.*

Chapter Twenty

—∿—

$\mathcal{S}$ ince that last evening with Serena, Charles had done his best to stay busy, and for the most part he'd been successful. Any day that Sir Roland dismissed him early, he would call on two or three tradesmen, as he'd promised Serena he'd do. Busyness served a twofold purpose. On the one hand, it served as a convenient excuse to avoid sightseeing excursions with his family, even though he did join them for dinner most evenings before he had to attend sessions of Parliament. And second, it gave him something to focus on besides thoughts of Serena and her outrageous proposition. Although, truthfully, it was never far from his mind.

He now had the names of two dozen tradesmen, including (thanks to Latimer's help) a half dozen printing businesses. Serena would be pleased with his efforts. The information could easily be conveyed to Serena in a note, but as he was very well aware, it also offered an excuse to call on her.

So with questionable good sense, he decided to deliver the list of names in person. However, he arrived at the Huntington residence, only to be met with a bitter sense of disappointment when Menken informed him that Lady Serena and Master Jem were out.

"I expect they will return shortly, if you would care to wait in the sitting room for them," the butler informed him.

Charles hesitated, wondering if he should take her absence as a sign from the universe that this was a bad idea, and he should simply leave now.

Sensing his indecision, Menken added, "Master Jem has been most eager for you to call again. He has a special surprise he wishes to show you."

"In that case, Menken, I'll await their return." He justified this decision content in the knowledge that Jem's presence would ensure that no improprieties could occur between himself and Serena.

Left by himself, Charles wandered over to the window, realizing he ought to have anticipated when he agreed to wait that he'd be assailed with memories of the last time he was in this room with Serena. *Idiot*.

To his relief, a welcome distraction in the form of Jem's kitten, Tabitha, emerged from behind the draperies and circled around his ankles, rubbing her head against his legs before leaping onto a nearby chair and staring at him intently with those bright blue cat eyes of hers.

"Are you trying to tell me you want some attention?" Charles asked. Almost as if she understood the question, Tabitha let out a plaintive "meow" and tilted her head.

He'd almost swear she was smiling at him, if such a thing were possible.

"I think you want some pets," he murmured, reaching out and scratching her head between her ears. This gesture was met with the low rumble of contented purring as she half-closed her eyes and slowly tipped her head from side to side so that he could better access her cheeks or her chin, depending on where she wished to be scratched. After a few minutes of this though, she'd evidently had enough petting because she leaped down and ran across the room, darting beneath the couch and out of his sight.

It was then that he noticed an elaborate bouquet in a vase on one of the side tables that flanked the green velvet sofa. He could see a small rectangular card next to the vase. It looked very much like the type of card that accompanied an offering of flowers sent by suitor.

Jealousy speared him, even though it was none of his business if Serena had received flowers from an admirer. Wasn't it what he wanted for her? That she find happiness with a man whose suitability far outweighed his own? He ought to be glad that she'd received a bouquet from an admirer, not staring at the blooms, burning with envy and resentment at whomever had sent them to her.

Or was he only the worst of hypocrites—saying he couldn't have her, but then taking what he had no right to take.

He'd been a fool to come here this afternoon. He strode to the door but stopped short before stepping into the hall. He turned, his gaze going to the card sitting beside the vase. A quick glance at it could satisfy his curiosity as to the identity of the sender.

Damning himself for being such a lovesick fool, he retraced his steps.

The card read:

> *My fondest regards,*
> *Mannering*

Frowning, he recalled that Mannering was one of the gentlemen with whom Serena had danced at the Peytons' ball. He hadn't found it remarkable at the time. Mannering was a shallow young puppy newly out of university, not at all the type of man who would interest Serena. Or so Charles thought.

Had the man been calling upon Serena? The idea didn't please Charles even if he did suspect the interest was entirely one-sided.

Whatever the case, it had been a mistake for him to call today. He was suddenly glad Serena wasn't home to witness this petty jealousy of his. With one last baleful glare directed at the flowers (because she wasn't here, so he could indulge his feelings, however unworthy they might be), he exited the sitting room.

Spotting a footman coming down the stairs, he went over to the servant. "Would you see that Lady Serena gets this?" he asked, handing the servant the folded sheet of paper on which he'd listed the names of the London tradesmen. "Tell her Mr. Townshend wished her to have this."

"Very good, sir." The footman dipped his chin as he accepted the paper from Charles.

"I can see myself out."

Once outside, he headed down Princes Street toward Oxford until he spotted a hackney and flagged it down.

"Gentleman Jackson's Boxing Salon, please," he instructed the driver. He was in the mood to punch something.

He didn't arrive at his rented rooms until shortly past nine o'clock. He'd run into Ambrose-Stone at Gentleman Jackson's and after a few rounds of sparring to work off his frustrations, he and Brosey had gone to White's for a bite to eat and while there they'd joined Phillip Hurst, Gilbert Ogilvy, and a few others in the card room. Several hands of vingt-et-un and a few brandies later, his mood had mellowed enough that he decided he was ready to face the emptiness of his lodgings.

He was surprised to be met by Miss Leticia, the elder of his two landladies, and doubly surprised by her flushed cheeks and the smell of sherry on her breath. "There's a gentleman waiting in the parlor who wishes to see you," she informed him as he drew off his hat and gloves in the entry hall. "We've been keeping him entertained while he waited for you to arrive home. Or perhaps I should say Mr. Wiggins has been entertaining us with a seemingly inexhaustible supply of society *on dits*." She gave a little (sherry-induced?) titter. "That man could write for the scandal sheets. He knows all the latest gossip."

This was odd. Charles didn't know anyone by the name of Wiggins, so the fact that the man had shown up at his lodgings out of the blue struck him as faintly ominous. And yet, surely if the man had come for nefarious reasons he wouldn't have bothered being such an entertaining guest. Could the reason Wiggins was here have something to do with Jem or Borland? Best to hear what the man had to say and then send him on his way.

As soon as he entered the parlor, however, he recognized

"Wiggins" despite the attempt at disguise. Wiggins was none other than Serena wearing a rather shapeless great-coat over masculine attire. Her hair was tied back with a black ribbon in an old-fashioned queue that disappeared beneath the collar of the coat she wore. A good thing too, because her thick, lustrous hair undoubtedly fell farther down her back then any true gentleman's would.

If not for the late hour, he doubted his landladies would have been fooled by a female dressed as a man, no matter how creditably done the disguise. But a room lighted by only a few candles worked in favor of Serena pulling it off.

What was she up to? He understood her reasons for the disguise. A lady did not call on a bachelor at his place of residence. Not unless she was related to him, or he had female relations who lived under the same roof as he, and whom she could ostensibly be visiting. None of that applied here. So why had she come?

She smiled as she came to her feet and her eyes gleamed with mischief, as if daring him to reveal her identity.

"Wiggins," he said, shaking the hand that she reached out to him, the gesture causing the front of her coat to open wider. Involuntarily, his gaze dipped to her bosom. There was only a faint swelling beneath the waistcoat she wore, and since he was quite familiar with the generous shape of her breasts, he wondered if she'd bound them with rags to minimize her bosom.

"This is a surprise," he continued, letting go of her hand and lifting his gaze to meet hers once more. "You really shouldn't have come out on such a messy night." A steady rain had started falling in the late afternoon hours and had continued throughout the evening.

She shrugged. "My evening plans were changed, and I found myself with time on my hands. So here I am."

She spoke in a lower, slightly husky voice that he found wildly seductive, and not especially masculine-sounding in his opinion, but close enough to fool his landladies apparently. He wondered if she'd changed her plans because of his visit to her home that afternoon. Had she guessed the reason for his abrupt departure after he'd told Menken he'd wait for her return?

"Indeed, here you are." Hoping to keep their conversation private, he led her to a seat on the far side of the room well away from his landladies. "The question is what to do with you," he murmured, a hint of exasperation in his voice.

"As to that…" She gave him an impish smile. "I have plenty of suggestions. Perhaps we should withdraw to your private rooms and discuss them."

His pulse quickened. He could imagine precisely what those suggestions of hers would be. "I think not," he said firmly.

"Why, yes, I'd love to see your living quarters." She spoke loudly now to ensure his landladies would hear her, and came to her feet as if he'd just offered to show them to her.

The minx.

He glanced toward his landladies. Both had pulled out their knitting and were now knitting with such rapidity that their needles were soft blurs as their fingers nimbly performed the rhythmic pattern of the stitches. They looked up and smiled indulgently. He imagined their expressions would be far different with regard to taking his guest up to his rooms if they knew that Wiggins was a member of the fairer sex.

"I'm afraid you misunderstood, Wiggins. I said my rooms are too messy for a tour this evening."

Miss Leticia gave a disapproving cluck. She often chided her boarders if she saw their rooms in a state of disarray.

Serena gave him a narrow-eyed look, but she sat back down. "A game then? I do like games."

"As long as it's a game we can play in front of my landladies," he said in a low voice.

"Really, Charles, you can be such a spoilsport." She gave an exaggerated sigh. "Very well. I enjoy draughts." She nodded toward a draughts board sitting ready on a small game table.

"Draughts it is," he said, slightly annoyed with himself that he felt more disappointed than relieved that she'd so easily given up on her effort to visit his rooms.

They took seats opposite each other, but it quickly became clear to Charles that draughts wasn't the only game being played. Beneath the table, Serena's legs had a way of brushing against his.

He looked to see if the Abbott sisters noticed this under-the-table-mischief, but they were still busily knitting and paying them no attention.

One corner of Serena's mouth hitched up in a teasingly suggestive smile. "Is something wrong? It's your move you know."

He turned back toward the checkered game board. "You're distracting me."

"Oh, good," she murmured. "That was my goal."

He slid a red piece to a new position.

She briefly considered the board before placing one slim finger on a black piece and slowly sliding it to another square. She raised her gaze to meet his, her eyes studying his face with a lazy, knowing look. She knew precisely how she was affecting him, and she was reveling in it.

He swallowed and absently moved another game piece. "What are you about?"

She tilted her head. "Playing a game with you." She licked her lips. "Though not the game I'd like to be playing."

"We're not playing those kinds of games anymore. We can't."

She jumped one of his pieces, placing it off to the side. "What would it take for you to say 'yes, we can'?"

With long-denied desires roaring to life? He was quite sure she could secure his capitulation with very little effort.

"I have no intention of taking you upstairs tonight," he said, pleased that he managed to imbue the words with a convincing amount of conviction, even if the truth was he'd like nothing better than to whisk her off to his bedroom and spend the rest of the night making love to her.

"Very well, then. Tonight is off the table." She rested her arms on the game table and leaned forward. As she did so the scent of her jasmine cologne teased his senses. "But what of the future? I put a proposition to you and you said no, and yet it's obvious to both of us that you'd really like to say yes. I understand your concerns, Charles, but what would it take to alleviate them?"

"If you could wave a magic wand and rewrite the past and erase my bastardy, that would be a step in the right direction. But you can't, so for that reason alone, my answer must always be no."

She pursed her lips. "Magic wands only work in fairy tales, unfortunately. However, we don't need to rewrite the past, we just need to keep it from intruding into the present. And it's still your move, by the way."

He slid a piece forward and she promptly jumped him.

"Thank heavens you don't play piquet so abominably," she remarked.

"Undoubtedly, I'd be a dreadful piquet player if you were able to get away with this behavior at parties," he said dryly. "You know precisely how you're affecting me."

Her lips curved into a self-satisfied smile and she tilted her head to the side. "Do I? Why don't you tell me *precisely* how you're affected?"

He just shook his head and pretended to study the pieces before him, but he could still feel her gaze on him.

"You drive me utterly mad, do you know that?" she asked at last.

"So what else is new?" Finally he moved one of his pieces, she moved one of hers, he countered, and she jumped him again.

"I don't mean in the sense of aggravating me, although there is that. I mean that I find you, your stubborn insistence on doing what is right to be insanely arousing."

He blinked. That wasn't what he expected to hear. "Well, that isn't my intention," he said.

"I know. But all the same it just makes me want to do things with you and to you. I can't because we currently have company...but if we didn't...I'd like nothing more than to climb over this table and settle myself on your lap and kiss you until both of us are breathless. And then..." She paused, gratified to see his eyes had turned hot and hungry. "Shall I go on?"

His jaw tightened, but for some insane reason he nodded. God help him, he was like the child who'd been warned about the dangers of playing with fire and then did it anyway.

"And then I expect your kisses would make me squirm with delight while I was perched upon your lap and naturally your body would respond by—"

"I know how it would respond," Charles said. "You don't have to say it."

"I was merely going to say it would respond by showing a, er, certain appreciation for the pleasurable sensations created by my squirming."

His body was responding in precisely that way just at the *thought* of the behavior she was describing.

She slanted a glance toward his landladies. "Miss Minerva appears to have nodded off, and Miss Leticia looks like she's not far behind." She returned her gaze to his face. "But don't worry. I won't take more than verbal liberties with you. Now where was I? Oh, yes, pleasurable sensations."

She sucked in her bottom lip and contemplated him thoughtfully. "Well, following this kissing and squirming, I think we'd have to divest ourselves of some of our clothing to better facilitate further exploration."

He was breathing hard now, fully enthralled with the sound of her voice as she wove a sensuous haze around him using only her words.

"Since turnabout is fair play, and I was the only one with clothing awry last time, I think your clothes should go first. So off would go your jacket and your waistcoat. But then I think I'd unwind your neckcloth slowly to better to heighten the anticipation. Naturally this would all be interspersed with more kissing and touching and well, let's be honest, more squirming."

"Serena." He groaned, his voice rough with passion.

"Yes, Charles?" she asked, her voice innocent, but her gaze was one of wicked possibility.

"Do you know what you're doing to me?"

"I have a fair idea. Because I suspect I'm feeling much the same way."

"As long as I'm not the only one being tortured," he muttered.

Her lips turned up in wry amusement. "Trust me. You aren't. And if we were actually engaging in what I've described, this would be the moment where things might get frantic." She gave a little laugh. "Almost assuredly things would get frantic and—"

"We both know none of this can ever come to pass," Charles said.

They stared at each other for a long moment, and even though no words were spoken, it was almost as if they were engaged in a silent battle of wills.

"Not unless I can change your mind," she said at last.

He shook his head. "As much as I want to, I just can't. For all the reasons I've already described."

"I was truly hoping tonight would end differently," she said. "I won't push you into surrender. I see you battling with yourself... conscience against inclination... but until you're truly ready for what I'm offering, you'll be sure to suffer from regret the next morning, and I don't want to be the indulgence you regret, Charles." She leaned forward, her face strained with emotion, and whispered, "I want so much more than that."

"Serena," he said. "I..." But then he couldn't think

how to express what he was feeling beyond simply saying her name. And that seemed to be enough because she nodded and let out a long exhale, the warm rush of her breath a caress against his lips, his cheeks.

"I should be going," she said. They both stood up. Miss Minerva and Miss Leticia still dozed in their chairs.

"I'll see you out," he said.

"There's no need. I'll have one of the servants alert my coachman. He's been waiting at an inn yard two blocks away. After I leave, you should probably wake up your landladies, and send them off to their beds. Tell them Wiggins thanks them for their hospitality tonight, won't you?"

"Wig...?" he began, momentarily forgetting her subterfuge despite the fact that she stood before him clad in male attire. "Er, um, yes, of course," he finished.

Once she'd departed, he went out into the empty hall, pacing for several minutes to release some of his tension, and once he was in a calmer, more presentable state, he reentered the parlor and gently roused the Abbott sisters.

"Oh, my, I hope Mr. Wiggins didn't think us unpardonably rude to nod off like that. Did you enjoy your game?" Miss Minerva asked.

"Well, enough," Charles said. "And Wiggins didn't mind in the least that you dozed off."

"You seemed to be quite engrossed in whatever you were discussing," Miss Leticia remarked.

"As you said earlier, he's a very entertaining conversationalist," Charles said. "Now off to bed with the pair of you. I'll tend to the embers in the hearth and snuff the candles."

Miss Minerva patted his cheek. "You're a dear boy.

Thank you. We'll see you in the morning. And the next time you see Wiggins, tell him we hope to see him again."

"I will do that, ma'am," Charles promised.

Alone in the parlor, he blew out a long breath and slowly completed the tasks as he'd said he would. He wasn't eager to go up to his rooms and be alone with his thoughts and his raging emotions.

"Dammit, Serena," he muttered as he climbed the stairs.

Once he reached his bedroom, he couldn't help but laugh. Not with hilarity. No, more of a wryly resigned, *why-the-hell-am-I-even-going-to-try-to-sleep* laugh.

Nonetheless, he pulled back the covers and climbed in bed. He just hoped thoughts of him caused Serena's night to be as restless as his was sure to be.

Chapter Twenty-One

*Charles gritted his teeth. His head was beginning to pound, no doubt a result of his poor night's sleep coupled with a growing sense of anger and frustration as he watched Mannering practically slavering over Serena as they stood together across the room from him. Damn the man, with his fawning attentions and his wandering gaze that dropped far too often to ogle her bosom.

"Terrific crush tonight, isn't it?" Phillip Hurst remarked.

"That it is," Charles said. His attention was still riveted on Serena and Mannering. The bounder had placed a hand on the wall next to Serena's head and was leaning in toward her.

"I only came because of the refreshments," Hurst continued in a confiding tone. "The Montfords' cook is exceptional."

Charles replied with a noncommittal, "Hmmm." He wasn't in the mood for idle conversation. Or any sort of conversation, really. Shortly after arriving at the Mont-fords' rout he'd spotted Serena in Mannering's company. His first instinct had been to go over and tell Mannering to get lost. But surely if Serena wished to rid herself of the man's company, she would. So here he was, nursing his grievance like a sulky school boy.

"You know, if you don't like Mannering drooling over her like that, why don't you go over and do something about it?" Hurst remarked dryly.

"Not really my place," Charles replied. "Besides she's capable of dealing with him herself. That she hasn't seems to imply she doesn't mind overmuch."

"Maybe she doesn't want to make a scene."

Charles gave a humorless laugh. "Serena? I wouldn't be too sure about that."

Hurst gave him a keen glance. "Perhaps you're right," he said before adding under his breath, "none of my business anyway."

They lapsed into a companionable silence. Or silence, at any rate. There was a stiffness to Hurst's posture that implied he found Charles's company anything but com-panionable. Charles regretted his snappish tone.

After a few minutes of this, Hurst could evidently take no more. "Dash it all, Townshend," he said with great vehemence. "Either go over and stake your claim or wipe that jealous glower off your face. Has it occurred to you she might not be discouraging the fellow because she likes to see you stew in your own juices?"

He wanted to argue that Serena wasn't like that, be-cause she *wasn't* like that. He'd never known her to play feminine games. But Hurst didn't deserve to be subjected to Charles's black mood.

"I think I could do with some fresh air," Charles said. Then he turned on his heel and left. He doubted Hurst was sorry to see him go.

If he could, he'd leave the party entirely. He was only here at Sir Roland's request. His employer wished to introduce him to Lord Byington, whose acquaintance, Sir Roland claimed, would be exceedingly useful for Charles's career prospects.

"If Byington likes you, you're as good as there," Sir Roland had told him, referring to Charles's expressed wish for a posting to Aix-la-Chapelle.

There'd been no sign of Byington when they'd arrived, so he and Sir Roland had separated when his employer declared a desire to have a smoke. Since Charles had never acquired the habit, and wasn't eager to spend time wreathed in smoke in the room set aside for this male pastime, they'd agreed to rejoin each other later in the evening.

Abruptly, Charles reconsidered his decision to seek some fresh air in the gardens. Finding Sir Roland ought to be his prime objective. The sooner he did that, the sooner the introduction to Byington could occur, and that meant Charles would be free to leave.

Since it had been over an hour since he'd parted from Sir Roland, he suspected his employer was already circulating somewhere in the crush of people. Nonetheless, he made a brief stop at the smoking room, unsurprised to find no sign of the man there. Charles continued to make his way through the crowded rooms, but failed to spot Sir Roland in any of them. Perhaps staying in one place was the better strategy.

Therefore, he headed for one of the main receiving

rooms, deliberately avoiding the one where Serena and Mannering had been holding their cozy tête-à-tête. Still in a foul mood, he chose a position near a large potted palm where he could unobtrusively monitor the guests entering and leaving the room. He'd maintained his post only a few minutes when Ambrose-Stone entered, and spotting Charles, headed in his direction.

"Townshend! Just the man I was looking for. Hurst told me you were here." Charles wondered if Lord Hurst had also mentioned what poor company he was this evening. "I was just on my way to get some refreshments. Join me? I need to discuss something with you."

Charles wasn't hungry, but he agreed to Brosey's suggestion. It seemed as likely he'd come across Sir Roland in the location where food was available as anywhere else at the rout. Reaching the room where the refreshments were being served, they joined the line of people making their way along the length of the table upon which platters and silver epergnes held a varied selection of food.

"Not partaking?" Brosey asked as he helped himself to some of the delicacies set before them.

"Not particularly hungry at the moment," Charles replied.

Ambrose-Stone nodded and, having filled his plate, proceeded to lead the way over to the tall tables that had been set up for guests to consume their food, which given their dimensions, forced the guests to eat while standing. Charles presumed this had been done to encourage people to finish their food and not continue congregating too long in here. Ambrose-Stone chose an empty table in the corner.

"Listen, plans have changed concerning Ronald," Ambrose-Stone said.

"Changed how?" Charles asked.

"He's not going to be standing for election as the representative from Rainsley."

"But that's been the plan during the whole time I've served. Has he balked at doing so?" Charles wouldn't find this to be completely unexpected, since at his core, Ronald Dixon was shallow and self-centered enough to throw away such a promising opportunity if it involved any sort of effort on his part.

"Not exactly," his friend replied grimly.

Ambrose-Stone glanced around, as if to gauge whether those nearby were paying attention to their conversation.

"The idiot fought a duel this morning and gravely wounded Viscount Stallings. I hope to God the man survives, but Ronald is on his way to the Continent as we speak." He gave Charles a pointed look. "Even if Stallings doesn't succumb to his injuries, Ronald won't be coming home any time soon, which means I'd like you to stand for reelection. You've served the borough well, and to be honest, if it weren't for Ronnie being my brother, I'd never have looked to replace you. As far as I'm concerned the seat is yours as long as you wish to serve in it. Even if Ronald comes back in a few months, and that's far from clear at the moment. But whenever he returns, he's going to have to find another means of occupying his time."

"I'm sorry your brother brought this upon himself. And you," Charles said.

Brosey snorted in disgust. "Do you want to hear what he dueled over?"

"If you wish to tell me," Charles said.

"The shine of his boots. Stallings disparaged them and Ronald, who was well into his cups—they both were, so I was told—demanded Stallings take it back, or he'd have satisfaction. Stallings wouldn't. Instead, he doubled down, and insulted my brother's clothing choices, the cut of his hair, his appearance in general. The two idiots met at dawn this morning. The bullet went through Stallings's side, causing extensive blood loss and damaging God knows what, though the surgeon sewed him up as best he could. It's touch and go right now."

"It would be a shame for two lives to be ruined over something so...frivolous," Charles said. But he wasn't surprised to hear that young Dixon had behaved foolishly over a silly slight.

Ambrose-Stone clapped Charles on the arm. "So what say you? Will you stay on as MP for the borough of Rainsley?"

Charles opened his mouth to decline the offer, then snapped it shut. Perhaps he shouldn't be too hasty about closing that door. He enjoyed serving in the House of Commons, and so far he had no other position lined up with which to replace it. Logic argued that the best course was to leave the possibility open for now.

Finally he said, "Actually, I've been making inquiries about joining the delegation to Aix-la-Chapelle."

"I beg you to consider dropping that idea," Ambrose-Stone said brusquely. "And not just because you're my choice to represent Rainsley, now that Ronald's out of the picture. Can't say I'm happy about how this has come to be, but I'm not sorry to be offering it to you again. I hope you know I mean that. You'll be wasting your talents going over to France, a peon in a sea of bureaucrats with no chance to make a real difference."

His friend had a point. But there was still Borland to consider. If Borland stayed in London, Charles needed to be elsewhere, and an MP was tied to London, at least while Parliament was in session.

"I'll need some time to think about it," Charles said. "But I'll..." He caught sight of Mannering entering the room and the burn of jealousy returned. He was somewhat mollified that the man wasn't accompanied by Serena. Maybe Hurst had been right and she'd tolerated Mannering's company only as long as Charles was watching. Could she have been trying to ignite a spark of jealousy within him? Perhaps hoping it would change his mind about them becoming lovers? He watched as Mannering and his companion strolled over to the refreshments table.

Ambrose-Stone shifted beside him, and Charles realized he hadn't finished his thought.

"And, um, well," he hedged, trying to recall what he'd started to say. "This development is quite unexpected. Not unwelcome, mind, but I just need time to consider... everything."

"Yes, of course," his friend replied. "I understand." He rubbed the back of his neck and gave Charles a sheepish grin. "I'd hoped you leap at the chance to stay put as the MP from Rainsley, but seeing how I was the one that chased you toward other opportunities, I can hardly quibble if you wish to weigh them against continuing to serve in the House of Commons."

Ambrose-Stone turned his attention to his plate, selecting a fruit tartlet, and popped the whole thing into his mouth.

Charles continued to watch Mannering, who'd drifted

over to an adjacent table along with his companion, a
fellow named Groton. Charles had occasionally crossed
paths with Groton at Gentleman Jackson's boxing establishment, where he knew Groton as a flat-footed fighter
with slow hands. Charles avoided having him as a sparring
partner because it was too much work trying *not* to win
the bout in the first few minutes.

Thanks to a blow to the head (though not one delivered
by Charles), Groton was also hard of hearing in one ear,
so anyone speaking with him had to raise their voice so
he could hear what they were saying. Which was why, a
few seconds later, upon overhearing a comment of Mannering's, Charles grabbed the man by the jacket lapels and
pushed him up against the wall.

"If no one ever taught you how to speak of a lady,
I'll be happy to do so," Charles ground out between
clenched teeth. "How dare you speak of her in those
disparaging terms when she's tolerated the addresses of an
empty-headed addlepate like you. Now, would you like to
reconsider what you just said? Or do you need me to teach
you that lesson?"

Mannering's mouth was open, trying to form words,
but nothing was coming out.

"Answer me," Charles said. Or not. He was itching to
plant a fist in the middle of Mannering's face.

"I don't think he can with your hand on his throat like
that," Ambrose-Stone said quietly.

Since fair was fair, Charles loosened his hold slightly.

"You're crazy," Mannering rasped.

"Wrong answer," Charles said, pulling back his hand.
His fist met Mannering's nose with a satisfying crunch.

Groton tried to intervene, but before he could deliver a

punch, he met a similar fate to Mannering's, except that it was Ambrose-Stone who delivered the blow.

Charles was vaguely aware of ladies shrieking and gentlemen shouting. Mannering was slumped over on the floor, cradling his face with his hands, and Groton was lying on his back, moaning.

"Here, Mannering." Charles held out a hand to the man. "Let's go somewhere more private and have someone tend to you." His gesture was less about having concern for Mannering's welfare and more a means to escape those gawking at them, but it was still the decent thing to do.

Turning to a nearby footman holding a tray of empty plates and glassware, he said, "Can you bring up some ice from the kitchen?" He assumed there must be a supply below stairs, since he'd seen chunks of it floating in the punch bowl. "And some rags or towels to wrap it in."

"Yes, sir." The footman turned and beat a hasty retreat.

"Go to hell," Mannering replied, his voice thick, thanks to his rapidly swelling nose. Blood dripped down onto his cravat. He swatted away Charles's outstretched hand. "Who do you think you are?"

"I'm a gentleman. As you should be, Mannering. I suggest you remember that in the future."

"Come on," Ambrose-Stone said. "They got what they deserved. The Montfords' servants will see to them."

Groton had managed to sit up, but he refused to meet either of their eyes.

So much for meeting with Sir Roland's contacts. Charles wasn't going to hang around and subject himself to questioning stares and whispers as news of the altercation made the rounds among the guests. He could only hope no one else had overheard Mannering's remark and that the only *on dit* from the incident would be about the fight, not what precipitated it.

Out in the hallway, Charles turned to Brosey. "I think it's time for me to go. Will you let Lady Serena know what happened, and warn her I may have made the situation worse, depending upon who heard what Mannering said."

"I will do that," Ambrose-Stone promised. "If it's any consolation I could barely hear Mannering's comment over the rest of the conversation in the room, and no one else was closer that we were."

Charles nodded, slightly encouraged that perhaps they'd been the only ones to overhear Mannering's remark. "I also need you to give Sir Roland Bellamy a message for me," he said. "Tell him what happened, and that I felt it was best to leave before the Montfords asked me to go."

His friend shook his head. "They'd be more likely to throw Mannering out if they knew how he spoke of Lady Serena. Montford cries friends with her father."

"Thank you for making my excuses," Charles said. "I'll be in touch about your offer. Unless you've changed your mind?"

"Not at all." Ambrose-Stone gave him a rueful smile. "It was good to see that right hook of yours again. 'Twas the reason I always put my money on you during our Cambridge days. You put it to excellent use tonight. Mannering is an ass."

Charles didn't disagree, merely nodded and turned toward the back of the house, intending to take the back staircase and thereby avoid running into anyone who might hinder a swift exit. The plan worked. The only person he came across was the footman he'd sent to the kitchen earlier and who was now returning from there with a bowl of ice in one hand and with a stack of towels balanced on the other. The servant gave him a wide berth in the stairs, and Charles couldn't really blame him.

Once outside, Charles began walking. The air was chilly, cooling both his skin and his overheated emotions. He'd made a spectacle of himself, and he wasn't proud of that. But when Mannering told Groton he'd "like to have a spirited filly like Lady Serena in his bed night after night" Charles had felt a red-hot rage rip through him.

His reaction had been instinctual, and very probably had been the wrong one, because by now the story of the contretemps would have traveled among those attending the rout. If anyone else had heard Mannering's comment, that had probably made the rounds as well.

He started to hail a hackney but then decided to walk home, the better to vent his seething anger. By the time he reached Nassau Street, he was chilled through, his irregular departure having meant he'd left his hat and gloves behind at the Montford residence. He hurried to the front door of 4 Nassau Street and knocked. No one answered. The servants must be abed already, and he'd have to go around to the back, where a key was hidden beneath the shrubbery that flanked the rear entrance.

"Blast it," he muttered under his breath, for it meant he must walk all the way around the block. Oh, well. There was no other way to gain admittance, and he'd already spent nearly two hours walking home. What was another fifteen minutes or so?

He reached the alley that ran behind Nassau Street, and had just turned down it when he heard a sound behind him. Before he could turn to see what it was, stars exploded before his eyes, and that was the last he knew for a while.

His head was pounding. He groaned as he came to, confused for a moment as to why he was lying on the hard ground, before he recalled the blow to the back of his head.

Gingerly, he sat up. A wave of nausea washed over him and for a moment he thought he was going to be sick. He clamped his mouth shut, not wanting to cast up his accounts here in the alley. Once the nausea passed, he took stock of himself.

His pocket watch was gone as well as the few coins he carried when he was out. Tentatively, he probed the spot on the back of his head where he'd been hit. As he'd expected, there was a rapidly swelling lump and his hair was matted and sticky.

Was it a simple robbery? Or was it related to the earlier altercation with Mannering? In a carriage, a friend of Mannering's could have reached Nassau Street well before Charles, since he'd walked home. But they could hardly have known the door would be locked and he'd have to go around to the back. He hadn't seen anyone hanging about as he'd walked around the block.

But then again, he hadn't been paying close attention. His mind had been occupied by the events of the evening, the potential ramifications of it.

At any rate, it was too cold to be sitting out here contemplating the attack. He felt well enough to stand, so he stiffly came to his feet. He gave himself a moment, then proceeded down the alleyway, passing the doors of other residences on the block before coming to his own.

As he bent down, a wave of dizziness assailed him and he dropped to his knees and waited until his head felt clearer before groping around the ground beneath one of the bushes. Nothing. He tried the bush on the other side of the doorway, and was relieved to find a small leather pouch partially buried in the dirt. He pulled it free and extracted the key from inside it.

After he unlocked the door, he returned the key to its hiding place before entering. Once inside, he made his way upstairs as quietly as he could, pausing every so often when the dizziness intensified. Finally reaching his rooms, he made a beeline for the washbasin. Glancing at his reflection in the mirror, he was surprised to find he looked better than he felt. A little wan, perhaps, and his hair was a bit mussed, but he didn't look like someone who'd been conked over the head in a dark alley.

He poured some water in the basin, wet a cloth, and cleaned away the blood from the back of his head as best he could. His head was beginning to throb, and a heavy drowsiness came over him. He undressed, dropping his clothes onto a chair, too weary to put them away properly. Then he climbed into bed, hoping he didn't feel like hell in the morning.

"You look like the devil this morning," Sir Roland remarked when Charles, responding to his employer's summons, entered Sir Roland's office. "Can't say I'm surprised. I heard about your dustup with Mannering. It was the *on dit* of the evening."

Naturally.

"I apologize, sir. I'm not proud of my actions." It

was on the tip of his tongue to say that Mannering had deserved some sort of reckoning, but he couldn't bring himself to offer an excuse for his actions. Fighting in the midst of polite company was, ultimately, inexcusable, no matter what the provocation. He and Mannering should have taken it elsewhere.

Sir Roland shook his head. "Mannering is a young fool. Ambrose-Stone assured me that your actions were entirely justified."

"I'm afraid that my manner of...handling it only served to amplify the incident, which was the last thing I wanted to do."

"If you're worried that people condemn your actions, they don't. The scuttlebutt going around was Mannering spoke disparagingly about a lady, though no one seemed sure of precisely which lady, and that you took exception to it, as any gentleman should. Public opinion is running in your favor."

Charles stared at him. Of course, he should have known Sir Roland would divine what had worried him most about the incident.

Sir Roland continued, "I doubt Mannering or Groton will be showing their faces in polite company any time soon." He shuffled through some papers on his desk. "So, we'll say no more about it."

"Yes, sir," Charles said.

Sir Roland leaned back in his chair. "Let's talk about your future."

"I hope I didn't mess that up too badly last night," Charles remarked. "But I won't blame you one bit if you no longer wish to support my quest to obtain a spot on the delegation."

"I admit. I'm having second thoughts about it, but not because of your fight."

"Oh?" Charles said, wondering what he'd done to bring around this change of heart. "Would I be out of line to ask why?"

Sir Roland drummed his fingers on the desktop and studied Charles with an appraising look. "No, although I ask that you hear me out without interrupting because I anticipate you will want to. Interrupt, that is."

"I can bite my tongue with the best of them, I suppose," Charles said dryly.

Sir Roland chuckled. "Sit down, then, and I'll speak my piece. And we'll see how well you can remain silent."

Charles did, settling into the leather armchair before Sir Roland's desk.

"Well, my boy, it hasn't been lost to me that your enthusiasm for a diplomatic career has been lacking, shall we say, whenever I've brought it up over the past year. In fact, it's only been in the last couple of weeks that you've expressed more than a polite promise to consider it."

Charles wanted to point out that one could change one's mind, but he'd promised to listen, so he did.

"Ah, very good." Sir Roland smiled. "I could see you wanted to offer a response, but refrained." He sighed. "You could have made a career of being a diplomat. Do you know how rare the ability to *not* speak is among men?"

Charles merely shrugged.

"Anyway, back to my main point," Sir Roland continued. "I had to ask myself, what could have caused this change in attitude? I should probably preface my next remarks by saying that I'm aware that you have a...soft spot for Lady Serena Wynter. And have for some time, though you've done a creditable job of hiding it. I don't think many are aware of it, but I am."

Again, this didn't really surprise Charles. His employer was a perceptive man. But were any of his secrets safe from him? Or had Sir Roland figured out the truth of his birth as well? Somehow he wouldn't be shocked to find that he had.

Charles crossed his arms and waited for Sir Roland to go on. There was really no point in denying the truth, and he'd promised not to interrupt.

"And so I added all the facts up...your feelings for her, how you've been spending more time in her company of late helping her with that young lad, and your change in attitude. They're connected, I'm sure of it." Sir Roland rested his elbows on the arms of his chair and steepled his fingers. "But why the eagerness to put distance between the two of you all of a sudden? What, I asked myself, had come between you?" He shook his head. "A disagreement? You've had those in the past, haven't you? A particular sort of disagreement? A lovers' quarrel, perhaps?"

Charles worked to maintain a neutral expression on his face because, for the love of heaven, he didn't want Sir Roland to guess the real reason—that he and Serena had crossed all sorts of boundaries they never should have crossed.

"Since I'm curious, I give you leave to answer that if you wish." Sir Roland studied him over his steepled fingers.

"The reasons for my interest in a posting to France are complicated. Lady Serena and I had a difference of opinion, it's true, but not what one could describe as a quarrel." Ironically, one of his motivations for going to

France stemmed from them getting on rather too well. The distance would ensure he didn't lose his head and engage in even more egregious acts of intimacy with her. "And that's all I can really say on the matter."

"Well, let's jump to last night's brawl at the Montfords' rout. Some might see that as highly uncharacteristic of you, since you're not a hothead. Far from it, in fact. You are remarkably coolheaded and sensible, one of the reasons I'll be sorry to lose you as my secretary someday. Therefore, I must conclude that Mannering spoke disparagingly of Lady Serena, and you reacted to his comment."

"As you said earlier, any gentleman would leap to a lady's defense."

"Yes, but not everyone would do so by breaking the bounder's nose. That speaks to strong passions, which brings me to the main thing I wish to say to you. I can't, in good conscience, help you hie yourself off to France and throw away a chance at happiness. I may be a crusty old bachelor myself, but I'd hate to see you end up as one. Especially since you're blind to the lady's regard for you. You think your affections are unrequited, but they are not."

"Whatever she feels for me, it's not love." Charles spoke with quiet vehemence, the words scarcely audible.

"And that's where I think you're wrong, my boy. Very, very wrong. I don't think I'm being immodest when I say I'm a shrewd judge of character, and I'm quite certain she's a lady in love." Seeing that Charles had opened his mouth to protest, Sir Roland held up one finger to silence him. "With you. Not Mannering. Nor any of the other young men who occasionally buzz around her. Now whatever your difference of opinion was about, I suggest the two of you find a way to reconcile it." He smiled and leaned back in his chair. "And when you have, you can thank me for being an interfering old fool and invite me to the wedding."

After Sir Roland dismissed him, Charles returned to his own desk. But he had no work to do, since he'd taken no dictation this morning, and he wondered if that had been deliberate on his employer's part, knowing that with nothing else to occupy him, Charles would stew over Sir Roland's pronouncement that Serena was in love with him.

Although, even with work to occupy him, he would likely stew over it and make a hash of whatever task he might attempt to complete. He wanted Sir Roland to be correct. Wanted it so badly he ached with the wanting.

But on the other hand, what did her being in love with him change? Borland was still hanging about London, his very presence a continual threat to expose his secret. And then there was the wide gap between Charles's social status and hers. Even if he were willing to ignore the latter, he refused to contemplate offering for her until he found a satisfactory solution to the former.

And right now, he didn't see what that solution might be. He would forever be illegitimate; there was no getting around that. But if the threat Borland posed was somehow eliminated...His heart began to hammer in his chest, even though he knew the possibility of that happening would take a miracle.

"Don't be a fool," he muttered.

And yet, he couldn't shake the feeling it was time to pray for a miracle.

Chapter Twenty-Two

◦

$\mathcal{S}$erena was outside pushing Jem in the swing she'd had hung from a branch of the oak tree in their back garden when a footman informed her that a Mrs. Avery had come to call. Normally, she wouldn't interrupt her playtime with Jem to receive a caller, but considering who it was she'd make an exception. She left Jem in the servant's care, and the sound of the boy's laughter followed her as she hastened to the back door. The young footman was delighting Jem by running beneath the swing as he shot it skyward.

Although the footman had supplied no information beyond the name of the caller, Serena had to conclude Mrs. Avery was Charles's mother. The reasons behind the woman's call were a bit of a mystery since they'd never been introduced, and calling upon someone that you'd never even met was such a breach of etiquette that it almost never happened.

Nonetheless, Serena was eager to meet the lady. She was more than a little curious about her, having drawn her own conclusions regarding the lady's character based upon what she knew about the way she'd kept the truth from Charles for all those years. Now she had a chance to see if those conclusions were correct based upon a face-to-face meeting.

"Mrs. Avery, what a lovely surprise," Serena said. She gave Charles's mother a warm smile as she came into the sitting room. Mrs. Avery, rising from her chair, however, didn't return her smile.

So this wasn't a friendly social call. Somehow this didn't surprise Serena much. Or give her any reason to revise her opinion of the woman.

Still, as she took a seat across from Mrs. Avery, she retained her smile of polite interest in the face of the other woman's thinly veiled hostility. She smoothed her skirts, folded her hands in her lap, and said, "It's a pleasure to make your acquaintance at last. I trust you're enjoying your visit to London," Serena said.

"Not nearly as much I'd like." Mrs. Avery's expression turned accusing.

"I'm sorry to hear that," Serena said.

"Are you? *Are* you really?"

Serena was taken aback by this open hostility on Mrs. Avery's part, wondering what she could possibly have done to earn it. "Well...yes. I'm afraid I don't quite grasp why you would think otherwise."

There was a beat of silence as a flicker of uncertainty chased across Mrs. Avery's face, as if she were reconsidering her desire to confront Serena. But then she pressed her lips together, squared her shoulders, and began, "I'd hoped to have a share of my son's attention while we were in town. More than just seeing him briefly at dinnertime. As soon as he eats, he bolts. To your side, unless I'm much mistaken." She practically spat out the words of her last sentence.

Serena was surprised to hear that this was the reason for Mrs. Avery's anger. She'd assumed she and Jem had seen less of Charles because of his family's visit. And heartened by it because it meant he wasn't spending time with Miss Lewis.

"As it happens, you are very much mistaken," she said coolly. "Charles hasn't called upon me in quite some time. I believed this was because he's been visiting with you and the rest of his family these past few days, so I can't imagine why this hasn't been the case." This wasn't the time to admit she'd visited him at his bachelor's lodgings. Besides which she didn't believe she owed an explanation to Mrs. Avery.

Mrs. Avery frowned and looked as if she didn't want to believe Serena. They stared at each other for several seconds, and Serena imagined the woman's thoughts mirrored her own. If Charles weren't spending his time with either of them, what had he been doing? Serena's instinct was that Charles was avoiding both of them, and if she had to hazard a guess, she'd lay the blame on Miss Lewis's presence, since she knew he held his family in a great deal of affection.

"I want to believe you," Mrs. Avery said at last. "And if you're lying, you're doing so very convincingly."

The irony of Mrs. Avery, a woman who had lied to

Charles his entire life, doubting Serena's veracity was rich. But understandable, given one tends to judge others by one's own behavior.

"You may believe me or not, but I'm telling you the truth."

"Then how do you explain my son acting completely out of character and brawling in public? He refuses to say why, but everyone thinks it was over a lady. And I believe that lady was you. He's become fascinated by you, but we both know there's no future in it for him." Mrs. Avery's voice had risen to a shrill pitch during this speech and she was practically vibrating with outrage.

"Mrs. Avery, I beg you not to overset yourself. Think of your health." The last thing Serena wanted was to cause a heart episode. How would she explain that to Charles?

"Think of my... what? I don't know why my health is of any concern to you, but I've no intention of allowing you to wriggle out of this discussion by treating me as if I'm some hysterical female."

"But..." Serena began, puzzled by the other woman's lack of caution given the doctor's admonitions about avoiding excitability so as not to stress her heart. When Charles confronted her, had Mrs. Avery exaggerated her attack? It was unthinkable that she would have employed such a tactic to manipulate those around her and yet...

Did she even have a heart condition? Serena wondered. The doctors thought so, because Charles said they'd been warned about it before he tried seeking the truth about his parentage.

"I beg your pardon, if I misspoke. I was under the impression becoming agitated could be dangerous to you. I assure you I'm not trying to evade anything."

Mrs. Avery leaned forward, a palpable tension radiating from the stiff lines of her posture. "*Is* there an understanding between you and my son?"

"Mrs. Avery, I think that's a question you should ask Charles rather than me," Serena said quietly. What had Charles said or done to give his mother the idea that there was some sort of agreement between them? Hope flared in her chest.

The corners of the other woman's mouth turned down as she glared at Serena. "My son is not rational where you are concerned. He's so enthralled with you, that he won't listen to any criticism of you, no matter how well deserved it might be. I may be what you'd consider provincial, living outside of London as I do, but I read the London papers, and I'm not unaware that you have a reputation as a bold and headstrong girl, and that's a kinder characterization than some have made."

"In that case, elucidate me. What is the more unkind characterization?"

At this question, Mrs. Avery's nostrils flared slightly. "That you are fast. That you associate with other ladies who are considered fast. In short, that you don't behave very much like a lady should."

"Well, I can't argue with that because I simply don't accept all the tenets that encompass how many believe a lady should behave. Maybe if those tenets applied equally to gentlemen I would be more accepting of them. I offer no apologies for my beliefs or actions in that regard."

"I'm not here to collect an apology from you." She waved a hand agitatedly through the air. "I merely want you to stop luring my son into your orbit."

"I assure you I'm not luring him anywhere. If he chooses to spend time with me, that is entirely by his own choice."

"I suppose it's no use appealing to your better nature, but on the chance that there is I beseech you to let him go. Until you do, he's not going to notice what's right in front of him, a young lady who holds a great deal of affection for him, who would make him happy in life if she but had the chance to do so."

"And you believe there could be a future for him with this lady if I would only get out of the way?" Serena asked.

"Yes, I believe it with my whole heart." Serena didn't share her conviction, but she didn't contradict her. "He and Miss Lewis are quite compatible, come from similar family backgrounds, and would, in all likelihood make each other very happy." Mrs. Avery leaned forward, her expression beseeching. "I want my son to be happy. Is that too much for a mother to ask?"

"I completely understand a mother's desire to see her children happy. But I must disagree with you on a key point."

Mrs. Avery's mouth thinned into an unhappy line, but she offered no comment.

Serena continued, "I don't accept your premise that there can be no future happiness between Charles and me, but whether there is or isn't, it's not up to you to decide. It may be that Miss Lewis would make a good wife for him, but only Charles can make that call."

"I'm not trying to make his decisions for him, Lady Serena. Quite the contrary. However, I don't think he can make a clearheaded decision if you're in the picture. He's become quite...bewitched by you, and I don't want to see him throw away a chance at happiness chasing after a girl who's...well, I'll say it plainly, so far above his touch that it's ludicrous for him to even entertain the idea of winning you."

"Again, I must disagree with your conclusions."

"Are you saying that if he asked you to marry him, you'd say yes? You, the daughter of an earl, and he, an honorable man, but without a distinguished family name or wealth to recommend him to someone like you. I don't believe you would. Or even if *you* would, that your father would allow the marriage to take place."

"Since I am of age, my father would have little say in that decision, but I have no doubt that where Charles is concerned he would counsel me to follow the dictates of my heart."

"So you *would* marry my son if he asked you?" the other woman pressed.

Serena looked down at her hands still clasped in her lap. She didn't want to answer such an intrusive question, nor did she entirely trust the woman's motives in asking it. She clearly didn't support a match between them, and it was obvious she wanted to hear that Serena would turn him down.

But would she turn him down if he proposed? After Thomas died, Serena had dismissed the idea of marriage, not believing she'd ever find a love like that again. But had she been deluding herself recently, thinking that all she wanted from Charles was a man in her bed? Did she actually want more than that?

Oh, my God, I do.

How horrified would Mrs. Avery be to discover that by

pressing Serena to give her an answer, she'd made Serena realize she couldn't honestly say that she wouldn't accept a proposal from him. And now that she realized it, she could only wonder why it hadn't been clear to her before.

Because now it seemed so obvious. She'd been so blind to the truth, stubbornly hanging on to the belief that her feelings were based in lust, not love.

She'd been a fool.

"Well?" Mrs. Avery pressed.

"I'm afraid that I don't intend to answer that question for you. How I would answer a man proposing marriage to me is too private to share with you, even if the man in question is your son. However, you're free to ask him if he plans to offer me a proposal. If he says no, that should put your mind at ease, shouldn't it?"

"Hardly," she snapped. "I know the lengths ladies go to when ensnaring a man."

Her words made Serena wonder what methods Miss Lewis might employ to snag someone like Charles. Or even what tactics his mother might use to prevent Serena from "ensnaring" him.

"What a poor opinion you have of your own sex," Serena said coolly. "Not to mention your own son."

"There are women who will stoop to any means necessary. I've seen it, and so have you, whether you want to acknowledge it or not."

"I'll concede there are those of both genders who stoop to less-than-honorable means to secure the hand of their target. However, I assure you I'm not such a person. *If*, and I must stress this is merely speculative, but if Charles and I were to become betrothed, there would be no trickery. Merely a decision that we wished to be together. I don't know whether that eases your mind, but it's the best I can offer."

"So you will not cut off your association with Charles?" Mrs. Avery demanded.

"I will not," Serena said firmly.

"Such headstrong obstinance is most unbecoming, Lady Serena. *Most* unbecoming. You should be ashamed of yourself, but of course, some people have no shame."

With that biting remark, Mrs. Avery stood up. "Unfortunately, nothing about this conversation has changed my opinion of you. I'd hoped you'd be reasonable, but I can see that was a futile hope, and I've wasted my time. You may be able to deceive my son, but you don't deceive me."

"If anyone knows about deception, it would be you, wouldn't it, Mrs. Avery?" Serena asked quietly.

"I . . . I don't know what you mean," the other woman said. Despite the hauteur in her voice, Serena didn't miss the flicker of uncertainty in her eyes. Or the momentary glimpse of panic that had followed it.

"You've deceived Charles for years. Perhaps it was too painful for you to admit the circumstances. Or perhaps you were too ashamed to own up to your own actions. Either way, you've denied him the truth for far too long. No matter what story you spun for others, surely he deserved to know the truth."

Mrs. Avery's mouth curled into a sneer of disdain. "I don't know who you've been listening to, but whatever stories they've told you, they're lies."

"The only person I've talked to is Charles. He told me the truth—as much of it as he knows at any rate. But the incredible resemblance between your son and a man named Edgar Borland is convincing evidence that you've never told the truth about Charles's parentage. He is the son of Edgar's father, Casper Borland, is he not?"

"I will not stand here and let you insult me like this."

In a way, Serena had to admire the haughty lift of the chin and the look of utter outrage Mrs. Avery had assumed. She was the picture of a female wrongly accused, but Serena didn't believe the performance for a minute, convincing as it was. She'd seen the truth earlier, when she'd caught Mrs. Avery off guard by suggesting she'd been deceptive.

"Nothing I've said is meant to be an insult, Mrs. Avery. I assure you that your secret is safe with me, but you should know that it may come to light anyway if people question the resemblance between Charles and Edgar Borland. I urged Charles to brazen it out and laugh it off as an extraordinary coincidence, but he won't. That's why he's planning to go to France. Not because he wants to. Rather because he believes he must to save you from embarrassment. Perhaps you can make up for a lifetime of lying, and convince him to stay in England."

Mrs. Avery didn't answer right away. "If he and this Edgar Borland resemble each other, it can only be through a coincidence. Or ancestors so distant the connection has been lost to memory. John Townshend was Charles's father."

For a moment, Serena almost questioned her belief that Mrs. Avery was lying. She was very, *very* convincing.

"Then I don't believe there's anything more for us to discuss," Serena said. "Good day, Mrs. Avery."

The other woman swept out of the room without another word.

Would she try to convince Charles to stay? Or would she urge him to go in the hope that it would put an end to any blossoming relationship between Serena and Charles?

Well, no matter. Serena had put plans in motion, and if worse came to worse...

She spoke French fluently.

Scarcely half an hour had gone by before Menken ushered the Duchess of Rochester into the room. Apparently it was a day for unexpected visitors.

"Grace." Serena, who'd been attending to correspondence at her desk, rose to greet her friend.

"I have news about Edwina," Grace said, waving a folded note in the air. "You can read it for yourself. This was on your hall table and I took it upon myself to bring it up with me. I too received a note from her, so I can tell you what mine said if you like. Or you can read yours. It's up to you." She handed the note to Serena.

Serena glanced at it, recognizing Edwina's handwriting.

"You can tell me," she said. They both took a seat, Grace in a chintz-covered armchair, Serena on the green velvet love seat.

"Edwina and Mr. Latimer have departed London. They're on their way to Latimer's property near Oxford where they'll be married by special license." Grace smiled broadly and her eyes danced with merriment.

"She never breathed a word." Serena held up her unopened note. "I mean I'm not surprised they decided to marry. But to spirit themselves out of town...it's so very impetuous."

Grace nodded. "It is, but as I suspected there is a

need for haste." She accompanied these words with a meaningful look.

"Her stomach issues?" Serena said. "So they weren't indigestion. I'd begun to wonder."

Grace nodded. "I thought you had. I think the only reason Edwina hadn't figured it out yet was because Beasley and her doctor had convinced her she was the reason they'd remained childless during their marriage. After all, Beasley had supposedly fathered a child with one of his mistresses."

"I never did think that child resembled Beasley very much," Serena said. "Now I'm curious if his mistress didn't have another lover. It would be a kind of poetic justice for all the grief he caused Edwina."

"I'm so happy for Edwina." Grace clapped her hands together in delight. "She's finally going to have the child she longed for all those years she was married to that philanderer."

"I'm beyond happy for her. Latimer adores her. I have no doubts that this will be a very happy marriage," Serena said. Impulsively, she jumped up and hugged the duchess because she had to hug somebody. This truly was wonderful news.

"Does she say how far along she is?"

"No," Grace replied. "Though it's possible she told you details that she left out of my note."

Serena broke the wax seal and unfolded the page. The note was brief and included little more than what Grace had already told her. Only the post script, written by Jason Latimer, added another detail. He apologized for temporarily setting aside his efforts to find a way to entice Borland to Canada.

*We're taking a day or two to honeymoon before we
return to London. Will deal with Borland then.*

"It looks as if we shouldn't expect to see the newlyweds for a few days, at least," Serena said. "Jason was
helping me with a certain matter and he added a post script
to Edwina's note letting me know they intend to enjoy a
short honeymoon."

"I can host the Wednesday Afternoon Social Club in
the meantime," Grace offered.

"As can I," Serena said. She refolded the note and
walked over to her writing desk and tucked it under the
blotter. She was thrilled for Edwina, but she was concerned this would delay her plan to dispatch Borland to
some distant shore as quickly as possible.

"I'm sure we'll manage to carry on in Edwina's
absence."

"I wonder if Charlotte knows," Serena mused.

"I sent her a note in case Edwina hadn't."

"We should serve champagne at a Wednesday Afternoon Social Club meeting when she returns."

"Absolutely," Grace agreed. "We'll have a little celebration."

Serena offered to ring for tea, but Grace declined
the offer.

"I can only stay a moment. Phoebe and I have fittings at
the modiste. I really just stopped by to make sure you knew
of Edwina's news. Since I'm here though, perhaps you can
tell me what prompted Mr. Townshend's fisticuffs with
Mannering. It generated a great deal of gossip and yet the
details are still vague. But putting two and two together, I
have to conclude it had something to do with you."

"I suspect Mannering said something about me that

Charles took exception to. Menken has been instructed to turn Mannering away should he come to call, though I doubt he will," Serena said dryly. "A step I planned to take in any case. I've no interest in Mannering's pursuit."

"Well, of course," Grace said. "Mannering is a bland bore at the best of times."

Serena sighed. "He is, but I'm human enough that I enjoyed the way his attention enflamed Charles's jealousy. I feel I'm partly to blame for what happened at the Montfords' rout. I could tell Charles disliked the attention Mannering paid to me, and even though I found the man's chatter quite tedious, I continued to endure it only because I loved seeing Charles glower at the two of us."

It had been vain and silly of her and completely unfair to Charles. If she'd hoped it would prod Charles into changing his mind about their relationship, it appeared to have failed. She'd heard nothing from him since then, and the silence was deafening.

She regretted her actions, and hoped Charles didn't pay too great of a price for them. He had to be hating all the attention it was bringing him. Particularly since his main goal lately was to *not* attract attention.

"I still like it when Miles shows a bit of jealousy. I want him to remember a man should never take a lady for granted," Grace admitted. "But just a bit. Too much jealousy becomes ugly and stifling." She placed her hands on her knees, as if about to rise from the chair, but paused to say, "I should be going, but let me leave you with this thought...now that Edwina is off to find her happily-ever-after, don't you think it's time you and Mr. Townshend made progress in that direction?" She came to her feet then.

Serena rose and accompanied her friend to the doorway. "I think, Grace, that maybe it is, but Charles is...resistant."

"A resistance that shouldn't be too hard to overcome," Grace said with a reassuring smile.

Serena hoped she was right.

After Grace left, Serena reread Edwina's note. "Good for you, Edwina," Serena murmured. "Better late than never."

But what of herself? Would she find the same sort of happiness her friends had? Or had she irrevocably ruined things between herself and Charles with her folly the other night?

A mixture of hope and dread filled her.

Only time would tell, but the one thing she did know. She wasn't going down without a fight.

Chapter Twenty-Three

*E*vidently, Lord Mannering was not one of the *ton's* more popular figures. At least that was the conclusion Charles came to during a visit to White's on the following evening. He was clapped on the back and he couldn't possibly consume all the drinks sent over to his table. Luckily, he had company to help him out on that front. Ambrose-Stone, Farrars, and Plumley were drinking with him after a round of billiards.

And sensing his reluctance to talk about the incident, his companions had refrained from quizzing him, though they'd been more than happy to help consume the whiskies and brandies that had been sent to the table.

"Borland, you filthy cheat. I thought we made it clear you weren't to show your face here again." The words, with their faintly slurred pronunciation of *shlow* and *fash* signaled the inebriated state of the speaker.

Charles looked around, as did the others, surprised that Borland, his name thoroughly blackened earlier, when he'd been caught cheating at a hand of cards, had had the audacity to return the club. Or that the doorman had even let him in.

"I'm shpeaking to you, you shoundrel."

A hand clapped on Charles's shoulder and spun him around. He barely had time to register the fist plowing toward his face, much less respond with an effective feint.

Once again, Serena prepared to pay a call to Number 4 Nassau Street, though this evening she was going as herself. No subterfuge. No disguise.

Tonight she wore one of her favorite gowns, an emerald silk that flattered her coloring and made her eyes look an interesting shade of light green rather than plain gray. Perhaps more importantly, the bodice accentuated her bosom quite nicely. It wouldn't hurt to remind Charles that (1) she had a very nice bosom, and that (2) he'd rather delighted in exploring it not so very long ago.

Despite this, she had no intention of trying to tempt him into anything tonight. She simply wished to speak with him, and then depending on his response...

Well, she refused to let her mind contemplate that yet.

Nervous energy was making it hard to sit still while Giselle finished fixing her hair in one of those elaborate styles that Serena usually avoided because no matter how flattering they were, she couldn't help feeling the time spent creating them could be put to better use. However, tonight was important and for once she didn't care how long it took to have her looking her best.

As Giselle worked her magic, Serena reread the note she'd received earlier from the Abbott sisters.

> *Heavens, dear, we don't hold your deception against you. We found Mr. Wiggins quite a kindred spirit, and frankly, we're not all that surprised to find out "he" turned out to be a "she." As enthusiastic adherents to the philosophies of Mary Wollstonecraft, we aren't the sort of spinsters who would be close-minded to the idea of a lady calling on a gentleman. But you couldn't have known that before you came to call. We are thrilled to be your accomplices tonight and will have everything in readiness.*

Obtaining their cooperation had been surprisingly easy, and she hoped that boded well for what else she wished to accomplish tonight. Mrs. Avery's visit—ironically—had given her the clarity she needed, and combined with Charles's determination to take himself off to France...Perhaps it was the impulsive side of her nature, but she simply couldn't wait another day. Besides, she didn't trust that Mrs. Avery wouldn't resort to something drastic to drive a wedge between Charles and herself.

So it was rather anticlimactic to arrive at Nassau Street and find that Charles wasn't there. All that heart-pounding anticipation during the carriage ride over had been for naught. Her fault, she supposed, for assuming he would be. His life didn't revolve around her alone.

"Everything is in place," Miss Minerva said as she

led Serena to the parlor. "We warned our other gentlemen boarders that this room is off-limits for tonight, as
we had a special guest visiting us. When Mr. Townshend
gets home, we'll bring him in and then make ourselves
scarce."

"Thank you," Serena said. "I rather hoped he'd be here
by now. I thought seven o'clock a good time to catch him
because he'd either be in for the evening, or if he had
plans, would still be getting ready to go out. But you say
he hasn't been here at all since he left this morning?"

Miss Minerva shook her head. "No, which *is* unusual
for him."

"True," Miss Leticia said, "but not unheard of. We
don't offer dinner to our boarders, so they must go elsewhere for their evening meal. Perhaps he's lingering over
his food tonight."

Or visiting with his family. It was only yesterday
that Mrs. Avery had called upon her, and she'd made
no mention of an imminent departure. If anything, their
meeting had probably compelled the woman to redouble
her efforts to push Miss Lewis in Charles's direction. Not
that Serena saw the girl as a rival, but nonetheless her
stomach clenched at the idea of the two of them being
thrown together.

"Whatever the reason, I've got nowhere to go," Serena
said, sounding calm despite the pulse pounding in her ears.
She drew in a long breath.

Miss Leticia, who had stationed herself by the window
that overlooked the street, said, "When his hackney arrives, I'll intercept him on the front stairs and bring him
in here."

The excitement in the room was palpable for the first

hour they waited. It started to flag during the second hour, even though the Abbott sisters tried to fortify all of their spirits with tea and cake, and any sense of anticipation had quite disappeared by the time the third hour rolled around. The mantel clock was chiming ten o'clock when Serena gently shook the dozing Abbott sisters awake and urged them off to their beds.

"Really, dear," Miss Minerva said, blinking several times to rouse herself. "We don't mind keeping you company until he arrives."

"No, we don't mind at all," Miss Leticia added, before daintily placing a hand in front of her mouth to cover a yawn.

"That's very sweet of you, but *I'd* mind keeping such staunch allies from getting a good night's rest." Serena made a shooing motion with her hands. "Now off to bed with the two of you. If Charles doesn't arrive soon, I'll be off myself."

"If you decide to leave before Mr. Townshend returns, you can send Donald round to the inn yard where your coachman is waiting," Miss Leticia said. Donald, a gangly young man who served as a sort of footman-handyman-messenger was the only servant still awake. "And then remind him to lock up after you."

"I will," Serena assured her.

Miss Minerva came over and patted Serena's cheek. "Good luck, my dear. And if you end up staying the night, don't forget to drape a handkerchief on the doorknob and we'll make sure the maid skips Mr. Townshend's room in the morning." With a roguish wink, she turned and headed for the door.

"I can't wait to extend my felicitations to the two of

you," Miss Leticia said. She gave Serena a fond wave and then she followed her sister out of the parlor.

Serena smiled, less sure of this prediction than the older lady. She was ready to roll out her most persuasive arguments to win Charles over to her way of thinking, but aside from one, which she hoped would prove particularly compelling, she feared he would still think the obstacles too great to consider anything more than friendship.

She wished to solve the Borland issue with Mr. Latimer's help, but he and Edwina still weren't back in London, and there was no way to make progress on that particular impediment until they were.

There was nothing she could do about the gap between Charles's station in life and her own, but why he kept insisting it was insurmountable when there were examples to the contrary even within their circle of friends...Grace, with her relatively humble origins had married a duke, after all...was frustrating, but surely he'd see this was a hurdle only if they allowed it to be.

Serena paced about the parlor for a bit, but the creaky floorboards sounded abnormally loud in the silence of the sleeping household, so she chose a periodical from a side table and took a seat by the fireplace, idly flipping through the pages, all the while wondering what Charles was doing.

Each minute that ticked off the clock made her more certain she'd come on a fool's errand. It was late, and who knew how much later he'd be? Better to leave and broach what she had to say to him another time.

Except she didn't want to put it off any longer. Didn't want to leave the words unsaid until tomorrow, or the day after, or even next week. Once she'd realized that only

Charles could fill the place in her heart that had been left empty since Thomas had died, she knew she had to make him aware of how she felt. So what was another hour or two?

Perhaps she should let Donald know she wouldn't fault him if he wished to doze, since it might be a while yet until he could seek his bed. She stepped out into the hallway and smiled.

There was Donald seated in a chair, eyes closed, elbow resting on the hall table with his head propped on one hand. Soft snores escaped his parted lips. Except for being a couple of feet taller and about ten years older, he reminded her of a sleeping Jem.

She turned and went back into the parlor, content to know she wasn't keeping him up. She wandered back to the fireplace, and took a seat in one of the armchairs that flanked it. Now what? Sitting around waiting was not her forte. She stared at the glowing coals, idly drumming her fingers on the nubby upholstery of the chair's arms.

At some point, she must have fallen asleep because the next thing she knew someone was gently shaking her shoulder. She opened her eyes, expecting to see Donald, but instead it was Charles standing before her, his expression serious, his eyes unreadable in the low light of the room, though to be fair, one was puffy and on its way to swelling shut.

The battered state of his face chased away any lingering vestiges of drowsiness. "Good heavens, Charles," she said, coming to her feet. "Who did that to you?" She moved closer to him to get a better look at his injury. Make that injuries. Because she could see the beginnings of a bruise on the cheek below his good eye.

"Calm down," he said, taking a step backward to avoid her ministrations. "I wasn't attacked. Well, I *was* attacked, but not on the street this time. It was at White's."

"This time?" she asked. "Were you attacked before this? My God, what is this city coming to? You never … I didn't know …" Her hands trembled before her, not quite reaching for him, but wanting to. "Why didn't you tell me?"

"It was only a robbery. The other night on my way home from the Montfords' someone knocked me on the head … well, knocked me unconscious and stole my pocket watch and money. I had a muddled head and a devil of a headache, that's all. Well, and a garish lump. That is, I assume it was garish. I couldn't see it on the back of my head, but I could feel it, and anything the size of an egg must certainly be garish."

"Oh, Charles." She swallowed back the fear that had risen in her throat at the thought he could have been more severely injured. "And tonight? At your club? Was it Mannering?" She took another step toward him, and this time grabbed hold of his upper arms so that he couldn't step away from her. "Or some of his cronies?"

"This had nothing to do with Mannering." His mouth twisted into a rueful smile. "I was mistaken for Borland."

"What? Why did a case of mistaken identity result in a rapidly swelling eye and a bruised face?" She drew in a swift breath. "Unless someone made the connection between the two of you and said something untoward. Oh, Charles. I told you to laugh off any unseemly speculation. Fighting only confirms people's worst conclusions. Nonetheless, we can find a way to fix this."

"It might surprise you that, one, there was nothing I could do to avoid this, and, two, it was purely a case of mistaken identity. Once the melee was over, no one seemed to question *why* I resembled Borland. Everyone simply agreed that Donovan—the fellow who punched me in the first place—had made an unfortunate mistake."

"Unfortunate for you," she said indignantly.

"For him as well. Farrars came to my aid and pulled him away, then Ambrose-Stone landed him with a punch that laid him flat on the floor. I'm not sure when he came to because the place descended into chaos again."

"What do you mean by *again*?"

"Just that there'd already been a clubwide melee earlier in the evening. One that centered around Borland and accusations of cheating. That's why Donovan reacted the way he did when he mistook me for...well, my brother."

"Only a half-brother," Serena cut in vehemently. "One who inherited none of the admirable qualities that you have in great abundance."

One corner of his mouth quirked and his good eye gleamed with amusement and something else. Something that warmed her insides and made her heart knock about in her chest. She felt the corners of her own mouth tip up in response.

"Shall I tell you the rest of the story or do you wish to continue singing my praises?"

"For now, I want to hear the rest of the story," she said.

Despite their words, they continued to stand there, simply drinking in the other's smile. During those few seconds though, she was quite sure something had shifted between them. And in a good way. A tentative step forward that gave her hope that maybe, just maybe, Charles would be glad to hear what she had to say.

Finally, he cleared his throat and said, "Back to what

I was saying. Earlier in the day, Borland had been playing cards in the card room. I heard he showed up with Bunbury and Leggins, that the bets at the table were large and reckless, but that Borland was on a lucky streak. He'd won several of the hands before Gilly Ogilvy, of all people, accused him of cheating. Naturally, Borland denied it, but Gilly insisted he was cheating, and the argument culminated in Gilly grabbing Borland's wrist and pushing up his cuff.

"When an ace fell out, Gilly snatched up Borland's winnings sitting on the table. Being Gilly, he wasn't interested in finding satisfaction on the dueling green. He just wanted the winnings he believed were rightfully his."

"Quite a sensible choice," Serena said.

"I agree, but apparently that's when the first contretemps broke out."

"So you didn't actually witness the altercation between Gilly and Borland?"

He shook his head. "No, I was in another room playing billiards with Farrars, Plumley, and Ambrose-Stone. I think we were on our fourth or fifth game. I confess, I can't remember precisely because I'd had rather a lot to drink. Anyway, that's neither here nor there, the upshot is the brawl which originated in the card room spilled out of there to the rest of the club. I've never seen anything like it. Men were throwing punches, overturning furniture, wrestling on the floor, and I'm not even sure many knew the reason behind the mayhem. They were just caught up in the fracas."

"Good heavens," Serena said. "And men are in charge of running the world. Honestly."

Charles reached out and cradled her cheek with one

hand. "Well, my little firebrand, I'm not sure a club where a great deal of drinking is going on is the best place to measure a man's worthiness for leadership, but I get your point."

"So was any of the damage to your face acquired during this first brawl? Or was it only later, when Donovan came at you?"

He grinned, then winced slightly. "I made it through that first brawl relatively unscathed. It didn't hurt that I, along with my companions, were in possession of billiard cues. Turns out they're quite handy for discouraging any belligerents who appeared threatening. Once things calmed down, we resumed our billiards game."

"But I'm still unclear about why Lord Donovan came after you. Had Borland cheated him as well?"

"I honestly have no idea. All I know is that Borland had been run off the premises during that first brawl, and when Donovan confused me for him, he was determined to make it clear that I—that is, Borland—wasn't welcome there. But there are two important things in all this. One, when the dust settled for a second time, no one appeared to find it unusual that I have such a close resemblance to Borland, and two, I don't think that Borland will be showing his face around London any time soon."

Relief flooded through her. "Does that mean what I think it means?"

"What do you think it means?" he asked, looking hard into her eyes.

"I hope it means you and I can come to some sort of understanding now."

He nodded. "I hope so too." But for some reason he

still looked hesitant. "Although, I should add that much will depend upon the nature of our understanding."

Her heart began to hammer in her chest. "Then I suppose it's most fortuitous that the reason I came here tonight was to discuss exactly that. I've had a bit of a change of heart, you see."

A slight frown creased his brow and she realized that he might have interpreted her words to mean she wished a return to mere friendship when in fact the complete opposite was true.

She reached for his hands, entwining her fingers with his, and he winced slightly. "Oh, Charles. I'm sorry." Despite his facial injuries, she'd forgotten that his hands would also feel the effects of tonight's fight. She immediately tried let go, but he resisted her effort, instead tightening his grip in response.

"No, it's fine," he said. "It's worth a little pain to hold your hands in mine." He swallowed and drew in a long breath. "Serena, I can no longer stand the suspense. You see, Sir Roland told me recently that he believed you were in love with me, and I need to know if he…that is to say, I fervently hope that he was correct in his assessment."

Serena's heart pounded hard in her chest. "Then I must tell you, Mr. Townshend," she began, teasing him a bit by addressing him so formally, "that he is entirely correct and I am in love with you, though I admit it's taken me a while to see the truth. My friends would attribute it to my stubborn nature and they might be right."

The words had no sooner come out of her mouth then he drew her into his arms and held her tightly against him, and if it caused him any pain, he gave no sign of it.

"You shouldn't," he whispered against her ear, "but I'm awfully glad you do."

"Don't you have something you wish to say to me?" she prompted. Because if they were going to be making declarations of love...well, she was more than ready to hear his.

"I do," he murmured. Then he stepped back and started to go down on one knee.

No! That was not how she'd planned this to go.

"Charles," she said, reaching for his hands and pulling him back to his feet. "Not so fast. We'll get to that part, but not yet."

"Managing me already, are you?"

"It's not as if you didn't already know I'm a very managing female. And at this moment, I also happen to be a female who's told you how I feel, and before we proceed any further, I'd very much like to hear how you feel about me."

"As if you don't know that I'm hopelessly in love with you." He pulled her close. "And I have been for quite some time. Even though you ought to send a fellow like me packing for having the gall to feel that way about you." He nuzzled his lips against her ear. "I love you, Serena. I have for the longest time."

"Charles," she breathed, letting her head fall to the side, because he was kissing her neck in a way that was sending shivers through her body. "I'm so glad you've come to your senses."

"More like lost them, but we can quibble about that later." He kissed a path along her jaw to her mouth. "First things first," he whispered.

His kiss was fierce and hungry. Greedy. Possessive.

Far too soon he pulled away. "Lovely as that is, I must make something clear to you." His gaze was serious, or as serious as it could be, considering one eye was a mere slit by now.

"Very well," she replied. "And then I have a few things I'd like to say to you." And then, depending on his response, she had several things she wished to *do* to him.

"I'm not interested in a love affair, Serena. As much as your offer tempts me, I can't say yes to it. I know you're far above my touch, and my connection to Borland could still prove embarrassing if anyone ever does guess the truth..."

"Borland is *not* a consideration," she said. "Nor is he an impediment."

"Perhaps you should consider that I'm unlikely to ever earn a salary that will be able to keep you in the style to which you're accustomed," he warned.

"Don't worry. My dowry is quite generous. We'll manage."

"Then there's my mother. She used every weapon in her arsenal to persuade me to make an offer to Miss Lewis—tears, guilt, anger. It's unlikely she's going to welcome you to the family." His mouth tightened into a grimace. "I hate to say it, but when you meet her, don't be surprised if you encounter some...hostility on her part."

"In light of her calling on me yesterday, I'm already aware that she doesn't have a favorable opinion of me," Serena said. "But I can live with that." One day she'd share the details of their meeting and let Charles reach his own conclusions on whether his mother's heart condition was as serious as the family had been led to believe. But not today.

Charles's face flushed, adding another layer of color in addition to his bruises. "She oughtn't to have done that, and I will speak to her."

"There's no need, Charles. I can fight my own battles with her, if necessary, although I hope she comes around eventually."

"I know you can, but I still intend to make her understand how I expect her to treat you." He reached up and brushed her cheek with the back of his fingers. "Since you're about to become the most important person in my life. Although that's been true for quite some time now, even if I've tried to hide it." He gave her a rueful look. "I don't think I've been very good at it of late."

"Have you heard me complaining?" she teased, raising up on tiptoe and placing her mouth within reach of his. "And since you don't need to keep your feelings hidden away any longer…"

Charles took the hint and conversation was halted while he quite capably showed precisely how he felt about her. Breathlessness finally forced them to draw apart.

"I think it's time for me to ask you an important question, Serena."

"No," she said.

"No?"

"While I'm not one to draw out a discussion when we could be getting to, shall we say, more pleasurable activities, there are still a few more things I want us to be clear on."

He nodded. "All right."

"I've no intention of changing how I live my life.

If you find me aggravating and unbiddable now, know that this isn't going to change. I intend to carry on with my work."

A small chuckle escaped him. "Believe me, I'm not foolish enough to think that would change."

"I figured you were smart enough to know that, but it's best to be thoroughly clear about these matters."

"As long as you know, I'll continue to try to rein in your worst instincts."

She gave him a wry smile. "I figured as much. We leopards and our spots, after all. And I suppose if our natural tendencies lead to the occasional argument, we can enjoy the way we patch things up between us."

"I think that sounds like a plan I can live with," he said. "Is there anything else we need to be clear on?"

"You should know that I plan to raise Jem myself."

"I saw that coming from the moment we took him back to your home."

"Initially, I had good intentions to find him a home elsewhere. Truly, I did. But he's become so dear to me. I couldn't part with him now."

"Would it surprise you to know I'm not unhappy to hear this? Jem wormed his way into my affections as well."

She playfully swatted his arm. "You never told me that."

"Things changed once I decided to let you make an honest man of me."

"Then perhaps we should get to that..."

"Gladly," he said, taking her hands into his own.

But before he could go down on one knee again, she said, "Let's do things differently, you and I," she said. "Starting with who asks whom."

He looked amused. "The floor is yours, madam."

"I love you, Charles Townshend. Love you, lust for you, want to spend all my tomorrows with you. Will you marry me?"

"I will, Serena. God help me, I will."

His arms went around her, drawing her tight against him, and as his mouth lowered to hers, her emotions were less about wanting his kisses, although there was that. There would always be that. But what she overwhelmingly felt was that she'd been on a long journey and she'd finally made her way home.

At last, she drew back. Once again, she needed to catch her breath, and besides, they hadn't quite finished their business.

"Well," she said. "I think it's time to ask you one last question."

He tilted his head and waited for her to go on.

"Are you free this Friday morning?"

His brows shot up at her question. "I think that could be arranged. Why?"

"I thought it would be a nice day for our wedding. We can go to Doctors' Commons in the morning and get a special license. And that will also give you a little time to look at the preliminary marriage settlement I directed Papa's solicitor to draw up, just in case tonight went as I wished. Plus, we can take advantage of your family being in town."

"I like that plan. A long engagement would likely kill me." At her questioning look, he continued. "I've already waited this long for you. I'm going to wait until we're properly married."

She sighed. "I had a feeling you'd say something like that."

$\mathcal{J}$hey were married at the Huntington residence in a very simple ceremony. Only a small circle of friends and family witnessed their exchange of vows. The wedding breakfast, on the other hand, was held at Edwina's residence and was attended by nearly a hundred people. A small army of servants converted Edwina's music room into a flower-draped space with tables and chairs set with fine china. A quartet of musicians played music on the small raised stage at one end of the long room.

In addition to the family and friends who'd been at the wedding, the guests at the wedding breakfast included several members of the Wednesday Afternoon Social Club, and some of Charles's friends, including Ambrose-Stone, Farrars, and Plumley. Sir Roland attended, of course. And even Gilly Ogilvy was present, since he'd had a large hand in solving the problem of Edgar Borland, who'd apparently fled to the Continent once again. Not that Gilly had any idea that's why he'd been invited, but Serena and Charles had thought it fitting to include him in the festivities.

Serena was incandescently happy, and she saw her happiness reflected in the faces of their guests. Oh, there were a few exceptions, to be sure. Mrs. Avery's expression was frequently closer to resignation rather than joy, although Serena did catch glimpses of her smiling in a stiff, *trying-to-appear-happy-even-if-she-wasn't* sort of way. And once or twice, Serena saw a look of wistful sadness cross Miss Lewis's countenance. The rest of the Avery family, however, seemed truly happy for them. Even Charles's half-brother Lawrence had made the trip from Eton to join in the celebrations.

"How much longer until you and I can have a more private celebration? One that requires much less attire?" Charles murmured in her ear.

She turned to him with a rueful smile. His dear face still bore the vestiges of that brawl from a few days ago, but she found his current disreputable rake look rather endearing.

"I'm afraid it will still be a while, my love," she said. "We can hardly leave before the meal is served. And we'll have to get Jem settled in before we depart."

Jem had been ecstatic to hear that Serena and Charles were to marry, and when Serena had asked him if he'd like for her and Charles to be his Mama and Papa, he'd thrown himself into her arms and wrapped his arms tightly around her neck in a long hug.

Not understanding the nature of a honeymoon, he'd initially been disappointed to hear that Serena and Charles would be leaving without him right after the wedding breakfast. They were to spend a week at a property in Hampstead Heath owned by the Duke of Rochester. It was chosen for its proximity to London—close enough to minimize their time on the road, but far enough away to seem like a proper wedding trip.

However, when Serena informed Jem that he had been invited to stay with the Rochester children for the first few days, his disappointment at being excluded from the honeymoon quickly turned to excitement. She looked toward the table where he and Grace's children were seated under the watchful eye of their nursemaids. Sitting next to Peregrine, Jem was laughing, and the faces of both boys glowed with mischievous delight. The two of them had become fast friends and partners in all kinds of boyish hijinks. In contrast, Peregrine's sister Agatha, who was frequently the target of said hijinks, sat across from them with her chin tilted up at a haughty angle and her mouth pursed into a superior smirk, as if she found them far too silly for her to deign to associate with them.

"Do you think he'll even miss us while we're gone?" Charles said, running his hand down her back in a light caress. A delicious shiver of awareness ran through her.

"Probably not," she said. "Between spending the first half of the week with his friends and the latter half being entertained by my father, Jem will be too busy to notice our absence much. Papa has embraced his role as a grandfather figure by clearing his social calendar and planning an ambitious number of activities for the two of them to do together while we're gone. I've been told there's to be a trip to Astley's, a picnic in the park, a trip to the Royal

Menagerie. Oh, and did I mention a pony is supposed to be joining my father's stables before we return?"

"Then it's a good thing we won't be away any longer than a week, or Jem will become hopelessly spoiled," he remarked.

"I fear that's going to happen regardless," Serena said. "Papa was delighted when I told him that you and I wished to raise Jem as our own. I think he finds babies to be mystifying creatures, but an eight-year-old boy is someone he can relate to. An instant grandchild, if you will."

He slipped one hand around her and gently squeezed her waist. "Remind me what plans you've made for *us* this coming week," he murmured.

"Just the usual things one plans for a honeymoon," she replied. "A great deal of vigorous activity involving a large bed. Or a chaise longue. A desk, perhaps." She gave him a considering look. "Possibly even up against the wall. If the weather is fine, maybe we'll search out a secluded spot for a wicked rendezvous."

His breathing quickened and his voice sounded faintly hoarse as he said, "And tell me again, how much longer must we remain here?"

"Let me speak to Edwina and see how soon the food can be served," she said.

By dinnertime, they were pulling up in front of a three-story, rambling red brick structure with a crenelated roofline and round towers built at the front corners of the house.

"When you told me we were staying at a place called Evermore Cottage, I somehow envisioned something much more modest and, well, cottage-like," Charles remarked, peering out of the carriage window.

A pair of footmen hurried down the front steps to open the door and help them alight. Charles descended first and turned to take Serena's hand to assist her.

"It is rather imposing," Serena agreed as she stepped down beside him. They mounted the steps hand in hand.

Mrs. Alberts, the housekeeper, met them at the front door with a curtsey. "Welcome, my lady. Sir. As you requested, a simple dinner has been prepared to be sent up to your room. Would you like it delivered now, or would you prefer to get settled in first? Since you sent your luggage ahead, that has already been unpacked for you."

Serena glanced at Charles, whose eyes held a hungry look, but not necessarily for food. "Now, please," she said. While Charles had been adamant that they wait for a bedroom to consummate their marriage, they'd indulged in a great deal of delicious foreplay during the drive.

There had been plenty of passionate kissing and groping, and although both had remained clothed the entire time, his nimble fingers had found their way under her traveling gown and had brought her to two thundering orgasms. The poor man probably had plenty of pent-up passion waiting to be released because he'd refused her repeated offers to return the favor. She knew they wouldn't want the servants interrupting their privacy once they reached their bedroom.

"Yes, ma'am." Mrs. Alberts curtsied again and directed that a footman named Robert show them to their room. As they followed Robert up the stairs, Charles slipped his hand around her waist, kissed her ear, and whispered, "I hope the food arrives quickly. I have more pressing needs than meat and potatoes at present."

"And whose fault is that?" she asked.

"Never mind that," he growled in her ear. "I just want to dispense with the servants as quickly as possible."

"As do I, my darling. As do I."

Fortunately, a pair of maids brought in the food trays from the kitchen just after Robert had departed. Serena instructed them to put them on the small table that had obviously been placed in the bedroom for just that purpose. The maids arranged the plates at the two places already set with crystal goblets and silverware, but Serena stopped them when they began to remove the silver covers from the plates.

"That's not necessary, thank you. We don't wish to eat quite yet."

"Yes, ma'am. Just ring when you're ready to have the dishes cleared away."

"Thank you, but I doubt that we'll need any further attentions this evening."

"I see." The maid inclined her head. "In that case, have a good evening."

After the door closed, Serena and Charles could hear their giggles in the hallway.

Serena closed the distance between them, lightly grasping the lapels of Charles's jacket as she smiled up at him.

"Well, Mr. Townshend. Here we are at long last. Just the two of us, a lovely four-poster bed. What is your pleasure? Shall I change into one of the lovely night rails I brought?"

His eyes darkened to a deep blue as he pulled her against him. She didn't miss the hard ridge in his trousers. "I think donning a nightgown would only be a waste of time, since all I want at present is to get you out of your clothes."

"A sentiment that mirrors my desires as well," she

murmured, coming up on tiptoe to kiss his mouth before pulling away. She reached for his hand and pulled him over toward the bed, then she turned and presented her back to him. "You'll have to undo the buttons for me."

"With pleasure," he said. Once he had the buttons undone, he pushed the sleeves from her shoulders so that the bodice of her gown fell forward, exposing her stays. His fingers went to free the laces. Finally divested of the stays, she turned back toward him, untied the tapes of her skirt, and stepped out of her gown. Impatiently, she reached down and flung it on a nearby chair.

His gaze traveled down her body and his breathing quickened. She was clad only in her stockings and a thin chemise, the gauzy, semitransparent fabric doing little to protect her modesty. She reached down for the hem and drew it over her head.

Nude except for her silk stockings and embroidered garters, she smiled. "Your turn. I've waited a very long time to see you without your clothes."

It was a hasty matter, undressing him. Neither, it seemed, wished to prolong it any more than necessary. They were hungry for each other, and much too eager to reach that final joining of sexual union to tease out the anticipation.

Once they'd completely divested themselves of their garments, Charles hurriedly pulled back the covers and together they fell onto the soft mattress of the large four-poster bed. Serena rolled on her back, and Charles was atop her, his arms braced against the mattress on either side of her.

She grasped his buttocks, pulling him firmly against her, adjusting her position so that he could enter her easily.

As he slowly eased into her, his jaw tightened and his breathing became harsh and labored, his face strained as he tried to maintain his self-control.

"Serena, I don't think...I vowed I'd take my time...make it good for you...but it's been so long..."

Though Serena enjoyed foreplay, she was in no mood for it now. She didn't want finesse, just a hot, frantic coupling. "I don't want restraint, Charles. I want you. *Now*."

His eyes, hooded with passion, looked hard into her own, but he took her words to heart, and it wasn't long before they each found release. Sated, neither one of them moved for a few minutes. Serena's arms were wrapped around Charles as he lay on top of her, her legs entangled with his, and the sheets tangled around them both.

"That was..." she began.

"...humbling," he said, finishing the sentence for her. "I'm sorry. I'd hoped to do better."

"Darling, I didn't last any longer than you did, and I'd already reached *la petite mort* twice earlier in the day. Perhaps I should be the one feeling humble." But she didn't. She felt *wonderful*, and she hoped to feel wonderful at least once more tonight.

He moved his head slightly so that he could kiss her temple. "You are magnificent. Always."

She narrowed her eyes and looked at him skeptically. "I'll have to remind you of that the next time you disapprove of something I do."

He kissed her cheek. "I thought..." he said. *Kiss.* "That we put any such behavior behind us." *Kiss.* "I know I heard you promise to obey me during the wedding ceremony." *Kiss.* And then he laughed, the wretched man.

"And I told you"—she gave his shoulder a light nip—
"to ignore that, since the vicar obstately refused to
excise it from the vows." She ran one hand down along
the skin of his back to his buttock and gave that part of
his anatomy a firm squeeze. "In other words, when I made
that particular declaration, *I lied*. It was the price I had to
pay to marry you, and so I did. Gladly."

He rolled off her then and gathered her close to his side,
one hand caressing her breast. "And I will be eternally
grateful that you did marry me."

"Did you notice that one of the Mr. Longhughs—I'm
not sure which, because they look so similar—seemed
to be paying rather close attention to Miss Lewis at the
wedding breakfast?" she asked.

"Is that really what you want to talk about right now?"
he asked. "Miss Lewis and a potential swain?"

"I feel a little sorry for her. Especially after you told me
about her fiancé jilting her two years ago. Do you think he
would make a good suitor for her?"

"I don't even know which Mr. Longhugh we're discussing, since you can't tell one brother apart from the
other."

"Well, would either of them make a good suitor? They
were your fellow boarders, after all, so surely you have
an opinion."

"They both seem decent-enough fellows. I didn't know
them all that well. Aside from at breakfast, I rarely saw
them."

"Hmmm," she murmured, ready to drop the subject
because he continued to caress her breast and it was causing other parts of her to ache for his touch as well. She
reached for his hand and guided it lower.

"We can discuss it later," she said. "I have a more urgent task I wish you to attend to."

It was some time later that Charles's stomach growled audibly as they lay snuggled in the bed together. Serena giggled, and he gave her a reproving look. "What? Can I help it if all this activity has caused me to work up an appetite?"

They'd had a lively—and noisy—lovemaking session. He kissed the crown of her head. "Do you think there's any chance the food is still warm? I'm starving."

"So I gathered." She rolled away from him and slipped out of the bed, presenting him with a view of her very shapely backside. She walked across the room to a large armoire, threw open the doors, and after a moment's perusal, pulled out a silk dressing gown, wrapping it around herself. She reached inside the armoire again, and when she turned around he saw his navy dressing gown dangling from her finger, but instead of tossing it to him, she gave him a saucy smile and walked over to the table, where she draped the garment over the back of one of the chairs.

Grinning, he threw back the covers and walked over to her, enjoying her frank study of him as he did so. He did love her boldness. He pulled out the chair for her before going over to his own. He put on his dressing gown and took a seat.

They lifted the covers off their plates to reveal roast chicken and vegetables and began to eat. The food wasn't completely cold, but it would have been much better had they consumed it earlier. Nonetheless, they both finished every bite. Done, Serena pushed back her plate and then walked around the table to stand beside his chair. "Do you remember our draughts game?"

"Memories of it have tortured me every night since," Charles said. "Although as draughts games go, it wasn't very memorable."

She grinned. Roguishly. Wickedly. "Well, I was being a naughty girl and not letting you concentrate," she said. "We should have a rematch. Although I can't promise that I won't be naughty again."

He grinned. "I would hope not. Provided, that is, we're playing in the privacy of our own home."

She raised a brow, which he took to mean she wasn't making any promises. "Anyway, this is what I really wanted to do that evening. Scoot your chair back a bit, won't you?"

He did and she settled herself on his lap, facing him with her legs straddled on either side of him.

The week passed quickly and Charles was surprised when he realized it was the last day before they must head back to London. Even though it was short, he couldn't imagine a more sublime honeymoon than the one they'd had. He discovered (and this wasn't necessarily a surprise) that his wife had a boundless imagination when it came to lovemaking and, further, she had no inhibitions.

He might still blush over the memory of one lovemaking session outdoors when they'd nearly been discovered by a goatherd searching for a lost nanny goat named Samantha, but Serena just laughed and said, "Admit it, Charles. The threat of discovery just made it that much better."

One thing he did know. She made his life so much better. He watched her sleeping beside him, her hair spread out across the pillow, blankets pushed down to her waist, exposing her naked breasts to his view. Since it was midafternoon, and the curtains were only partially closed, he could drink in the sight of her to his heart's content.

She opened her eyes and gave him a drowsy smile. "Why, Mr. Townshend, you're getting that look on your face again."

He leaned down and kissed her. "What look is that?" he asked, playfully biting on her earlobe and giving it a tug. She squirmed beside him. It drove her crazy when he nibbled her ears and throat.

"That *I want to ravish you* look."

"And do you wish to be ravished?" he whispered, placing a trail of kisses along her throat.

"I think I do." She sighed and reached her hands above her head, stretching her arms in a way that gave him ideas. "Even though I was pretty thoroughly ravished not that long ago."

"As you wish." He reached up and with one hand, captured her wrists in a firm grip.

"Mmm." She moaned as his mouth closed over one breast. "I do like it when you take command."

"I know," he murmured.

And take command he did.

Chapter Twenty-Five

The next day they returned to London, arriving at the Huntington residence in the early afternoon to find both her father and Jem not at home.

"Lord Huntington and Master Jem are sailing boats at the park," Menken informed them. "Afterward, I believe, they planned to stop at Gunter's."

"When do you expect them back?" Serena asked, slightly disappointed. She'd missed Jem during the past week, and she knew Charles had as well, though neither of them was sorry to leave him behind for the honeymoon.

"I doubt they'd return before four o'clock at the earliest, my lady," the butler replied.

Serena glanced at Charles. "In that case, I think we'll take a rest from our journey," she told Menken. "Please tell the footmen there's no need to bring the luggage up until later."

"Very well, my lady."

Serena thought she caught a twinkle of amusement in the butler's eyes before he dipped his head slightly and took himself off to carry out her instructions. She strongly suspected the servant knew exactly what she meant by "take a rest" and that it had nothing to do with going to sleep. She turned to Charles, whose wickedly suggestive gaze indicated he also knew what she'd meant.

"Shall we?" she asked. She reached for his hand, but he gave a slight shake of his head, and then surprised her by sweeping her up into his arms to carry her upstairs like a bridegroom.

"Let's do this properly," he said.

She wrapped a hand around his neck and pulled his face toward hers for a kiss. "As long as once we're in the bedroom, we do things most improperly."

"My thoughts, exactly," he said.

Later that evening, after dinner as they were gathered in the sitting room, Lord Huntington announced that he intended to stay with his cousin Archibald until Serena and Charles took up residence in the new lodgings they'd rented.

Serena looked up from the game of spillikins she was playing with Jem. "But, Papa, we can't move in until the lease is up for the current occupants and that won't be for nearly a month."

"I know. I know," her father said, brushing aside this concern with a wave of his hand.

"There's no need for you to do that, sir," Charles said. He and her father were seated across from each other in the pair of armchairs that flanked the fireplace. "It's very thoughtful of you, but please don't feel it's necessary.

Serena and I don't wish for you to have to vacate your own house on our behalf."

A wistful half-smile formed on her father's face. "I want to. I was a newlywed once, you know." He turned to Serena. "After our elopement, your mother and I came directly back from Scotland and went to visit her parents so we could collect some more of your mother's possessions, and try to smooth things out with her mother and father. But the day we arrived was the start of a weeklong period of heavy rain every day. We ended up having to stay another two weeks while we waited for the roads to dry out enough to make carriage travel possible. It's not an experience I'd wish upon any pair of newlyweds. Consider my absence a kind of wedding gift, if you like."

"Well, Papa, of course, under those circumstances it would be awkward. But that's not the case here. I think you're glad Charles is taking me off your hands."

Her father snorted at that, and Charles let out a wry chuckle.

"You're too much your own female for either of us to be under any illusion that I'm passing you off to him. Am I right, Charles?"

"Completely," Charles agreed with a grin.

"At any rate," her father continued, "your grandparents accepted our marriage quite well once it was *fait accompli*. In fact, your grandfather seemed quite pleased about it. I think it was your grandmother who so strongly opposed the match. She favored a certain duke who'd courted her daughter, but your mother would have a love match or nothing." He sighed. "I do miss my Gwen."

"I know, Papa," Serena said. "I do too." After a minute,

she added, "I never knew you had a rival. Which duke had his eye on Mama?"

Her father winked at her. "No names, daughter. He took his loss like a good sport and we're friends now."

Jem, who'd been listening to their conversation this whole time, got up and went to lean against the arm of her father's chair. Papa put his arm around the boy, a gesture that brought tears to Serena's eyes. She was so glad to see the growing affection between the pair of them.

"Can I come stay with you for a few days, like when I went visiting to Peregrine's house?" Jem asked.

"Why, certainly, my boy. I'd enjoy it."

A glance passed between Serena and Charles, a tacit acknowledgment that they'd enjoy having the house to themselves, even if only for a few days.

For the week and a half after their return to London, Serena spent every afternoon helping with preparations for the Wednesday Afternoon Social Club's subscription ball hosted by the Duke and Duchess of Rochester. She felt guilty for not doing her fair share this year to get everything ready.

Grace, with the help of Phoebe, had been working on preparations for several weeks now, and many of the tasks needed to bring off a social event of this magnitude had been completed while Serena had been in Hampstead Heath with Charles. But there was still a great deal of last-minute details that needed to be attended to, and so any members of the Wednesday Afternoon Social Club who were free in the afternoons had been meeting at the Rochester residence to work on completing them.

Once again they'd sold every one of tickets and the

club's coffers were in excellent shape as a result. But even here, Serena had failed to do her part. She hadn't managed to sell all of her allotment, so she'd bought the remaining ones herself and given four of them to Charles's family. His younger two half-brothers, Stuart and David, were too young to attend, but when she offered tickets to his mother, stepfather, Miss Lewis, and his brother Lawrence, they were happily accepted.

She also sent four tickets around to 4 Nassau Street, a pair of them were for Miss Minerva and Miss Leticia, who, after initially protesting they didn't have anything to wear to such a grand occasion, had been persuaded to attend. And two were given to the Longhugh brothers, who seemed quite tickled to receive them.

She hoped whichever of the brothers who'd been enamored with Miss Lewis would take advantage of the opportunity to further his suit. When she'd told Charles about it, he'd rolled his eyes and asked if this was practice for eventually becoming one of those obnoxious matchmaking mamas.

He'd made this comment while lounging on their bed late one evening waiting for her to finish her nightly toilette. He'd paid for his remark though, because she'd scampered over to the bed, leaped on top of him, and plied her own particular type of torture to him. Which in the end, he didn't seem to mind at all.

The morning of the ball dawned clear and mild. The temperature during the day felt more like late spring and Grace fretted that they wouldn't have enough ice to keep the refreshments from Gunter's frozen. It had cooled somewhat by evening, but in the end it didn't matter because Jason Latimer had somehow managed to secure an additional supply of ice, even on such late notice, and so Grace's worries had been assuaged.

The ball was a smashing success. The Rochester ballroom was crowded with guests, even though, thanks to the still-mild night air, a fair number of them had spilled out onto the garden terrace.

Serena and Charles loitered near the open French doors, eating ices. Serena's was raspberry flavored and in the shape of a rose. Or rather it had been before she'd consumed half of it. Charles had already finished his vanilla ice.

Just then, Grace and her husband stepped through the set of the French doors nearest Serena and Charles. Serena thought her friend's coiffure looked a bit more mussed than it had a short time ago.

Catching sight of her, Grace flushed slightly. The duke must have been kissing his wife out in the gardens.

"Have you seen Phoebe?" Grace asked.

"I saw her out on the dance floor earlier," Serena said. "Were you looking for her outside?"

Miles gave Serena a sardonic look. "We were looking for a spot to cool off."

"Then I don't think you succeeded," Serena said, causing Grace's cheek to turn pinker.

Miles laughed and gave her a wink. "Maybe not, but perhaps some of Gunter's ices will do the trick." He gave her a quick a kiss on the cheek. "I'll be right back with some, darling."

"It's a shame Charlotte wasn't feeling well enough to come tonight," Grace said. "But she is getting close to the baby's anticipated arrival. I can see why an evening spent mostly on her feet didn't hold a great deal of appeal."

At that moment, Edwina and Jason stepped through the farthest set of French doors.

"Is everybody going out into the gardens?" Serena asked.

"It's presently rather hard to find a private spot," Grace admitted. "I just wonder where Phoebe has gotten off to," she added a bit impatiently.

"I'm sure she has the good sense not to go outside," Serena said, addressing her friend's unspoken worry. The words had no sooner left her mouth than she spied the girl waltzing in the arms of a tall, dark-haired gentleman. His back was to them, so she couldn't tell who it was. She pointed her out to Grace.

"I wonder who that young man is," Grace said, looking intently in the direction of the waltzing pair. She straightened. "Although...I think it might be...yes, it is. The gentleman from the bookshop. The one whose identity I said we should learn."

"Well, I can supply that for you," Serena said. "It's Simon Trentwell, the Duke of Penwarren's grandson."

"Oh, good heavens," Grace gasped. "That nice, unassuming gentleman is Simon Trentwell, the notorious rakehell? She shouldn't be dancing with him. And what is she doing dancing with him? They haven't been properly introduced! Not that I'd want her dancing with him even then. What would Anne say if she knew?"

"Anne would probably say 'hooray,'" Serena said dryly. "Since his brother died, Trentwell is the duke's heir presumptive and the Marquess of Trenton, although for some reason he's refusing to use that honorific. But I can see why Phoebe is drawn to him. Just look at him—tall, dark, and impossibly handsome. Not to mention that way he has of focusing those brown eyes on a female...one can't help but go all melty inside. I can understand why he's so successful in his conquests. If I weren't so in love with my husband"—she gave Charles a radiant smile—"I might feel like swooning over him myself."

"And precisely how much time have you spent around this fellow who sounds too luscious for words?" Charles asked.

"I've spoken with him only once or twice," Serena assured him. Finished with her ice now, she set the empty crystal bowl on one of the tray tables placed around the room for that purpose, and tucked a hand through his arm. "You have nothing to worry about."

"Who's too luscious for words that Charles needn't worry about?" Jason Latimer asked as he and Edwina joined them.

"Phoebe's current dance partner, Simon Trentwell," Grace said. She turned to Edwina. "He's the young man from the bookseller's I told you about."

"The one who sat by the window reading during your visits?"

"Yes," Grace said, sounding quite exasperated. "Who would expect a man who frequents a bookshop on a weekly basis, and who seems to have a love for reading...Well, who would expect a man like that to be a well-known rake?"

Jason shrugged. "The fact that he showed up regularly on the days you shopped there might have been a clue," he suggested. "Phoebe is a beautiful girl. Even though she's not officially out yet, she's attracting quite a bit of male notice. So it's not a surprise that she attracted Trentwell's."

"Trentwell is one man who can jolly well stop noticing," Grace declared.

Miles rejoined them carrying a dessert bowl in each hand. He handed one of them to his wife. "Here, darling. I don't know what has you so upset, but this can only help." Grace took the bowl from him.

"Phoebe is waltzing with Simon Trentwell and we must do something about it, Miles," Grace said.

"I think the best thing to do is to not overreact," the duke warned.

"He's right, Grace," Serena said. "Forbidden fruit is always the most tempting."

"If it makes you feel any better, Duchess," Jason Latimer said, "I don't think Trentwell's reputation is entirely representative of who he is. His wild ways didn't start until after his brother's death."

"What I'd like to know," Serena said, "is what he's doing here tonight. He doesn't typically appear at social functions like this. Who sold him his ticket, do you think?"

They all looked at one another and it was clear they all shared the same suspicion. *Phoebe.* But Serena didn't think the girl would have done so if she'd realized how upsetting it would be to her aunt.

On the other hand, the waltz was ending, so they might soon know how Phoebe came to be dancing with a man whose checkered reputation made him so unsuitable for her. Simon escorted Grace's niece over to them, relinquishing her to her aunt's care with a bow.

"Aunt Grace, Uncle Miles, may I introduce you to Mr. Trentwell? Mr. Trentwell, may I present my aunt and uncle, the Duchess and Duke of Rochester?"

The young man bowed. "It's a pleasure, Duchess." Grace nodded, but she looked as if she considered the meeting anything but a pleasure. She was studying the pair with no small amount of consternation. Turning to the duke, Trentwell added, "Your Grace, it's good to see you again."

"I confess it's something of a surprise to see you here, tonight," the duke responded. "You don't make it a habit of socializing in polite society." Although the duke's tone wasn't censorious, the rebuke was clear.

"However," the duke continued, "thank you for returning my niece to us." It was a clear dismissal, and Trentwell knew it. He bowed and made his farewells.

Phoebe looked quite taken aback by this exchange. "Uncle Miles—" she began.

"Phoebe, are you completely unaware of Mr. Trentwell's reputation?" Grace interrupted.

Phoebe looked surprised by the question, so it was clear to Serena that her answer was going to be yes, and it was.

"He's a rake, my dear," Grace said. "Completely unsuitable for a young woman like you. You mustn't encourage his attentions. He may look like the kind of man girls dream of marrying some day, but it's almost certain he would never be the kind of husband who would make you happy."

"Oh," Phoebe said. "Well, I'm glad to know that, but surely, Aunt Grace, you must admit he's behaved as a perfect gentleman toward me. It doesn't seem to be right to judge him on his reputation alone."

"Serena," Charles said, giving her a pointed look. "The musicians are tuning up for the next dance." He held out his hand to her. "Shall we?"

"Why, yes, Charles. I would love to," she replied. She knew Charles was right, and they should give Grace and Phoebe the opportunity to discuss Mr. Trentwell without the rest of them overhearing the discussion, but that didn't mean she wasn't curious to hear how it would go.

He led her over to join the line of dancers for the set. Edwina and Jason, evidently having the same idea, got in line beside them.

"They do make a lovely couple," Edwina said in a regretful voice. "But I know how disappointing it is to be married to a rake. I certainly wouldn't wish that on Phoebe."

"Nor would I," said Serena. "It's a shame, really, that it's next to impossible to reform a rake."

It was well after midnight when Serena and Charles returned home from the ball. As they made their way up the stairs to their bedroom, Charles turned to her and smiled. "Did my mother tell you that Nigel Longhugh asked her for permission to call upon Miss Lewis while they are here in London?"

"She did," Serena said. "To hear her tell it, it was all the result of her shrewd efforts to bring them together."

"Did you inform her that Mr. Longhugh was only in attendance tonight because of *your* efforts?"

"I did not." Serena slipped her arm around her husband's waist. He looked so handsome in his evening clothes, but she was rather eager to get him out of them. "I figured I'd let her claim this victory."

"I think she's trying to improve since I had my talk with her."

"I'm sure she is," Serena agreed. "At the very least, she

knows where you stand on things and what you expect of her."

Soon after their return from Hampstead Heath, Charles and his mother had had a long overdue heartfelt talk. It hadn't been entirely satisfactory on all fronts. Although her attitude toward Serena was less hostile, Mrs. Avery still hadn't acknowledged the truth of Charles's parentage or the lies she'd told to cover it up. And if Charles was willing to look past the woman's massive flaws, then Serena could do no less.

Arriving at their room, Charles opened the door and ushered her inside. Then he gave a head-splitting yawn.

"How tired are you?" she asked.

He slanted her a glance as he held out his arm for her to help with his jacket. "I'm tired, but what did you have in mind?"

She tugged on the arm of his jacket until he'd managed to work that arm free. One he removed the garment, she turned for him to undo the fastenings of her dress. They usually dispensed with the services of her lady's maid and his valet in the evenings, since that gave them more privacy to indulge their whims when it came to bedroom activities.

She turned back to face him. "Quick and frenzied could be fun."

He appeared to consider this before saying, "I believe I have enough energy for that."

"I'm confident you do," she said, giving him a wicked grin. She began to help undo the buttons of his waistcoat while he worked to loosen the knot of his cravat.

He leaned down and kissed her. "For you, I always do." His hands slid into her hair. "And I always will."

Find out what happens with Phoebe and Simon in the next Unconventional Ladies of Mayfair story

Sweet Dreams Are Made of Dukes

Available Spring 2023

About the Author

KATE PEMBROOKE is a lifelong reader whose path to becoming an author of Regency romance was forged when she first read Jane Austen's *Pride and Prejudice*. Kate lives with her family in the Midwest. She loves puttering around in her flower beds, taking beach vacations, and adding to her already extensive collection of cookbooks.

You can learn more at:
katepembrooke.com
Twitter @KatePembrooke
Facebook.com/KatePembrookeAuthor
Instagram.com/katepembrooke/

Get swept off your feet by charming dukes, sharp-witted ladies, and scandalous balls in Forever's historical romances!

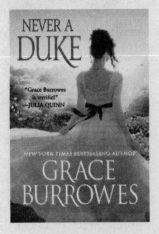

NEVER A DUKE
by Grace Burrowes

Ned Wentworth will be forever grateful to the family who plucked him from the streets and gave him a home, even though polite society still whispers years later about his questionable past. Precisely because of Ned's connections in low places, Lady Rosalind Kinwood approaches him to help her find a lady's maid who has disappeared. As the investigation becomes more dangerous, both Ned and Rosalind will have to risk everything—including their hearts—if they are to share the happily-ever-after that Mayfair's matchmakers have begrudged them both.

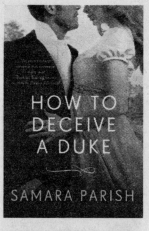

HOW TO DECEIVE A DUKE
by Samara Parish

Engineer Fiona McTavish has come to London under the guise of Finlay McTavish for one purpose—to find a distributor for her new invention. But when her plans go awry and she's arrested at a protest, the only person who can help is her ex-lover, Edward, Duke of Wildeforde. Only bailing "Finlay" out of jail comes at a cost: She must live under his roof. The sparks from their passionate affair many years before are quick to rekindle. But when Finlay becomes wanted for treason, will Edward protect her—or his heart?

SAY YOU'LL BE MY LADY
by Kate Pembrooke

Lady Serena Wynter doesn't mind flirting with a bit of scandal—she's determined to ignore Society's strictures and live life on her own terms. But there is one man who stirs Serena's deepest emotions, one who's irresistibly handsome, infuriatingly circumspect, and too honorable for his own good…Charles Townshend isn't immune to the attraction between them, but a shocking family secret prevents him from acting on his desires. Only it seems Lady Serena doesn't intend to let propriety stand in the way of a mutually satisfying dalliance.

THE REBEL AND THE RAKE
by Emily Sullivan

Though most women would be thrilled to catch the eye of a tall, dark, and dangerously handsome rake like Rafe Davies, Miss Sylvia Sparrow trusted the wrong man once and paid for it dearly. The fiery bluestocking is resolved to avoid Rafe, until a chance encounter reveals the man's unexpected depths—and an attraction impossible to ignore. But once Sylvia suspects she isn't the only one harboring secrets, she realizes that Rafe may pose a risk to far more than her heart…

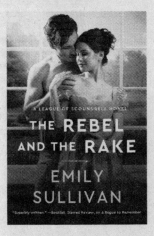

THE PERKS OF LOVING A WALLFLOWER
by Erica Ridley

As a master of disguise, Thomasina Wynchester can be a polite young lady—or a bawdy old man. Anything to solve the case—which this time requires masquerading as a charming baron. Her latest assignment unveils a top-secret military cipher covering up an enigma that goes back centuries. But Tommy's beautiful new client turns out to be the reserved, high-born bluestocking Miss Philippa York, with whom she's secretly smitten. As they decode clues and begin to fall for each other in the process, the mission—as well as their hearts—will be at stake...